PRAISE FOR THE NOVELS OF USA TODAY BESTSELLING AUTHOR, ALYSSA RICHARDS

"Having read Alyssa Richards other books, I knew I was in for a treat, even though this was a slightly different genre. And gothic suspense being one of my absolute favorites, I was extremely psyched to read this book. Fortunately, everything that I anticipated about how good this book would be, and how much I would enjoy it, came true.

At first glance, this might appear to be your average haunted house story. But in the hands of this very capable, and highly readable author, it becomes so much more. The haunting was unique and the story revolving around the haunting was very intriguing. I totally did not anticipate the way the story was going or how it was going to end up. This was a great first entry in a new genre that I hope the author will continue. This book, as well as everything else this author has written, comes highly recommended." — DT Chantel, book reviewer

"Man oh man! Alyssa Richards has seriously outdone herself with this trilogy. It encompasses love, passion, deception, heartache, reality and alternate reality. Just stunning from start to finish. This trilogy is awesome. If you're looking for a paranormal romance that's focused around psychics and time travel, definitely grab this trilogy. It's simply amazing!" —*Nay's Pink Bookshelf*

5.0 out of 5 stars "Now this is what I'm talking about...absofreakingamazing!

"It's authors like Ms. Richards that really opened up the portals to my world, and instilled/nurtured within me a love for reading. Hook, line and sinker you are pulled fast and hard into her storylines and are wrecked when you've reached the end...you just don't want it to be over. The Haunting of Alcott Manor is no different and has a wonderful mix of gothic suspense/mystery with a titter of romance that will captivate you..and the end...omg I so didn't see that coming. What a stunning conclusion!" —*K. Berry, Amazon Reviewer*

5.0 out of 5 stars That ending...!? Are you kidding me?!

"Like others, I'm sure, I`ve read hundred(s) of these types of books. This was a great read, great twists and turns. ...and the end...? WOW! What's really getting me right now though? Henry and Gemma at still with me....days after I've finished the book! I cried with them, I loved with them, and they touched me deeply! Great job! (This is the first time I have been inspired enough to write a review, too!)" *T. Vari-anon, Amazon Book Reviewer*

A MURDER AT ALCOTT MANOR

BOOK 2, THE ALCOTT MANOR TRILOGY

ALYSSA RICHARDS

Library of Congress Control Number: 2017918989
Ebook ISBN-13: 978-0-9991555-1-6
Editing by Peter Senftleben
Proofreading by Karen Boston

**Sign up for Alyssa's newsletter at to receive special offers and news
about her latest releases.**

You can follow her on:
Instagram

Contact Alyssa at:
authoralyssarichards@protonmail.com

1

"I know this must be hard for you," Layla's attorney said.

Billy Langmire sat composed, his tanned skin as smooth and flawless as his expensive navy blue suit. He would never understand just how hard this was for her.

She knew this from the polished and perfect gold band on his well-manicured ring finger. And she knew this from the silver framed photos of his beautiful blonde wife and little boy, on the dunes at the white sand beach. And she knew this from the trophy fish that was hung on the wall behind his desk. She often wondered if someone like him ever had real problems, or did he only have difficult choices.

She pinched the soft skin of her thigh beneath the teal green of her scrubs. Numbness was covering her inch by inch like a thick blanket and she hoped the sharp nip from her nails would snap her out of it. Guilt was swallowing her whole, as if a giant whale engulfed her into its dark, watery belly, and she descended into nothingness.

She hadn't felt this lost since the end of high school, when she had been accused of killing Brooke Williams—an event that caused Layla's life to jump its rails. It simultaneously destroyed her future with Mason, the man she thought she would marry. And it landed her in a marriage with Asher Cardill—her newly deceased husband who continued to ruin her life, even from the grave.

Back then, an entire summer of official charges and public humiliation had taken place before the police had ultimately proven her innocent. "There just isn't enough evidence to support the claims," the detectives had finally said.

But what the police and everyone else had never managed to figure out was that she had done it. She had killed Brooke Williams.

"Isn't there anything I can—" Emotion caught in her throat now. "There has to be something I can do to stop the bank from taking our house."

"I'm afraid not." His lips nearly disappeared into a sad smile he must have conjured for the most pathetic of situations. No lips, no teeth, no compassion. Just...unconcerned.

"There *has* to be something. We have nowhere to go. I have children—two girls who have lived in that home all their life." The hatred she had for that house bubbled up in sour grape flavor and swirled around her mouth. The bedrooms were too small, the kitchen too dated, the yard didn't have enough trees.

The small, two bedroom ranch-style house had been Asher's house before they married, never hers. Apparently, it was still his house because he never added her to the deed. That's what they sprung on her today.

She'd wanted to leave Asher's bachelor-era house so many times over the last ten years. Now she would. Not in the way she had wanted or expected, but she would go. She and her girls were all flying the coop, with no place to land.

"The bank cannot leave us homeless." Her voice sounded as though it came from someone else, from somewhere else in the room. She was disassociating. A psychologist described that reaction to her years ago and she knew the signs. Numbing out was one of them.

Billy pushed a letter toward her that was littered with numbers and harsh language. She'd seen the letter before, read it several times; she didn't need to see it again. So she ignored it and kept her eyes on his.

"Your husband's business owed the bank $552,000 on a line of credit. Since his company didn't have any revenue, they're entitled to seize his assets to settle his debt. He signed a personal guarantee with them." His pencil tapped a sentence at the bottom of the paper. She ignored that, too, and maintained eye contact. She was determined that he see her as a human being, that he help her with this.

"Your house is worth roughly $245,000. I've spoken with the bank, and they're willing to give you a discount of seven thousand dollars. But they're going to hold you to the remaining $300,000."

"How kind." She tried to tamp down her anger that was developing its own momentum, like a gallop that sped toward a cliff.

She was acutely aware of how anger could ruin your life. It could make you do things you later wished you hadn't. But the emotion she felt today was the special kind of anger that made her sprout fangs and claws and forced grown men to cower in her path. It grew its substantial roots on the day her first child was born, and its protective nature was bigger than she was. She called it her mama bear side, since it only reared itself when someone threatened the well-being of her children.

Right now, someone was taking away her children's

home. When she tapped her fingers on the table, she fully expected to hear claws on polished wood.

"I don't understand why *I* have to settle the rest of *his* business debt. Plus—" She dug through her purse for the papers she'd finally found this morning and slapped them on the desk. "We took out these life insurance policies for $500,000 each. His policy will cover most of what he owed the bank."

"Well." Billy lifted a stack of stapled papers from his open white file folder and passed it to her. "Does this look familiar?"

The top page read *Personal Guarantee and Loan Agreement*.

"This isn't mine."

He folded the first few pages over and pointed to her signature in blue ink next to the word 'co-signer'.

"Oh, no." She exhaled hard. "Asher had me sign this a long time ago. I'd forgotten."

"The bank remembered. You signed it three years ago." He underlined the date with his pencil.

She wondered how much trouble she would get in if she shoved that pencil up his nose. "The market was crap, and Asher's business was down. The bank was going to call his loan if he couldn't offer more collateral. I had some inheritance money from my grandparents socked away; of course, that ended up in Asher's business, too. The bank said if I co-signed on the line of credit that they would let him keep the loan."

Layla lowered her forehead into her palm. When she finally peeked up, she asked, "What about the insurance money?"

"I called the insurance company when you told me about them. And yes, his life insurance policy would have covered this debt, but he let it lapse over a year ago."

Her breath came faster now. As a nurse, she knew fast breathing increased anxiety. She'd counseled countless families of her patients to *slowwww* their breathing. But she couldn't manage to slow her own breath right now and it set its own pace.

"And your policy—" The attorney flipped through his folder of papers. "Was for three million. Not $500,000. Were you aware of that?"

Her rising mama bear anger dropped through an unexpected trap door. "Three? Three *million*? That's not right."

He slid the policy papers in front of her and she lowered her eyes to where he drew a light circle around the number.

"I don't understand. We bought half million dollar policies. Why would he increase the amount of mine?"

Billy leaned forward. "Layla, I don't know how well you knew your husband, but I'll just say this. If the situations were reversed and he had collected on your policy, the police would haul him down to the station faster than a barefoot jackrabbit on a greasy griddle."

"For what?"

"Suspicion."

"Suspicion of what?"

"Murder."

"Murder?"

"Yes, ma'am. Scuttlebutt is that he wanted to develop the Alcott Manor land through his property development company. You own part of the family stock that manages the manor and its property?"

"Yes. Quite a bit, because I'm a direct descendant of Benjamin Alcott. Only family members are entitled to have ownership."

"But he would have voting rights since y'all were married, right?"

"No. Only if there's a...death." A rush of white noise filled her ears while all the ways Asher might kill her passed before her eyes. Strangle...pummel...or smash her head...he was a man who would want to use his hands to finish her off.

Billy continued to talk, but his voice drifted away until she couldn't hear it at all. She floated in the space of the dark nothingness that surrounded her now. It wouldn't stop until it took over.

She didn't remember walking to the car, but once she was there she thought of her girls—how she needed to provide for them and their education and how Asher's debt would get in the way of doing just that.

Guilt, guilt and more guilt.

Standing outside the driver's side, she allowed a tiny ladybug to crawl onto her finger from the car's door handle. If Asher had been with her, he would have killed the bug just to see it die. If the girls hadn't been around to see him do it, that is.

If they had seen him find the ladybug, he would have made up some fantastic story and named the ladybug after them both in a hyphenated name. Half her eldest's name and half her youngest's.

"Let's call it Anna-Emma!"

She wondered if she were the only person on the planet to know Asher for who he truly was.

Deep belly breaths, she reminded herself and she crawled into her small car. She needed calm. Instead she got tears. Lots of them. She hadn't cried this hard since she'd discovered that Asher no longer loved her, not since she suspected he never really had, and not since she'd known she would have to pack up the girls and leave him.

The shrill ring of her cell phone startled her out of a deep, gut-wrenching sob.

Peyton.

Sisters knew somehow. They knew when you were in over your head and needed a helping hand. Though there was only so much she would tell her, Layla knew her sister would help. She wiped the running mascara from beneath her eyes and cleared her throat. "Hey."

"Hey. I just landed, did you get my texts?"

"No. My meeting ended only a few minutes ago."

"How did it go?"

White blooms from the crepe myrtle in front of her dipped and swayed in the wind. The sun bore down on the windshield, and she figured that somewhere, someone was talking about what a lovely day it was. Warm sun, nice breeze. Great day for a walk or a picnic. Her life was crumbling into too many pieces to count, and yet the world would simply go on.

"Worse than I expected, actually." She pressed her hand against the pain that throbbed at her temple.

"Oh, Layla. What happened?"

She went into detail about the lapsed insurance policy, how the bank was taking the house and how she'd have to pay off the rest of Asher's debt because he'd talked her into signing that personal guarantee. Oh, and it looked like he might have been planning to murder her for insurance money and her Alcott Manor stock.

Layla wiped a tear from her cheek. "How am I going to explain to the girls that we're losing our home?" She envisioned the house that would soon be just another case number for the bank. The twenty-year-old roof that needed replacing, the brown shutters that needed painting, and the weather-beaten front door that needed to be replaced.

Peyton's sigh was loud over the phone, and Layla could feel her sister's anger seethe. Peyton hated Asher.

"We'll figure this out. I'm on my way. Where are you right now?"

"Going to meet Tom Watson at the manor. Need to get myself together first." Layla thought of Tom, how kind and dedicated he was to their family and to their ancestral home. He worked for the Historic District Commission, but he had championed the completion of the restoration for several years now. Thanks to him, they were closer than they ever had been.

"Layla, I know this problem seems insurmountable, but remember you're stronger than you think."

Layla nodded and tried to take in her sister's encouragement. "Paying down that debt will be like a monthly payment for two mortgages. How in the heck am I going to afford that and keep a home for the girls and send them to college? How will I ever be able to retire?"

"Listen, honey. You of all people in the world deserve happiness. So, this is going to work out."

She wanted to believe her sister. Peyton had been blessed with courage to spare, and intelligence that catapulted her out of their hometown and away from their mother. Her determination was the gift that kept on giving, and Layla had never stopped wishing that she could have just a fraction of her sister's fearlessness. She started the engine and hoped that the drive to Alcott Manor would give her a fresh perspective.

"You've got the stock in the manor. That will pay off for you when the tours begin."

"The manor's a wreck. It might take a year or more for them to finish the repairs in that place."

"Why don't I meet you therer? I'm about forty-five minutes out," Peyton said.

Layla pressed the gas pedal. "I'll drive over to the public park and walk along the sand to the back of the house. Maybe we'll get there around the same time."

Layla's mind filled with sandy barefoot memories of her and her sister racing along the beach hand-in-hand and overflowing with giggles. It almost hurt to think of them, those far away good times.

"I'm on my way, Layla-pop."

Layla's heart softened for a twinkle of a moment at the sound of her childhood nickname. She could almost taste the sour apple lollipop she usually had in her mouth as a child. In the next second, she toughened up.

She had to—she was headed toward Alcott Manor.

Asher Cardill walked across the great hall and beneath the wide second story balcony where he had fallen to his death.

He watched Tom Watson and Mason Holloway while they met for their daily progress meeting on the manor. Mason was the newest builder to take on the manor's restorations, and it was obvious that he had no idea what he was getting into.

The two men inspected nearly everything in the room, from the oversized crystal chandelier, to the near-perfection of the gold paint, to the intricate balusters along the grand staircase that were being restored to their original design. Now they gathered around a mysterious spot on the floorboards, one that evoked bad memories and sent a cold sweat over Asher's skin.

Both men missed the fact that Asher paced to the outside of their meeting. If the house had been quiet, they might have heard his footsteps. But on this morning, Alcott Manor was filled with the construction noises of hammers banging, saws whirring, and men yelling, so they didn't notice him.

Asher rather liked it that way.

"It's disturbing," Mason said. "Every board within eight feet of where Asher died was completely replaced last week. These stains shouldn't be there."

Mason had a long history in Charleston where he had been born and raised, but he was new to the manor, so incidents like this caught him by surprise. It was fun to see him off balance. Because even though it had been ten years since they both graduated from high school, the unvoiced rivalry between Asher and Mason still ran strong.

Looks, women, money, success—those were the playing fields where they competed. Alcott Manor was their newest and final arena, where they would fight to the death to win one last prize—Layla Alcott. He knew that Mason couldn't possibly top his plans to win her. He had taken Layla away from him once before, and he was about to do it again. Seeing Mason lose this final round was something Asher would enjoy, maybe more than life itself.

He watched Tom squat near the wide dark stain and he chuckled at how little the two men knew about the manor's secrets. The reappearance of a blood stain should be the least of their concerns. Tom had worked at restoring the manor for years and though he knew more about its history than most, he still didn't know the half of what really went on around them.

Tom studied the area, then pressed two fingers into the shadowy marks. "It's sticky like blood. Smells like it, too."

"Can't be blood, there's too much of it," Mason said. "Has to be something else."

"The manor has a dark history that it can't let go of." He

showed Mason his fingertips which had blotches of red smudged on them.

"Houses don't feel. And that mess could be anything."

Tom clicked his tongue against the roof of his mouth. "Alcott Manor isn't a normal house. I warned you about that when you took this job. It doesn't let go of much, if anything. More time you spend around here, the more you'll see I'm right." He wiped the blood from his hand with a blue patterned handkerchief and squinted at the walls as though their ornamental beauty hid something dark and slithering. As if those walls filled to overflowing with an unseen dark energy and he couldn't protect himself.

"Be careful in the manor, nothing here is as it seems. I've had enough strange experiences in this place to know that this spot isn't just a stain. It's a sign. The manor is giving us notice of what's to come."

"I don't believe in any of that stuff. One of the workers probably spilled some paint, could even be food." Mason rested his hands on his hips and looked unimpressed.

A whiter shade of pale fell across Tom's face and he rubbed his forehead with the back of his hand. "People have lost their fortunes and their lives by underestimating this place. I would caution you against making the same mistake."

"So, what's this a sign of? Another death? The evil house takes another soul or something like that?"

Asher watched Mason chuckle.

"Hope not." Tom's broad shoulders seemed to drop slightly. "Right now, you need to think about how Layla will react when she sees this. She'll think we haven't cleaned up this mess since her ex-husband died here. She's the major shareholder in the family-owned business that runs this place. The one we need to keep happy, the one with all the influence."

Mason ran a hand over his face that was beginning to show signs of worry and fatigue. The job wasn't going as smoothly as he'd planned. Plus, he'd arrived at four-thirty that morning.

"Yeah, I remember. When is she coming?"

Tom glanced at his wristwatch. "About an hour. I'd tell you to throw a rug over this for the short-term, but the house will soil that, too. Get wood that's fresh from another location, none that's even been on this property. Trust me on that."

"We have a lumber delivery coming in later this morning. I'll have somebody tear this out in the meantime."

Asher watched Mason take his phone from his pocket and began to text while he walked away.

"Mason," Tom gestured to the stained flooring. "Once you get this wood out, burn it."

Mason shook his head as though he'd just been told to do the ridiculous.

When the two men left, Asher walked around his death site that the manor had re-marked. Yes. Now that Layla was coming, this blood was most definitely a sign. Someone else would die and the manor knew. The manor always knew.

One hour until Layla arrived. Asher couldn't wait.

3

L ayla was tired. Down to the marrow of her bones tired. Not just because of the stress, although that was a big part of her fatigue. She was tired because she hadn't slept. Because once again, the pattern was starting.

She'd woken up in the kitchen the night before, standing in front of the open refrigerator. Before she could fully understand where she was, she tasted the sugar-sweet icing from her daughter's red velvet birthday cake on her tongue. She had no memory of leaving her bed, no memory of walking to the kitchen and no memory of shoving that thick wedge of confectionary joy into her mouth.

And yet, there she was at two in the morning.

Sleepwalking.

Sleep eating.

That this had happened before was bad enough. That it was happening again troubled her.

Years ago, a psychologist had told her mother that teasing at school was the root cause of her sleepwalking. Bullying. Layla's unresolved stress would send her wandering right out into the night in her jammies and usually with a handful of cookies to munch along the way. Neighbors occasionally returned her home, though several times it had been the police.

Dr. Waters wasn't as dismayed over her sleepwalking and sleep eating behaviors as her mother. He said he liked that it was Layla's nature to try to work out her worries at night, and he recommended she learn a technique he used with most of his patients.

He called it lucid dreaming.

"Quite simply, lucid dreaming is your awareness of being in a dream state, while retaining your capacity to make choices. So, if you've ever been in a dream and you were aware that you were dreaming—then you have had a lucid dream.

"As a therapeutic treatment, I will teach you how to recreate your most distressing situations from school and life. You'll have the opportunity to control the outcome of these situations where typically you may not. You'll be able to handle conflicts with new strength and new creativity, and the sleep eating and sleepwalking will stop. Your confidence will rise, too."

When Dr. Waters began their sessions, he explained, "Dreams are a safe place where you can really let go of your inhibitions. You can sail to the moon on a cloud or run through fire without getting burned. You can even leap over tall buildings or fly with your own wings to Paris. You can feel true freedom, maybe for the first time in your life. Most importantly, I'll teach you how to recreate your problems within the safety of your dream world, and how to respond to that conflict in an empowered way."

He taught her how to wake up in her dreams without completely coming awake. With plenty of instruction and lots of practice, she finally got the hang of the process. It was all playtime at first. She could relax and have fun and learn without pressure. She flew to Paris with her own wings. She swam beneath the ocean without any scuba equipment— she often imagined herself a mermaid with a long blue green tail. Happily so.

Then it was time to work on the events that upset her the most. Like when someone harassed and bullied her at school. So, in her lucid dreams, she recreated the situation exactly as it had happened that day, down to the room, the time of day, and her bully, Brooke...only this time around, Layla was strong and confident when Brooke tried to humiliate her. Layla had witty and eloquent comebacks that left Brooke dumfounded and even apologetic.

Just as Dr. Waters promised, her personal power began to come back. There were fewer bullying incidents as a result, her stress levels lowered, and her sleep eating and sleepwalking stopped.

"There are limits to this technique," Dr. Waters warned. "Time limits with very real consequences. Hard limits. Your spirit actually leaves your body during lucid dreaming, and if your spirit stays away from your body too long, it won't find its way home. That would leave your body in a coma."

Dr. Waters gave her a suggestion to guard against that possibility: "Wear a watch and check the time before you fall asleep. It may sound silly, but many of your waking world details will cross over into your lucid dream. Awareness of time can be one of them and you can use that to your advantage. When you wake up in your dream, check the time again. You need to force yourself to wake up before the three-hour mark."

"I can force myself to wake up?" she asked.

"Yes. You can wake yourself up with a firm intent. As

long as your body isn't too tired, that is. In a lucid dream your body is sleeping. So, if your body is overly tired or fatigued, then you might not be able to wake yourself up as quickly as you would like. Don't wait until the last minute."

She hadn't used her lucid dreaming for a while, but now her physical and emotional exhaustion were catching up with her again. She needed a few minutes to recover from her morning, a lucid dream to tamp down the stress. She was early for her appointment with Tom and to meet Peyton, so she parked in the lot of a small county-run beach that was just below the Alcott property line. The manor was situated on sixty-five acres, almost an hour south of Charleston and along the coast.

With a glance toward Alcott Manor, she wondered if it were far enough away. Because usually, her lucid dreams were simply dreams. Beautiful, charmed experiences that healed like nothing else. But the manor had a dark history all its own that affected people's lives. Once, when she had fallen asleep close to the manor, something horrible happened. Something that destroyed her plans for a future with Mason. Something that changed her life forever.

She searched the horizon but the manor wasn't in sight. She wasn't even on Alcott property. She was fine, she reassured herself.

Perfectly fine.

The warm sun heated the interior of her car. Layla opened her eyes and checked her watch, then continued her deep breathing, just as Dr. Waters had taught her: inhaling white sparkling light, allowing it to fill the inside of her body, then exhaling dark smoke. Drifting further and further into the dream space, the other world where she felt most at home. Remembering his suggestions, following the path that was now familiar and well worn, deeper and deeper into her intent to recreate her morning, albeit with a different outcome this time.

A few breaths later, she opened her eyes and found herself just as she had intended to be: in her lucid dream, sitting in her attorney's office, at the highly polished desk with Billy across from her, folders and papers in front of him. He was giving her the bad news: that Asher had cancelled his insurance policy, hers had been increased, and she had to pay off Asher's bank debt. She noticed the several subtle clues that Dr. Waters had taught her to see. A tingly, electric feeling at her fingertips, a slight out-of-body sensation, and on occasion, image trails that followed certain movements.

She breathed deeply once again and prepared herself to respond differently this time. She would not get overwhelmed; instead, she would sit tall and ask what her options were. Wasn't there some form of bankruptcy she could file that would protect her? Wouldn't Billy call the bank again and negotiate something on her behalf?

She opened her mouth to ask these things with confidence, but a yank to her midsection dragged her ten feet away from her attorney's desk.

Billy looked at her wide-eyed and wondering, his mouth open and speechless.

Was she waking up already? Surely not yet. She'd only just begun.

She shook her head and cleared her throat. "Sorry. Not sure what that was." She scooted her chair toward the desk again, and she felt a warning: a tingling in her stomach where she had just been pulled, where something had a grip.

Like a giant fist, it quickly tightened and yanked her into the air this time, beyond the back wall and out of the office altogether. When she landed on her rear, it was in the one place she had spent most of the last ten years avoiding: Alcott Manor. She looked around the 1880s-style kitchen that boasted open shelves and light wood work tables in place of modern-day cabinets and countertops.

She grabbed ahold of the long rectangular table in the middle of the floor, her heart thumping hard, and her breath struggled to keep up. An older heavy-set woman in a frilly white apron chopped carrots, using the table as a cutting board.

Her spirit had been taken into the manor. This wasn't the same living space in the manor that other people could see. She knew this because the manor had brought her to this particular place during one of her lucid dreams before, a long time ago.

There were signs. Specific characteristics that she remembered and that were also here today. Like the air. In this part of the manor, it was quiet and thick on her skin—an inside-the-terrarium-like stillness. No breeze, no circulation.

It was a dead zone.

The screen door shut with a squeak and a slam—the sound of a well-loved home. Three blonde girls in bow-tied pigtails and red smocked dresses giggled and squealed and chased a brown terrier puppy with a red ball in its mouth. A tiny bell jingled on the dog's red collar. She leaned out of the way and watched them disappear around the corner.

That's the way it was in this dead zone. People and things from a different era appeared and disappeared. They passed through like they were unaware that they belonged somewhere else. Like she did. They were all here for a moment, while their beginnings and endings were some-place else.

A microwave sat on a table at the other end of the room, as well as a coffeemaker—two signs that the present wasn't too far away.

This place gave her a strange feeling of being neither here nor there, as if she had left the present but wasn't quite anywhere else either. Not the past, not the future. Just sort of hovering in the middle somewhere. Some place in time that only the manor could know. It was just like this house to have a toehold in some sort of netherworld.

Perched on an antique pedestal cake stand and on top of a white cloth doily was a thickly iced, double-layer chocolate cake. Obviously homemade and already carved substantial pieces, Layla's mouth watered. Cake was still her favorite security blanket, and without thinking twice, she helped herself. She had lost a substantial amount of weight in the last few years and sworn off sugar, but she didn't have to count calories in a dream. Three large crumbs spilled onto the smooth wooden surface of the table and she left them. She didn't have to clean in a dream either.

Voices murmured low and nondescript, like distant chattering at a cocktail party. "Uh-uh-uhhhh," one voice cautioned and rose slightly louder over the others.

Her heart stuttered with adrenaline at the sound. Whenever Asher caught her eating sweets, he used that parental expression with her while he wagged his finger at her face.

He was dead, she reminded herself. There was no need to be afraid.

When the tall, dark-haired man in the faded red T-shirt and jeans passed by the doorway, she put the cake on the table. Although she caught only a glimpse of his muscled physique, she recognized him in an instant.

She tip-toed quickly though the dining room, the foyer, and up to the grand staircase. Following the man she knew as Mason Holloway, she wondered why he would be at Alcott Manor. Tom hadn't mentioned anything about him to her.

Mason knelt on the third step from the bottom and sanded a small area of unfinished wood by hand. That was definitely the Mason she remembered—a perfectionist. Traditional. Classic. A genuine if-it's-worth-doing-it's-worth-doing-right kind of guy. His rhythmic scratching of the sandpaper against the raw wood kept perfect time. When she leaned close to the back of his neck, she found mixed scents of fresh citrusy sweat and something powdery.

"I've missed you," she whispered against his damp skin.

Mason stopped sanding and turned to face her, though she knew he couldn't see her.

His commanding presence reeled her in and swept her toward him. She couldn't help herself: she kissed his soft lips.

The tug in her midsection pulled her away from him. Her fingertips grazed his cheek before she was jerked backward in a rush, away from him and the manor. Back to her body that was asleep and dreaming in the car.

She was waking up.

MASON HOLLOWAY GLANCED around the main foyer where he had been sanding a step on bended knee. He could have sworn he'd felt a touch on his cheek; he could have sworn he'd felt a kiss on his lips; he could have sworn he'd heard Layla's voice.

Soft as a whisper, but clear as day.

4

L ayla stood behind Alcott Manor in her real life this time, her waking world where the ocean waves crashed onto the white sand beach and the soft grassy lawn stretched toward the manor. She remembered what the home was like when she was a little girl, when the white paint curled away from the house in long strips as though it tried to escape its destiny. Nothing stuck to the house at that time. Not paint or good fortune or restorations.

For many years, there had been a barbed wire and chain link fence around the property, with another one around the house, and heavy chains with locks at the gate because people had died here.

In fact, the house had a long history of death, from Anna Alcott, who was rumored to have been shot and killed by her husband Senator Benjamin Alcott, to more recent deaths like a young teenager and a restoration specialist, both of whom had fallen to their deaths under suspicious circumstances.

For those reasons and more, she had often wondered if

Alcott Manor was cursed like people said it was. But Asher died here. And that removed a curse from her life.

When the house was fully restored, the family would offer tours of the home and the property. The revenue from the tours would bring significant income for the entire Alcott family and she would get a big part of that. Peyton was right. She would have to push for a quick finish.

She passed the first two squares of rose gardens that had been recently renewed to the original glory she had seen in old photographs. The landscapers had done a beautiful job. Installing benches and gliding chairs was a lovely touch.

Ferns stretched long and lithe in the shade of ancient magnolias. A plentiful herb garden of echinacea, chamomile, and passionflower bloomed just shy of the back porch. The sweet scent of oleander reached her nose before she finally spotted the shoulder-high bushes in a gathering closer to the water. The perfume from the small white flowers reminded her of the neighborhood potluck picnics of her childhood where several families would meet near the banks of the Ashley River.

They brought with them enough meatloaf sandwiches, casseroles, potato salad, and brownies to feed an army. The floral essence of the oleander always caught the breeze and flavored their gatherings. It still made her think of Southern ladies in wide-brimmed sun hats who wore stockings and drank sweet tea. It was the scent of a more innocent time in her life, and she inhaled the fragrance deeply.

She walked along the pebble path that led to the portico where Tom stood waving. She waved back. Because of the number of shares she held in the private family corporation, Tom needed to have her buy-in and support on this—hope-fully—last restoration. This one *had* to go smoothly since there wasn't any more funding for another one.

Her former husband had led a resistance to the restoration within the group of Alcott family members. He had them convinced that tearing down the manor and selling it to developers would cost less and yield more. Some of his believers remained in the family. At Tom's request, and as the largest stockholder in the family-wide investment, she became the liaison between Tom's restoration work and the family. Sort of a restoration advocate, which she always had been anyway.

In these final stages, he wanted her onsite as much as possible—taking pictures of finished areas, being educated and up-to-date on everything that had been completed. Touting the positive and squashing the negative.

"Layla, you look amazing, sweetheart." The top section of Tom's blond hair lifted in the breeze and revealed a receding hairline. She guessed that he'd probably lost most of his hair trying to restore her ancestral home.

She felt a smile pull at the corners of her mouth, which she would have thought impossible given her dreadful morning. But she was nothing if not polite; in her book, manners were a consideration for others. "Thirty pounds so far this year and sixty overall."

"If only I were twenty years younger." Tom kissed her on both cheeks. "I appreciate you coming out, darlin'. I know this must be hard for you right now."

That was the second time someone had said those words to her this morning.

Tom finger combed the top part of his hair and she thought that made it look puffy.

"Not as hard as some other things. I'll be fine."

"Come on in." He patted her back when they walked through the kitchen door. "Coffee?"

"Yes. Please. Make mine a double."

The kitchen appeared just as it had in her dream, a rehabilitated snapshot frozen in time. It had a war-torn feeling, seeping from the walls like an endless fatigue. The manor had been through a lot over the years. She could relate.

He took two mugs from the lowest shelf and filled them to the brim.

She thought for a moment about how her dead husband had let his insurance policy lapse and increased hers to the max. He had two things on his mind—murder and money. The hot coffee hit her empty stomach and she struggled to keep it down.

She eyed the cake on the side table and caught her breath. A piece on the table had a bite taken out of it and three crumbs had fallen to the side.

Tom gestured to the cake. "Here. Help yourself. One slice won't hurt you. Two probably won't either. I have no idea how this got here, maybe one of the workers brought it in. Looks like someone already took a bite. Sorry about that. House full of men around here. You know how that goes."

Tom put a slice on a plate and handed it to her, and she took a bite. It tasted just as chocolatey as it had in her dream.

Tom went on about how he had hired a new builder who was taking care of the final repairs. She chewed her cake and nodded, but Tom's voice became almost inaudible. The half-eaten piece of cake on the table was exactly like the one she'd left in her lucid dream. A shiver of nerves and vulnerability twitched through her.

The cake competed with the numbers that were crowding her brain like traffic on the freeway at rush hour. In her typical style of delayed reaction, she realized that with Asher's quarter of a million dollars of debt following her around, she'd never be able to buy another house for her and her girls.

No one would give her a mortgage with that kind of debt. It would take her thirty years or more to clear it from her name. For the rest of the time that she had the girls with her, they would be crammed into whatever tiny apartment she could afford. Her girls were going to hate that. They were used to having a yard and a swing set and room to run.

She helped herself to another bite of cake. The fudgy chocolate taste was an old friend. The flavor worked its culinary magic and coated the prickly edges of her regrets.

Tom's voice cut into her thoughts. "All that to say I appreciate you taking the lead with your family organization. I really do want to finish up this restoration. For you. For the entire family." He squinted slightly and appeared to study her face.

She was sure he could tell she had been crying. Before she'd left her car, she checked her face in the rearview mirror and saw that her eyes were red. Her make-up was gone. Her lips were swollen, and she had that red blotch on the end of her nose that showed up when she had a hard cry.

Her ever-ready make-up bag was stocked full to the zipper, and she had reapplied her face as best she could. There wasn't anything she could have done about her red eyes.

The very thought of all that debt felt like a locomotive heading straight toward her in a dark tunnel. She took another bite. This was maybe the best cake she had ever eaten. Definitely not from a box.

"How did your meeting go this morning?" Tom sipped his coffee.

Yesterday she had told Tom she couldn't meet with him

first thing this morning, that she had to meet with her attorney first.

"Ah, well. Not as good as I'd hoped. Seems Asher let his life insurance policy lapse, and he left us about half a million dollars in debt. So, the bank is taking the house and I get to pay back the remaining three hundred thousand." She said the last bit of news as if she'd just won an award or gotten a promotion.

Tom's face sagged with worry. "Layla, I'm so sorry."

A memory of Asher's throaty laugh echoed through the crowded hallways of her mind. He was never happier than when Layla was burdened with a task that kept her at home or kept her weighted down.

"Where are you and the girls going to go?"

The absence of his life insurance policy made her want to scream. She chewed the last bite slowly. The taste and the texture covered the helpless feelings and made them less noticeable. But it also covered her teeth, so she put her hand over her mouth before she said, "Not sure yet. I'm gonna have to figure that out."

She smiled her professional closed-lip nurse's smile, the one that covered all potential concerns. Usually that expression was a comfort to patients' families, but Tom didn't appear to be comforted. Neither did he return her smile.

He shifted his position to lean against a work table, and his studious expression deepened with lines of concern. After a while he said, "You know, as a true Southerner, I can't help but think about how my mother would skin my hind end if I didn't help a woman in distress. Especially a woman with children. A good woman."

"No, Tom. I can handle this. Don't you worry, I'll work this out. I'll get money from the tours when the restoration is done. I have my nursing job. I shouldn't have said anything. This is all just so fresh."

"Money from the tours is a long way off. Listen—"

She pressed her lips together in a polite smile.

"The builder and I were just talking about bringing someone on who would be a caretaker for the property. We'd like for them to live here, give the house more of a homey feel. Maybe you'd want to take that job. It would give you and the girls a place to stay, for a while anyway. It's a short-term solution, but maybe this would give you a chance to get back on your feet."

"Gracious, I don't know anything about taking care of a historical property. I'm not handy. Most I could do to help around here would be to put in an IV or administer meds. Maybe take someone's pulse."

"We just need a—um, consistent presence here. The house has a dark history, as you know. That's part of what we think has attracted the ghosts and hauntings over the years. We've been told that having a regular presence throughout the manor would help us keep a more, ah, *positive* environment. We need people here around the clock. Stirs the energy up, apparently. In a good way. You and the girls could really help."

She didn't say anything, but she gave him a look that said that she questioned what he was saying, a look she'd honed over her many years as a mother.

"What I'm telling you is true," Tom said. "Now, I know this could be a little awkward, given that Asher died here. So, I'll understand if you just can't. But it's a huge house, you could effectively avoid that area if you wanted. I'd just like to help you however I can."

She felt everything about her soften in light of Tom's kindness. Trusting someone else for help didn't come easily to her these days, not after Asher. Not after a lot of things in life. Though she didn't think she could push away a helping hand, not now.

Someone yelled Tom's name from the front of the house. He patted the table between them once and hard, like a that's-that slap and turned to leave. "You think about it."

She squeezed her eyes tight for a moment. She and the girls had nowhere to go, and it was her responsibility to provide a safe home for them. "I'll take it temporarily. Just until the restoration is complete."

His broad smile was as bright and honest as the sun, and the warmth of it reached her heart. "Good deal."

The text alarm dinged on Tom's phone and he glanced at the screen. "I have to sign for a lumber delivery." He paused at the doorway that led to the main areas of the house and pointed to her. "Stay there. I'll be right back and we'll discuss details."

"Will do." She gave him a mock salute.

The distant hammerings in the house banged in counterpoint to one another, and she was certain she could feel their impact on the inside of her head. Heck of a morning.

Electric saws whirred. Men yelled unintelligible words to one another from other parts of the house.

Three hundred thousand dollars.

No life insurance.

The short curtains that framed the kitchen window ballooned on a breeze, and she thought she heard the distant echo of Asher's laughter.

The cake helped assuage some anger. She hadn't eaten any sweets since she started losing the weight—sleep eating aside. Today was a special occasion. Yes, very special. She cut a half slice this time and took a giant bite.

"Uh-uh-uhhh..." she heard Asher say. His no-no-nos to

her were stronger than a memory, but not as loud as an actual voice. She took a huge bite that nearly filled her cheeks.

"Tom—oh, hey. Sorry. I was looking for Tom."

A fit and fabulous ginger-eyed man waved and smiled from the doorway. His equally fabulous white-toothed grin plowed into her like a speeding truck.

"Mmfm." She knew him immediately but remembered her mouth was full of chocolate cake and pressed her lips together.

Adrenaline shot through her body like a spray of fireworks. This was the Mason she'd grown up with, the one she went to senior prom with, the one who had been her best friend since they were in junior high together. The one she had secretly hoped to marry.

She couldn't blame him for not recognizing her, it had been ten years since they had seen one another. And aside from her significant weight loss, she had grown her hair down to her elbows, and, oh, dyed it light blonde.

The short sleeves of Mason's red T-shirt were stretched to accommodate his oversized biceps. When he extended his hand, she noticed the substantial muscles on his forearm, and here she was with cake in her mouth. He probably never ate cake.

"I'm Mason Holloway."

His confident smile radiated, and his chest puffed when he strolled—cool and self-assured—in her direction. If she hadn't known all the other sides of him, she would have thought him vain, showing off his best attributes front and center. He displayed every good look he had to offer like a fisherman's lure, trying to attract his target. He'd never approached her like that before, and that only sped the fireworks inside of her.

His hand reached for her face and a faraway memory of prom night revisited her. He'd reached for her then, too. He'd touched the back of her neck, brought her to him and kissed her full on the lips. Their first kiss.

Her first kiss ever.

Her heart remembered that night and jump started into a rat-a-tat-tat.

His eyes shifted from hers to the side of her face. He picked something from the side of her mouth.

"You like cake?" He held the substantial crumb for her to see, then tossed it into his mouth. Another grin.

"Mmm." She fought the rest of the chocolate that covered the front parts of her teeth. "Always have," she said from behind her hand.

His expression softened, like he saw something familiar but wasn't able to place what it was. "I think chocolate cake just became my new favorite dessert."

It was like being at a masked ball where you knew your suitor, but they had no idea who you were. She rather liked this arrangement.

Tom rounded the corner. "Sorry about that, Layla—oh, I see you've met Mason, our builder. He and his team are doing all the heavy lifting for the final repairs."

"I knew that was you!" Mason's accent had remained Southern strong. His grin widened into open-mouthed surprise.

With her lips together, she continued to run her tongue over the front of her teeth to clear away all traces of the treat she wasn't supposed to have. Then she finally said, "Hey, Mason."

His smile was a life preserver from her past, tossed to her in this sea of chaos. She remembered everything about him, but the hug she especially recognized.

Everyone hugged differently, especially men when they hugged a female friend. Some kept a little distance, others squeezed and swayed, some patted repetitively like a nervous habit or a dog with an itch.

Mason went for full contact, body to body. Then he held you there, gentle and snug against the upper half of him that was firm and strong. This time he topped off his signature hug with a kiss to her cheek, as though she'd just returned from vacation.

She also remembered the guilt she used to feel when she was around him. At least toward the end.

"My goodness, sweetheart. Don't you look amazing!"

With her hands in his, he extended her arms and looked down and up again. "Unbelievable. How long has it been?"

"Well, hopefully not *that* unbelievable."

"No, I just meant—"

"It's okay." She ran her hand along the front of her scrubs, pleased that she was down six (SIX!!) clothing sizes since the last time he saw her. She was even more pleased that her transformation left him tripping over his tongue.

This was almost one of those dream come true moments —where the boy you crushed on for half your life shows up unexpectedly and you look terrific.

"With long hair—and blonde, no less? You're out to break hearts, Layla-pop." He clicked his tongue against the roof of his mouth.

"I told her as much myself. How do y'all know each other?" Tom asked.

Mason ran his hand over his short brown hair and dusted the back of it with his palm, as if the teacher had just scolded him to keep his hands to himself. A boyish move, and just the way he would have done it ten or fifteen years ago. "We grew up together. Playmates, fishing buddies, partners in crime. Thick as thieves until—uh. Well, I guess going off to college separated us."

That obviously wasn't the reason, but she knew he hadn't forgotten. The end of their friendship had been as traumatic as any romantic breakup.

"This world is just one big small town some days." Tom rested his hands on his hips and shifted his glance between the two of them. "Mason, you must not have realized it, but *this* is who agreed to serve as our liaison with the rest of the Alcott family members. She's the largest stockholder in the family."

"Wow. Okay. It *is* a small world."

"She has been a strong voice for the benefits of our continued restoration. So far we haven't had any more...resistance."

Tom turned to Layla. "Sorry, sweetheart. I was trying not to bring him up." His voice was low and tinged with regret for her.

She shrugged. "It is what it is."

"Well, anyway." He sidled close to her and hugged her twice. "I've offered her the caretaker position we discussed and she's accepted. She has two young girls, so there will be lots of activity throughout the manor while they're around."

"That's great. Really good."

He sounded genuinely pleased at the news, and her nerves settled a little. The fireworks didn't.

"So, you're the builder?" she said.

"Yeah, took over my dad's business."

"Wow." A slow squiggle of guilt and panic wormed through her insides. "What happened to New York?"

"Change of heart. Change of plans. Long story. So, you're going to live here for a while, huh?"

"Yeah, for a little while." Her heart broke into a jog, and

she caught herself glancing at the door that led to the outside. Run. She wanted to run. She wanted cake and a quick escape.

"That's great. Well, I'm here all day long and half the night. It'd be great to catch up."

"She's going to keep an eye on things for us," Tom said. "Keep the energy moving in the right direction."

"Tom brought Dixie in to try to figure out how to keep the manor's more mystical events to a minimum. Right, Tom?" Mason's tone held just the slightest mocking flavor.

"I know how you feel about psychics and the paranormal in general, Mason. But your mother was quite good." Tom turned to Layla. "Regular activity in every room, every day is supposed to keep the energy fresh and active. We were going to put a plant in each room to remind us to water it. But she wanted us to have *a lot* of regular activity throughout the house. Not just an in and out of a few rooms here and there. House needs to feel loved and lived in."

"I don't think houses *feel* anything," Mason scoffed, and his handsome face hardened just enough to show he didn't think anything was funny.

"Rooms can get stagnant when no one has been in them for a while. I've heard that emptiness can breed a sort of negative energy that attracts ghosts," Layla said.

"Neither of you have seen some of the things that have happened in this house like I have. If you had, you might be a little more believing," Tom said.

"Not me." Mason winked at Layla.

He obviously assumed she would agree with him. So she smiled her sweet smile, the one she often used in new situations, the one that covered what she really believed. Deep down, another wriggle of panic reminded her that Mason had never been able to flow with anything that wasn't logical.

Tom waved Mason off. "Never mind him. Let's talk about when you can move in."

She ran her fingers around her lips, hoping there weren't any remaining crumbs. "I guess I'll need a few days to get everything packed."

"Let me know if you need any help." Yet another grin from Mason, one that came with a steady gaze that was downright flirty.

His behavior took her by surprise. So did the goosebumps that slid over her body. She had forgotten just how deeply certain smiles from him affected her.

The heavy front door opened with a groan.

"Layla?" Peyton's voice rang out.

Layla excused herself and called to her sister from the doorway to let her know where she was. "I hope you don't mind, I asked my sister to meet me here."

"No, no, no. Of course not." Tom's first no was the highest and the loudest. The two 'no's that followed dropped in tone like notes in a song. It was the tune of a Southern gentleman, and Tom was that through and though. "It's more your house than mine."

Layla knew how the reintroduction with Mason would go down, and she prepared herself emotionally. Peyton was a beautiful woman. Her slender figure, blunt cut long brown hair and bangs that grazed her soft brown eyes would assure that she garnered all the attention in the room.

"Sorry I'm late." Peyton breezed into the kitchen like she'd been in and out of the manor all her life, like she owned the space around her. She had her black on, her big city uniform that included a tailored suit jacket that said she was ready for business.

She kissed and hugged Layla first, her perfume drifting through the air like a quiet statement of elegance. "Look at you, you gorgeous thing." Peyton hugged her again. Then she spun around and began to shake hands. Tom, she'd met. But she hadn't seen him for some time, so she reintroduced herself.

When Peyton turned toward Mason, Layla felt a little twinge in her chest. She'd enjoyed the renewed connection she and Mason had shared. She didn't want to see Peyton take part in the same thing, though she knew Peyton would stun him into a near speechless stare. That was just the effect she had on men.

"Peyton. It's good to see you again." He kissed her on the cheek.

That was that.

No hugs, no lightning strikes or love songs floating through the air.

Layla decided she was the only one who was stunned. She definitely wasn't used to being the one who got all the attention.

"What a small world. Did you know Mason was working here?" Peyton asked Layla as if Mason weren't in the room.

"No, complete surprise. I thought he was still in New York."

"Your sister is staying on with us for a while." Mason nodded to Layla, and she felt her skin flush warm. She also noticed how quickly he had changed the subject.

"Here?" Peyton asked.

"She's really helping us out. She can tell you all about it." After a moment, Tom patted Mason on the shoulder twice. "Come on, Mason. You need to find a place for that lumber you ordered. It's on the front drive."

Mason nodded. "Layla, let me know if I can help you

with anything." He handed her his business card. "That's my cell phone number there on the front." He lingered a moment longer, then he and Tom stepped into the next room.

Layla reached to her sister and pinched her on the arm.

"Ow!" Peyton slapped her sister's hand. "What are you doing?"

"Nothing. Just making sure."

Layla felt an old familiar wind of harsh emotion sweep through her. As if it worked its way from the outside in. She'd felt it from Asher before and curiously whenever things turned positive. Like when she'd gotten a promotion at work, or when one of the girls' teachers complimented her or just when her flower garden birthed particularly beautiful blooms.

Her happiness sent him into a briar patch of severe insecurity. He never admitted as much, but her theory was that if she were happy and independent, he thought she might leave him.

When they met and married shortly thereafter, she had been close to eighty pounds overweight. Terribly low on confidence. She knew something about him preferred her that way. Without strength. Without hope. Without options.

Positive signs were flickering around her. Mason had reappeared in her life today. Someone who had always been kind, supportive and complimentary. Someone who had given her strength. At least up until the end. And Tom Watson had offered her an assist—a shelter in a storm.

If Asher's spirit were still around, all of those things would make him angry enough to not only take them away from her, but angry enough to work those people out of her life. Maybe even angry enough to do what he had obviously planned for some time now: murder.

A small dog bark sounded from the next room, and Layla and Peyton peered around the corner.

"Well, where'd you come from, little fella?" Tom held a small golden terrier that licked at his face.

Mason picked up a red rubber ball and tossed it lightly into the air. The dog barked and wagged his tail.

"Sure is cute. Does he have a tag?" Mason asked.

Tom spun the collar around. The tiny bell on its red collar jingled.

Layla shook her head and leaned against the wall.

"Are you okay?" Peyton asked.

"Yeah. I just—it's the manor. I need some air."

5

Asher paced slowly through the distinguished antebellum hallways of Alcott Manor. When he passed one of the wall sconces, he flicked a dangling crystal to watch it swing. The black and white marble floors were flanked with deep mahogany wainscoting. The walls and arched ceilings were inlaid with rose-colored marble and heavy crown moldings in a style that mimicked the finest European castles.

But as impressive as the manor's finishings had always been, Asher never gave them much of a thought. They never stirred his imagination or sense of family pride. Instead, it was the land that infatuated him. It sent him dreaming of a tourist resort with condos and all the money that would come from that development.

In fact, being at the manor usually reminded him of what he could have had, of what he didn't have. Being at the manor usually sent him into a rage. Because Layla stopped him time and again with a cruel flick of the vote in the wrong direction.

He had invested so much time with her, banking on the

fact that he could sway her vote. And for quite a few years he had her right where he wanted her. She bought his act without question—his camera-ready smile, the tailored button-down shirts in subtle, soft colors, his patient listening through hidden and gritted teeth.

But then, bit by bit, he realized his control over her was slipping. That's when he started to feel a slight burning in his gut, like heat rising from the cinders of his best laid plans.

The heat intensified when she once refused to make his evening tea. And it grew hotter still when she began to set her jaw just so, a blatantly defiant move. The burn spread through him like a wildfire when he heard her on the phone with a divorce attorney. And when she didn't vote her Alcott Manor stock the way he told her to, the burn became a liquid heat, like lava that churned, driving his rage to new heights.

He stopped his nightly stroll and pushed on the newel at the top of the stairs—back and forth. Anna Alcott had commissioned carved seahorses to sit at the top and bottom of the grand staircase. Tom and Mason had had them recreated beautifully. The more Asher loosened it, the more it became the hazard he wanted it to be.

Layla would be living at the manor soon, and as a pseudo-caretaker, she would make as many trips around the manor as he did. That gave him the perfect opportunity to line up a payback event. Something catastrophic and deadly that would bring her to him for a happily ever after they could share within the confines of the manor. It would also prove to Mason once and for all who had the final say in their ongoing competition.

The base of the newel gave way with a crack, and Asher felt a satisfying release. The seahorse wobbled, and he envisioned Layla leaning on it and taking a header down the staircase.

That made him think. What if one of his girls happened upon one of his traps he had intended for Layla? He crossed his arms and rubbed his middle finger along the base of his lower lip. The pendulum of the grandfather clock clicked slowly behind him as if his answer were being timed. Did he mind if one or both of his daughters took up residence with him in Alcott Manor?

Might not be a bad idea. Might be a nice family reunion. Might even be motivation for Layla to join them.

If none of his traps worked on Layla, he had a Plan B.

He could get to her through the magic combination of the manor and that special dreaming of hers.

He walked to the window at the end of the second floor hallway and opened it. He tried to lean into the ocean air, but he met a firm resistance. The house wouldn't allow him to go that far. He was stuck. The house owned him.

Soon, it would own Layla, too.

6

Mason hoisted the last bag of woodworking supplies into the back of his dad's old red pick-up truck and slammed the tail gate shut. All the building materials were housed at the manor. The sanding and staining items he used on the old Alcott kitchen work table were his own, though, and he had forgotten them today. So, he ran home to get them and looked forward to working on that project over his breaks and lunch hour. As usual.

Tom had suggested they take the table to a furniture restoration specialist in town. They had already taken several pieces to the business, and there was certainly room in the budget for one more. That way Mason wouldn't have to use his time and effort on restoring a table.

Mason refused the offer. He enjoyed the physical work of putting his hands on the wood, sanding away the old stain and imperfections and giving this gorgeous piece a second life. He was not only happy to spend his free time in that way, he looked forward to it.

Working with his hands was the one bright spot in his

work at the manor, the place where his life had gone askew over a decade ago. That was the night when his life broke from its close-to-perfect track and never quite recovered. That was the night when someone ruined the future he thought he might have had with Layla.

His mind dragged him back to that awful night: His former girlfriend Brooke in her sleeping bag, the back of her head smashed and sopped in blood. The police never figured out who did it, though Mason always suspected that it had been Asher. There had always been a strange competitiveness between the two of them. It seemed to peak around then.

He often thought how different his life would have been if they had never camped on the great lawn that night. Beautiful as it was, there was something deeply wrong with that house. As if its only legacy was death and the destruction of dreams.

He was there once again for one primary reason—Layla Alcott. After all this time, his dream for them was finally moving forward. He had bid to repair the destruction that was imposed on the historical home, with the specific intent to reconnect with her.

Her extended family had a business that owned and managed the property, its restoration, and, they hoped, the revenue it would bring in. Tom had mentioned that she served as the liaison between him and the family organization and that she had been a positive force for their efforts.

The papers had posted an older picture when they ran the story about Asher's death, one where she appeared to be just a slightly older version of the friend he knew and loved when they were growing up. When he met her in person, he hardly recognized her.

She had the same wry sense of humor and the same

beautiful smile. Though she was a smidgen of the size she used to be, her hair was longer and she had dyed it bright blonde. She looked like one of those models they featured on tourism commercials for visiting Charleston and their nearby beaches.

She didn't seem all that upset that Asher was dead and gone from her life. When Tom brought up Asher's name, and not in a positive way, she just shrugged. "It is what it is," she had said. So he guessed the shine from that jewel of a marriage had dulled a long time ago. Maybe she had used whatever disappointment there as a motivation to achieve her own personal goals. He hoped, anyway. He wanted her happy.

He threw his workout bag into the front seat, pushed the old knob gear shift down and into reverse, then sat there with his hands at ten and two on the wheel. He would ask her out for dinner. Today.

Question was, could she forgive him? He had a pretty big mistake to make up for. He had tried to make things right with her, though he hadn't succeeded.

Was the past really the past for her?

The way he felt about her today—his unwavering sense of finality and conviction that she was *the one* for him—might be difficult for anyone else to understand. Particularly since they hadn't seen one another for over a decade. Yet it made perfect sense to him. Finally, anyway.

He had been happiest when he was around Layla, and she had always been his person: the one he wanted to share everything with—his secrets, his celebrations, every bit of his free time. She had a gift for getting him out of his head, for broadening his horizons, for taking him on a guided tour beyond his comfort zone. His friendship with her was the most real, the truest happiness he'd ever known. Unfortunately, he had to lose her to realize that.

And there was that kiss. He'd had thousands of kisses from pretty girls in his lifetime, and none that he could remember all that clearly. But the first time he kissed Layla —that one never left his memory.

Nearly every detail replayed in his mind with haunting accuracy—beams of light that sparkled like flickering stars on the water, "Up Where We Belong" echoing across the lake from some neighbor's gathering, the feeling of forever dancing around them as easily and gently as every meant-to-be-moment did.

"Hey—"

Mason jumped so hard he thought he pulled a muscle. "Good grief, Mama." He placed his hand on his stomach. "Give a guy some notice, would you?"

His mother's toothy smile showed him that she didn't feel one bit sorry for the fact that she had startled him. In fact, her shoulders shook with a silent laugh. "Well, darlin', I'm parked right behind you, it's not like I was hidin'." She gestured to her dark blue Honda that was indeed parked right behind him. With the engine running, no less.

He knew she had just been to her morning yoga class at the YMCA. She wore her thick black leggings and a sleeveless, loose-fitting shirt. Her brown, naturally curly hair was twisted into a high ponytail, and loose ringlets framed her face.

He turned the engine off. "What's up?" He extended his arm toward her through the open window and she put her hand in his. He squeezed it. That was the closest he could get to giving her a hug right now.

"I heard something in my spirit this morning. Clear as day." She patted her heart three times for emphasis.

"Oh, Mama." He took his hand back and rested his head in it. "Not this again."

"No, now listen. This is important. Very important." Her soft brown curls danced around her face when she shook her head. He often wondered how she got them to move like a visual exclamation point.

"I'm late. Can we schedule some time to do this later? Or not at all?"

"I heard there's someone new in your life and that it's someone I know. Is that true?"

It wasn't lost on him that she ignored his objection completely. "No one said anything to you this morning about my personal life."

"I'm not going to debate with you about how I got my information. I just shared that so you won't think I'm being nosy or that I'm snooping."

"No, of course not." He flashed her a sarcastic smile that he knew would earn him a pinch on the arm.

And it did.

"She also said a few other things. Important things. As in there are some dangerous things going on at the manor." She pressed a finger against his arm to make a point. "But before I share those pieces of information, I want you to tell me if that's true about the first part."

Mason leaned toward the shiny steering wheel and banged his forehead against it several times. When he finally lifted it up again he said, "Why, Mama? You know I don't believe in this stuff. And honestly, you shouldn't either."

"Enough. Spill." She waved him off with a regal swipe of her hand.

He sighed, long and slow. "There isn't anyone new in my life." He put air quotes around the word 'new'. "Unless you're talking about Layla Alcott. I saw her at the manor this morning."

His mother gave a quiet gasp and pressed the tips of her fingers against her lips. "How did that go?"

"Well, first of all, she's not *in* my life. We've only just reconnected." He told her the story about how the bank took her house and how Tom offered her the caretaker position.

"Good. You know that caretaker position was my idea. You need lots of activity around that place day and night. It needs a new infusion of positive energy."

"Please don't bring it up."

"Listen. If she got hired for that caretaker position, then my work has helped you. This will give you a chance to spend time with her. Make things right. Move things forward. You haven't changed your mind about her, have you? I do think y'all are meant to be."

"No. I haven't. And I agree." He smiled his sweet smile this time and held his hand out to her again. She waited a beat before she put her hand in his. He gave it a little shake. "I do have to run, though."

"Alright. Are you coming for dinner tonight? I have a few other things I need to pass on to you. Important things. Safety issues. Has to do with Alcott Manor. I keep hearing there's some kind of threat—"

"I figured."

"All right. Here." She handed him several folded news-paper pages with the black and white crossword puzzle on the front. "I saved these for you from last week's paper."

"Thanks, Mama." She kissed him on the cheek and he took the crossword puzzles and placed them on the seat next to him. She had done things like this for him since he was a little boy. He was a little surprised he didn't see a stick of gum taped to the top puzzle.

"Oh, and when I come by tonight, I don't want to talk about whatever you heard about me. I really don't."

"See you about six-thirty?" She walked toward her car.

"Mama—"

She raised her arm over her head and waved behind her.

"Daddy always said that arguing with Dixie Holloway was just fighting a losing battle," he murmured.

He thought about how she tried to be more open about her gifts when he and his brother were in elementary school. She did a reading for the minister's wife, only that foray didn't go as well as she thought it would.

They learned that when Mrs. Milligan asked if her husband was cheating, she didn't really want an honest answer to that question. When word got out that Dixie had exposed Reverend Milligan's indiscretion, they also learned that the community was not nearly as accepting of her abilities as she thought they would be. He and his brother weren't invited back to their private school, the country club didn't renew their membership, and his father lost his biggest clients. Not to mention the neighbors became far less friendly and much more...condemningly curious.

His dad never said it was Dixie's fault that their lives as they knew it disappeared. Though he did say that the world was an insecure and judgmental place.

Mason's takeaway was that anything paranormal was an unnecessary and unadvised choice. Caused nothing but harm. Especially in today's world. Not to mention that he really didn't believe in it. So he continued, in vain apparently, to convince Dixie to stay away from it.

"I can't help that I have gifts," she would say.

From his side view mirror he watched her get in her car.

She waved sweetly with each of her fingers moving independently, then backed her car out of his driveway.

He really hadn't wanted his mom to know that he had spoken to Layla, at least not yet. Since she had known Layla so well when they were growing up, it wouldn't be unlike her to drop by the manor and ask way too many questions. Share too much.

He didn't want her at the manor again. Not yet. Not ever, really. The paranormal wrecked his life once before. Now he would do whatever he had to in order to keep that stuff out of his life forever.

7

The night wind howled against the outer walls of Alcott Manor.

It rattled the shutters and sent a subtle breeze past the warped glass of the windows and across the upper balcony of the interior. Tom tried to ignore the unsettling moan and instead made a note to replace the sealants on the upper floor windows.

He also tried to tune out the strange energy that crept about the manor like an invisible intruder. It was a presence that filled empty spaces and stalked his every move. If he had his choice, he would have left Alcott Manor a long time ago and never so much as looked at it in his rearview mirror. But he had made a promise to a dear friend that he would finish the restorations on this house, for the benefit of his company and all their employees. And so he would keep his word.

He scribbled a few more notes and wondered for probably the twentieth time if he should have extended that offer to Layla. She was a grown woman, he argued. She knew about the manor's history and how odd it could be. He couldn't have just stood there and offered her nothing but sympathy. Mason was here as much as, if not more than he was. He would tell him to keep a close watch on her, to help her with the evening rounds.

He looked up from his paper. A human-sized shadow shifted along the wall and disappeared behind an open door as quick as a blink. He stood rock solid still and stared at the wall where muted gold paint glimmered innocently. Like nothing had happened.

"Trick of the light," he said in a you-don't-scare-me tone. He side-stepped away from the top of the stairs just the same. Casually. Like he knew someone was watching him and he didn't want to let on how he really felt.

He had gone to West Point, served in the Army. He had faced down enemies that would make most grown men cry for their mamas. He was strong, he knew, and shouldn't feel afraid.

But the presence was there again, lurking nearby as it sometimes did when Tom walked the house alone. Like an uninvited guest, the presence was an interloper he couldn't quite explain. A ghost, maybe. The house had always had them.

He shook the newel at the top of the grand staircase. It wobbled like its stability had been worn by decades of use. He knew Mason had just repaired and reinstated all of the iron balusters and posts.

"Someone could get really hurt because of this."

He held his clipboard steady and scribbled yet another item on his repair list for Mason. The base would have to be rebuilt. There were nine items so far tonight, nine broken pieces that hadn't been in need of repair on the night before. He had yet to finish making his rounds, and he knew there might be another nine before he called it quits.

He glanced over the balcony, remembering in a flash how Asher's body looked after he'd fallen to his death.

He'd arrived at the manor on the morning after it happened, the detectives had shown him the digital pictures. The broken and bloody plank rose from Asher's midsection with valiant success, like the manor was proud to have removed an enemy. After a while, the house seemed to take on a new air. Something darker, something that had intent. Something that seemed to have a personal vendetta.

If Asher were dead and hanging out in this house, that was fine. For all the harm he had caused in the world, he should be sentenced to life as a ghost. Tom stared at the open door for a moment, then stormed toward it to prove a point. He yanked the door away from the wall and saw only the empty wall and freshly polished hardwood flooring. He exhaled.

Since the latest round of repairs had begun, Tom had committed to a nightly tour of the manor. He'd told Mason it was just to keep track of their progress—sort of like a one man oversight committee. But the reality was that he didn't trust Alcott Manor. Or who might be wandering around in it.

The ocean breeze blew harder this time, hard enough to rattle the panes. Only now the air carried a scent, one he'd smelled before. Cologne. Alcohol-based and too strong. It turned his stomach. Made him search the room.

He didn't see spirits. But now he wondered if the presence he sensed was Asher Cardill. If his spirit were still in the house, he could be the source of the strange smells, the shadows, and the unexplained damages.

"You're dead, Asher. Go home. Alcott Manor will never be yours."

Dixie had told him to say that whenever he thought he

might be in the presence of a spirit. "Sometimes they don't even know they're dead," she'd told him. "Sometimes letting them know that they're no longer alive can help to move them on."

Tom's shoes clicked across the hardwood as he left the area and headed toward the upstairs sitting area. If he hadn't been so well-grounded and open-minded, he might have questioned his sanity when he heard the distant cackle. He rubbed his hand against his chin. Maybe he really was somewhere in this house.

He would reach out to Dixie, to see if she could get rid of a resident ghost. If this was Asher, he was there to make trouble, just as he had been in life.

When he reached the carpeted hallway that led to the master bedrooms, the air chilled. He wasn't imagining it, it was several degrees cooler in this area. This was another sign Dixie had warned him about. The presence of a ghost often lowered the temperature.

"Your days here are numbered, Asher. You're yesterday's news." Tom pushed past the cold spot and opened the door to Anna Alcott's bedroom. Doors were supposed to be left open to completely air out the scent of paint and staining chemicals. He'd told the crew that time and again, and still the doors on this hallway remained closed. He made another note on his list for Mason: Leave all doors open!!!

Then he remembered that he would have to tell Layla the same thing.

That's when the thought occurred to him. *Layla.* What if Asher wasn't just in the manor as a squatter? What if he wasn't only trying to make trouble for them by continuing to ruin the final repairs? What if his real goal was to get to Layla?

Tom looked at some of the items on his list: loose newel,

broken step, frayed wires...Asher wasn't just trying to make trouble. He was setting the stage for an accident. A fatal one. He realized he couldn't let Layla stay at the manor now. He couldn't take the chance.

The sound of water running echoed through the otherwise quiet. There was splashing, like someone was filling a tub.

He would have to have the water turned off at all the access points on the top floor. First, he had to make a call. Tom pulled his phone from his pocket and dialed Layla's number. "Run all the water you want," Tom whispered into the empty bedroom. "I'm putting an end to this right now."

Tom's heart banged too hard against his rib cage and his chest started to ache. Why hadn't he made this connection between the ongoing damages and Asher sooner? Layla's phone rang two times, three times, four times...

"Dang it, girl. Pick up." Her voicemail answered and he hung up and dialed her number again. He hoped she wasn't on her way over to the manor with a load of belongings. She had told him she might drop a few things off tonight once she got the kids settled. He'd told her to call him first so he could let her in and help her carry a load or two. But he hadn't heard from her.

He also hoped she wasn't downstairs arranging things. Maybe Mason had come with her to let her in, help her out. An oily chill slid along his insides. He'd seen the spark between Mason and Layla. If Asher had seen it, too, then he would want her as dead as he was.

The water continued to pour in the tub next door, and Tom could see how the bathroom floor would be flooded soon.

"That's exactly what he wants. He wants me to hang up and go turn off that water. Meanwhile he'll go downstairs and get to her before I can." Layla's voicemail picked up again. "Layla, this is Tom. Listen. I need to tell you something. We've had a change in plans and I need you to call me right away. We're going to have to make other living arrangements for you. Don't come to the manor. Call me." He hung up and dialed her number again.

The splashing was quiet now, and he knew the water level must be high enough in the tub that the running water no longer made a noise. That meant it was probably overflowing. He thought quickly about which room was beneath Benjamin Alcott's master bath: the dining room. The one room with coffered ceilings and 14 carat gold accents, all of which would be ruined if water leaked on it from above.

With his phone still to his ear, Tom walked cautiously to Benjamin Alcott's master bedroom. The heavy wooden door was closed. The hinges groaned when he pushed the door open.

"Hello?"

"Layla? It's Tom, honey. Listen, I'm sorry to bother you so late, but this is important."

"I had my ringer off, and I just noticed that you called. Is everything okay?"

The master bedroom was drenched in red—from the curtains to the bed canopy to the carpet—and it was freezing. The cold landed hard on his skin and made him shiver. The bathroom door at the end of the bedroom was wide open, and the marble bathtub was in plain view.

The faucets were turned on all the way and water spilled over the edge of the outer rim of the oval-shaped tub. Water leaked from the tile floor into the bedroom, turning that area of the carpet a deeper shade of red.

"Tom?"

"Everything is fine, sweetheart." He felt nothing of the

sort. "Nothing to worry about. Just a little hitch in our caretaker arrangement, but I'll help you work something else
out."

"Oh?"

He could feel her panic through the phone. She was in a
bad spot and needed a place to live. Or maybe that was his
panic. The room was so cold he started to shake on the
inside.

"It's okay, I'll help you find another place in the meantime. This is probably just going to be a short delay." He
kept his voice calm. The wet carpet squished under his step.

The water ran soundlessly into the tub, and the overflow
splashed onto the tile floor and echoed off the white walls.
Yes, he'd get someone out here ASAP to get rid of Asher,
then everything would settle down.

He searched the bathroom. It was empty. No one in
sight. But he could feel Asher, feel his presence as if it were a
second skin. And he could feel Asher watching his every
move.

"Oh? Why's that?" Disappointment weighed heavy in
her voice.

With that he changed his mind, he *should* tell her his
theory that Asher was in the house, because that would
keep her away. He didn't want her to get hurt. He reached
over the tub, and the first lever squeaked when he moved it
to the off position.

"Well, I guess this might sound a little far-fetched to
someone who hasn't spent as much time in the manor as I
have, but I'll just ask you to keep an open mind here for a
minute."

ASHER STOOD close to Tom while he leaned over the tub on tiptoe to reach the levers. Flooding the bathroom had been easier than he thought it would. Moving things just took concentration, that's what he'd learned today. Extraordinary concentration with focused intent made things happen. But that was true no matter what your desire in life, right?

Like right now. He couldn't have Tom ruining what was left of his life. Layla was almost within his grasp.

Benjamin Alcott's bathtub was wide and raised, and Tom stretched over it oh so precariously. Perfect position.

Asher focused hard. He placed his palms on Tom's head. One... Two... Three. He shoved with all his might and Tom slipped and slammed his head against the side of the tub. A metallic tone rang into the room. The upper half of him slid into the water along with his phone. Tiny bubbles and a sinewy thread of blood rose to the surface.

Asher brushed his hands against one another. "Nothing to worry about," he said in the direction of Tom's phone, where Layla's name shone brightly on the screen. "Nothing to worry about."

8

P eyton and Layla stood on their mother's gray cement driveway with the red brick edging. Layla told Peyton about the insurance policy, the caretaker position, and finding Mason in the manor. In turn, her sister responded with bolstering, confidence-enhancing advice about how to handle this unexpected information, which largely boiled down to: Take the job! Move into the manor!

"I wonder if Jayne Ella feels any guilt over how she pressured me to marry Asher. Considering how all that turned out. Considering what his motives really were."

"If Jayne Ella feels any amount of guilt about anything, then there's hope for the world yet." Peyton side-hugged her two quick times.

Layla glanced at the darkened backyard where she and Peyton played for hours in the plastic pool with the tiny slide. Peyton would dutifully empty the pool whenever too many grass shavings floated in the water, and Layla would get the hose to refill it. Their mother had since replaced that area of the yard with a fancy in-ground pool that had a tanning ledge and a hot tub. For her granddaughters.

"What do you think about living at the manor? I know it's got that creepy history because people have died there. But Mason's working there and that could be a positive, right? He couldn't take his eyes off you at the manor." Peyton lifted her hair off the back of her neck and turned into the breeze.

"I think I ought to ask our mother for the money."

"Oh," Peyton said like she had been punched in the gut. "I don't think that's a good idea. In fact, I think that's a down-right bad idea."

"There isn't anyone else who has that kind of money," Layla said.

"She'll hold it over your head. If you borrow from her, she'll use the debt as a weapon to control you. You'll never be free of her."

"The bank's not any different. They'll own my soul until I pay them off."

"But they won't dole out emotional blackmail and send you on expensive guilt trips like Jayne Ella."

Layla pressed at a stress pain just over her eyebrow. If she looked in the mirror she was sure she'd see her mother's face over that spot. Jayne Ella had that kind of effect on a person.

"Then maybe she would pay off this debt as an advance on my inheritance."

"I can hear her now. 'Layla just couldn't wait until I was dead. She had to have my money now.'" Peyton's voice was high and her accent was heavily Southern when she imitated their mother.

"Better that you push hard to get the manor ready for

tours so you can have that income. Jayne Ella has been good with the girls?" Peyton asked.

"She's been better about helping with them than their father was." Asher, while he perfected the role of ideal dad when the girls were around, had a different point of view when she needed babysitting support. "You wanted 'em, you work out the childcare."

"A lot of men don't help. You weren't alone on that."

Weren't. Past tense. Relief flowed like she'd crossed the finish line in some sort of painful race. She survived her husband and a marriage that nearly took her down with it. She stretched her jaw open and it clicked.

When Asher proposed soon after they'd started dating, Jayne Ella told her: *Take it! Girls like you don't have many options! Take the offer!*

Peyton pressed her lips tightly together, and Layla knew her sister was working hard to hold in all the words that wanted to spill forth. She knew Peyton would much rather see her in Alcott Manor with all its creepiness than owe their mother anything.

"Look. I just want you to be able to take care of yourself, and you would save a ton of money by staying there. It's obviously not a perfect environment, but not having to pay rent, insurance, electricity, trash, recycling—that's probably, what? A thousand a month? Maybe more when it's all totaled?"

"Yes, but last time I was there I saw something--a few somethings, actually--that just sort of wigged me out."

"You're not looking to live there forever. By the time you move out, you'll have saved enough to put a down payment on a small house for you and the girls. We can all do what-ever we have to when it's short-term. Right? Particularly when there's a payoff at the end."

Layla had rationalized that seeing the dog and the cake were just weird coincidences. Remembering the cake crumbs sent a shimmy of adrenaline through her. They also reminded her she had to be careful. Because she'd learned the hard way a long time ago that her lucid dreaming at the manor made things happen in her waking world as well.

"And I have a bad history with the manor. None of it bodes well."

"Your history with the manor happened in high school. I doubt anyone still blames you for Brooke's death. The police cleared you. Not to mention if our mother gives you the money *that* would end up being a total nightmare."

Peyton's wide-eyed expressions were so much like their father's. Layla had very few memories of her father anymore, since he only spent time with his new family. She still referred to them as new, although after all this time his family wasn't that new anymore. "A nightmare at a distance, though. Which is better than sharing space with one."

"If you're feeling guilty, don't. Brooke's death and the way Mason acted, none of that was your fault."

Layla sighed. It actually was her fault. That guilt weighed heavy, like she carried a bag of rocks on her back.

"It was just an awful time, and I don't want to relive it. Not with Mason, or anyone. I have enough going on in my life right now. If Mom gives me a reasonable out, I'm taking it. It would be better than staying at the manor. Stuff just goes bad there."

Their mother and both of Layla's girls walked outside, each of them balancing a book on their head.

Jayne Ella's large bust, slender waist and tailored clothing made Layla think her mother was stuck in the 1950s. Everything about her was Sears catalog perfect.

"Oh! Peyton! Sweetheart!" Jayne Ella let the book slip

from her bottle-red head and gave her eldest daughter a kiss on each cheek and examined her outfit. "Welcome home, honey. Don't you just look *sharp*?!"

"Aunt Peyton!" Layla's daughters squealed.

"Emma! Gracious, honey. Even in a ponytail your hair is about to touch your waist," Peyton said. "And Anna Kate, good heavens, I'm almost looking right into your eyes you're so tall!"

"Have you lost more weight?" Jayne Ella ran her hand over the back of Layla's scrubs and pulled on the extra fabric at her waistline.

"A few pounds." Layla wiggled away from her mother's touch.

Jayne Ella used to pinch a roll around Layla's middle exclaiming: "This is fat. Just pure fat. How are you going to get rid of this?"

"Well, keep it goin', honey. Keep it goin'," her mother said in that cheer whisper that Layla hated. Encouragement in that particular tone was hollow, like she said the right thing but didn't really think Layla would win the battle of the bulge.

Jayne Ella returned the book to the top of her head, extended her well-manicured hands to the side and strolled across the driveway.

As awful as Jayne Ella had been to her over the years, at least she was far better with her grandchildren. In fact, she was almost ideal.

Because for as much as Layla didn't stick up for herself all that well, Jayne Ella knew that Layla would protect her girls until her dying breath. And like a mama grizzly, too.

"That's it, girls. Nice and tall. Chin just a little higher, Emma."

"What is this?" Layla held her building temper by the string of a frayed cord.

"Now, honey."

It wasn't the cheer whisper Layla hated, but it was close. Her tone was of the everyone-knows-this variety and it lit a fire deep in Layla's gut that made her crave more chocolate.

"Slouchy posture isn't good for the vital organs, right, girls?"

"She's right, Mama. You know they have standing desks now because sitting is so bad for you." Emma tapped her tummy with the fingertips of both hands.

"That's what Gramma's boyfriend is making. Stand up desks." Emma goosed her older sister in the ribs and dashed away. The books tumbled to the ground with a bang-bang.

Anna promptly rolled her eyes and gritted her teeth. "It's standing desks, not stand up desks, you—"

"Kind words, Anna Kate," Layla warned. "Hands to yourself." She'd said those words ten million times before today. Still their hands would be pinching and poking and pulling whatever they could to get back at the other. Just as she did with *her* sister when they were their age.

"Slouching is the new junk food. It's bad habit." Jayne Ella raised her eyebrows in a told-you-so-fashion. She mouthed the words "*It's lazy.*"

Layla teetered on the edge of a verbal barb. Then decided she couldn't refute what her mother was saying. But something about it put her on the hairy edge of irritation.

Maybe it was because she could still feel her mother's knuckle run down her spine. "Sit up straight. You'll look thinner," she'd said when Layla was younger and usually when they were out at a restaurant.

She decided it was that tone of assumed rejection that

bothered her. She had adopted that tone when their dad moved out.

Once inside, Jayne Ella poured sweet tea over ice for the two older girls while the two younger ones played outside. "Now, tell me, honey. How did the meeting go with your attorney? Did you get all that worked out with the insurance policy?"

Layla returned the glass on the table. "Not really. No."

She relayed the story in detail, how Asher had left a ton of debt that she had to pay off, how she was losing the house as a result and how she wondered if her mother would be willing to help. She intentionally left out the part about how Asher had raised the value of her policy. Her mother had a special gift for wearing her out and she just couldn't go over that again. Not right now.

"I've already accepted an offer from Tom to live at the manor. It's a caretaker position, but that's a very temporary solution. What I really want is to be as independent as possible. So I was wondering if you would buy a house for us? And then you could sell it a few years from now and keep the gains. Or maybe you could front me some money as an advance against my inheritance? I know it's a lot to ask. But Asher left us in a bad situation."

She left out how Mason was working at the manor and she wasn't sure how well it would go if the two of them shared such close quarters.

"Well, honey. Of course I'll help you." Her mother rubbed and patted her on the knee again. Several times. It was her mother's sure sign that she was all in.

"Thank you." Layla breathed a sigh of relief. "I never thought I'd ever have to ask you for money."

"Well, don't you worry, I'll take care of this. How soon do you have to be out of the house?"

"Sixty days."

"We can probably find something close by before then. And if we can't find something that suits, y'all can move in with me until we find what works."

"Here?" Layla's chest tightened. "We wouldn't want to crowd you."

"Nonsense. Family is always there for family, right?" Jayne Ella waved off Layla's concerns. "I'll clear out the guest room for the girls, and you can take your old room."

The very thought of moving back into her old room in her mother's house made her feel like the walls inched toward her. She could almost feel the bright yellow paint from her mother's living room walls on her skin.

The electric look in Peyton's eyes was part I-told-you-so and part run-for-your-life.

If Layla moved in, her girls would start to listen to their grandmother more than they did her. And wouldn't that make Jayne Ella so happy?

The manor wasn't a perfect option for several reasons. Though it was a far sight better than moving in with her mother.

"The girls could stay here for a few nights here and there, but I'd have to think about anything more lengthy than that. I need more of my own space." Hell would serve ice cream before she moved into her mother's house. "Maybe I ought to just stick with the caretaker job at the manor. The girls and I could live there until the restoration is complete."

"You don't have any experience in that area. I can't imagine you'd be very good at that. Alcott Manor is a family-wide project. If you mess anything up, you would catch the brunt end of your relatives' anger. I really wouldn't want to see you go through that. And what if the girls ruin something? How would you pay to replace it?"

It sounded like she was offering protection and sage advice, but she wasn't.

Peyton had been right.

Accepting their mother's handout was all wrong.

"Besides, the girls can't live there. Their father *died there*." She whispered her last two words.

"They don't know where he died. Only that he was on a job and that he had a bad fall. They can avoid that area of the house." Her mother had a point, though, and she began to mentally write her worst-mother-of-the-year acceptance speech. "But I think what you're really saying is that *you* think I'll screw it up and *you* don't want to be on the brunt end of our relatives' disappointments."

"Well, honey—" The end of her "honey" pitched up, like she had to placate something irrational that Layla had said.

"No, it's fine, Mom. Really. It doesn't matter, I've decided to go with Tom's offer."

Her mom sat speechless. Peyton stifled a smile.

9

They had seven rooms of living space in the manor. *Seven.*

That was more room than they'd had at Asher's house, and more than they would have had at her mother's house. She felt better about how well she was providing for her children.

The area was used as a space for storage when they moved in. Ladders, old chairs, a six foot tall gold frame without its print. Several bookcases with glass fronts were stacked in the front room. The paint on the walls was peeling, the overhead light fixtures were missing, though their medallions remained. Albeit cracked and chipped. The entire space reeked of bleach from an overturned container.

The ornate picture frame was tall enough to walk through. Tattered bits of painted canvas remained. Gold flourishes were chipped along the outer edges. The girls could have fun performing a skit inside of it, like it was the fancy outline to a stage.

She stacked everything else in a far corner. She draped a few sheets over the stack to keep it out of sight.

They had a lot of privacy. Tom gave them all of the summer quarters, which included the summer living room and the summer dining room, the old larder and kitchen, as well as a couple of spacious offices. In other words, he gave her and the girls the entire basement.

When Alcott Manor had been built in the early 1800s, there wasn't any air conditioning. It wasn't unusual for the family to cook and dine and relax in these cooler quarters during the warmer months. She imagined the far better shape this level must have been in back then—music and laughter and the scent of freshly cooked meals.

Layla wasn't wild about living in the—partial, anyway—underground; she definitely preferred brighter and airier rooms. She preferred living above ground.

There were some small square windows along the back of the house that faced east. They were bound to let in a good amount of morning light. Even if they hadn't had that to enjoy, artificial light would have been better than living with her mother. Anything was better than living with Asher. She was grateful for what they had. She was grateful for Tom and she would thank him again—

Tom.

She forgot that he—she covered her mouth with her hand. She closed her eyes against the horror of it all. She had been on the phone with him when it happened. Their call had been cut off. She couldn't get him back on the line, so she had called Mason. He was the one who went to the manor and found him.

She dropped her head into her hands and cried. Tom had been one of the last people on the planet who was on her side. Come what may. Now he was gone.

The police ruled Tom's death accidental. He slipped on the wet bathroom floor, knocked himself unconscious and drowned. No one could explain why the bathtub had been full of water.

Freak accident, the police said.

"I'm going to honor Tom's offer on the caretaker job. Don't you worry," Mason said. "And I'll finish the restoration for you and your family."

He didn't seem to know anything about what Tom had meant about "hitting a snag with the caretaker job."

She didn't bring it up.

Whatever problem Tom was going to tell her about, maybe it wasn't a big deal.

She pressed her hand over the ache in her chest. She looked around the room for something to do.

She left her iron bed behind. She had shared that with Asher. She refused to bring that baggage with her. She wiped the tears from her face and pulled an air mattress from its box.

She had been so trapped with Asher for the better part of the last decade, it was utterly liberating to pack up her life and the girls and simply drive away. She only wished that Asher had been alive when she did it. It would have been satisfying to see his face when she cut those ties.

She brought only the necessities and only the things she wanted to carry forward—all the girls' clothes and furnishings and toys. Kitchen stuff, towels and toiletries. When she cleaned out their too-tiny pantry, she brought the girls' favorite Pop-Tarts, chips, and cookies. The flour, eggs, and sugar. She deliberately left behind Asher's teas. Those stupid teas.

"Make me a tea, would you, Lay?"

"Don't call me that."

Oh, Lay. Let it go. It's just a sweet term of affection.

Sometimes he called her Layla-pup.

"I'm not a pup."

"You're my pup." He'd said with a greedy smile.

He'd expected her to function like a wife from the 1940s —with dinner and a drink ready in the evening. Although for him, the evening drink was hot herbal tea.

Once, after a long day of work, she said no, she wouldn't make his tea.

He'd responded with a plastic smile.

Then Layla felt the shift in the air.

Step by step he got closer.

She was proud of herself. She stood her ground.

"You don't want to make my tea." He nodded like a stupid bobblehead doll. "I hear you."

Unfortunately, the visual of his fat head and receding hairline wiggling with cheap plastic charm made her laugh.

He laughed, too.

Until his fist landed in her gut.

"Don't worry about it," he'd said. "Don't make the tea." He left the room.

When she finally stood upright, when the pain and nausea faded, she made his tea and left it on the counter.

Before she left that kitchen of his for the last time, she took the homemade bags of dried rose petals, lavender buds, and chamomile leaves and dumped them onto the floor. She spun the heel of her shoe on the tea leaves and left.

Flower tea, Asher had called it.

Sadly the girls wanted flower tea every night before bed.

Layla set the petals that were for Asher's tea aside in a strainer until he came home, so his tea would be hot and fresh.

She blew another breath into the inflatable mattress that would be her bed for the foreseeable future. The bank said they could have stayed in the house for another couple of months. Of course, the interest on the total amount she owed them would continue to accrue during that time.

She said no.

She sold her wedding rings, her wedding dress, and Asher's favorite armchair. She put the cash in the bank. The girls would need new school clothes. That money would come in handy.

Peyton walked in. She dropped a stack of blue folded sheets on a straight back armless chair. "I think you made the right call. Unless you're at all worried about being in the same home where Asher died."

"Nope." Layla never told Peyton that Asher hit her. Like a walking stereotype, she felt ashamed.

"Good. Make your own way. Stay away from the far end of Jayne Ella's emotional leash."

Layla pushed against the air mattress to test its firmness. It might be more comfortable than she originally thought.

She blew her nose. Then she and her sister tucked the sheets around the makeshift bed.

Her daughters ran down the hallway, laughing and squealing and chasing after the small golden terrier. The bell on the dog's collar jingled.

"I can't believe you got them a dog," Peyton said.

"He came with the manor," Layla said.

Peyton cocked her head. She seemed to notice that her sister had been crying. "This could be a new beginning for you. Mason looked incredibly handsome when I saw him last week. You know, sparks could fly."

Layla shook her head. "Stop."

She thought about her dream, how easy it had been to approach him, how wonderful it had been to be close to him again. And then there was that lovely kiss. But that wasn't real, since he didn't know she had kissed him. She had to remember that.

There was some sort of barrier between the dead zone and the real world, like a two-way mirror. When she was in the manor's dead zone, she could see the real world, but the real world couldn't see her.

"I don't know," Peyton said in a sing-song voice. "Seems like I remember you telling me about a romantic kiss after prom."

There had been two kisses, actually. One after prom. One a couple of days later at the lake where they used to swim.

In the locker room that week after gym class, Brooke plopped down next to her like they were friends. "Layla, I just don't know what to do." Brooke rested her hand in her head until Layla finally, reluctantly said, "Oh?"

Then Brooke would find a complaint to share. "Mason calls me *so* much." Or. "He wants me to spend all my time with him." Then she would make a face, like a grimace. Though it seemed a smile was not far away.

Then Brooke said, "You're so lucky that you don't have a boyfriend. It's such a burden to worry about things like this." She patted Layla on the leg, then pranced away while she adjusted her thong underwear.

Almost every one-sided conversation with Brooke went like that. It made Layla think that one of two things must be true. First, that she somehow knew about Layla's secret crush on Mason and was determined to show Layla how she didn't have a chance. Or two, that Brooke didn't like the friendship Mason and Layla shared and was determined to make her claim abundantly clear. Maybe both were true.

Layla and Mason were close. They had been for a long time. In public, he seemed pretty dedicated to Brooke. To hear Brooke talk about it, they were headed for the altar. But then Mason had kissed *her*. Twice. They weren't casual pecks either.

She'd originally thought that maybe they meant something. She'd thought maybe they were heading someplace. He had even said that he was planning to break up with Brooke right after the campout. He told her that after that was done, he wanted to ask her to dinner. And he hoped she would say yes.

Then Brooke died at the campout, and everyone blamed Layla, including Mason. They didn't speak to one another for ten years. She'd long ago decided that that kiss with Mason hadn't meant what she'd thought. It hadn't meant anything at all.

"That was prom, for crying out loud. High school. Hormones. A lifetime ago. I think he only took me because he felt sorry for me."

"He took you to prom because he enjoyed being with you."

"He took me because I didn't have a date, because he and Brooke were on the outs, and because she ditched him to go with Eric from the football team."

Layla didn't mention that they had made plans for the future.

Peyton clicked her tongue against the roof of her mouth. "Y'all always did have that lovely friendship."

"That's been over for a long while." She slung the last pillow into the depths of its case and propped it on the makeshift bed.

Memories took her down a path of sweet moments she and Mason had shared over the years: Saturday afternoon lake swimming complete with rope swing, church group camping, Friday night movie classics. There was even the occasional school skip day when they went back to the lake. They talked and swam until sunset. The times they shared were always her favorite, and they remained vivid in her mind.

A tingle sparked in her chest, one she hadn't felt in recent years. Definitely not with any man. She remembered it as her go-ahead feeling. Kind of a funny sensation she used to get when she knew the right direction to take— when something was meant to be.

"He's here. You're here. Maybe a little something could start up?"

"Mmm." The foreign warmth tickled at the inside of her chest like a cherished memory, like a happiness she had forgotten, like a sign that guided.

Why that meant-to-be tingling sprang to life in her chest, she didn't know. Either it had forgotten the fact that she had killed his girlfriend, the girl he was probably supposed to marry, or it was a faulty signal. Because she had gotten that feeling once before with Mason, a long time ago. It had been wrong then, too.

"I think you still have a soft spot for him. You deserve something positive for a change."

Peyton shrugged her shoulders and flipped her freshly blunt-cut hair with such confidence. It made her look like an expert on the topic. And, she was. She had never wanted for a boyfriend or a date or even attention. Boys were always clamoring over one another to get to her.

"That's just not my style. Plus, I'm not ready."

"This is about you having fun and enjoying life. You deserve a turn at being happy. This could be a new beginning."

"I don't think I could put myself out there like that with Mason. Or anyone right now." She waved her sister off.

"Sure you can. It's all about good marketing."

"No—"

"Layla. You're gorgeous. This would be good for you. Have a little confidence."

She sent her sister a lukewarm smile. "Plus, he's such a perfectionist...being in a relationship with that would just be a jail cell. Honestly, Pey, I'm not ready."

Peyton's smile was laced with a sister's love. "You've been through so much. I just thought you and Mason might finally—well, I'll stop pushing."

At the mention of his name, Mason's lightly-tanned face flashed in her mind's eye. While her sister spread a thin, worn patchwork quilt over the foot of the bed, Layla ran her fingers over her own lips. The memory of what it was like to kiss him all those years ago came back to her.

Peyton cleared her throat. "You're thinking of him."

Layla dropped her hand to her chest. "I know it doesn't make sense after all this time, but I do miss what we almost had." Her voice was whisper soft, like she didn't want anyone to hear her, like she didn't want her memory spoiled, like she cautiously hoped her fantasy might still come true. "Anyway." She swished her hand back and forth like she could wave away the regret.

"I know, sweetheart. We love who we love, sometimes we can't help it." Peyton rubbed her hand along her sister's arm. She gave it a light squeeze, then she unpacked another box. "Do you have any idea what his story is? Last I heard, he was a stockbroker in New York. How did he end up back in Charleston and running his father's homebuilding business?"

Layla wanted to refute her sister's insinuation that she loved Mason. She was a bit taken with him, that's all. The feeling would fade. "We haven't really spoken."

Peyton plugged in her sister's bedside table lamp. She turned it on and off and on again. "Well, you, my love, are just beginning the good times. I'm sure of it. The proceeds from the tours at this place will get you out of your financial mess. And maybe just keep an open mind where Mason's concerned. Okay?"

Layla shook her head. "You're hopeless."

"Look." Peyton backed up a few steps and gestured to the row of windows across the top of the room.

Layla stood with her sister, and together they watched Mason carry two long pieces of lumber across the great lawn. Hot and sweaty, fit and muscular, hard and hardworking. She thought his movements might have decelerated into slow motion, like a soft drink commercial.

"Gracious," Peyton said.

"Yeah," Layla breathed.

"You sure he isn't your happily ever after?" Peyton asked.

"I don't believe in happily ever after."

He dropped the lumber on the grass with a clatter and wiped the sweat from his forehead with the back of his hand.

In the other room, her daughters argued over closet space.

"There goes the peace," Layla said.

"Why don't I take them outside for some beach and swim time? I'll wear them out for you."

"Deal. I'll finish unpacking."

"Unpack later. Rest for a minute, first. Put your feet up. No offense, but you look like you could use it."

Layla passed on the opportunity to tell her that she was sleepwalking again. "Spoken like a woman without children. I have too much to do, and the girls have school tomorrow. Too much to organize."

"Layla-pop. I have to go back to Boston late tonight. Accept my help while you have it."

"Tonight? You're leaving so soon?"

"I have to get back to the office in the morning."

Layla hugged her sister. "Oh. I'll miss you."

"I'll miss you, too." Peyton kissed her cheek. "Now get just a little rest while you can."

Layla sighed. It wasn't the idea of resting that bothered her. She didn't even mind being a little disorganized. Her concern was the inevitable dreaming.

10

E mma and Anna made their way to the beach with their aunt. Layla couldn't see them, but she could hear them, and by the sound of the laughing and squealing she was sure there was a game of tag going on.

She had planned to unpack a few more boxes and organize their kitchen while the girls were out. She really did want the kitchen area usable before they had to make a school morning breakfast there tomorrow.

But then fatigue pulled at her.

It had been an incredibly stressful few days. She just needed to get horizontal for a minute. Besides, she would have to sleep sometime. If she slipped into a lucid dreaming state, she would be cautious. She could do that.

She laid down on her air mattress and closed her eyes. Her mind wandered restlessly through the manor: the foyer, the main hallway, the great hall. She thought about how she would need to walk through the manor again today. Then she thought about what path visitors would take when the tours began. Her mind's eye reached the music room, and her memories shot her to the great lawn: the overnight camping trip from a decade ago. The back of Brooke's blonde head, matted with dark red blood. Her face slack and pale like a corpse. Mason's fire red face screaming, "What have you done?!"

Layla's eyes flew open. Sweat prickled under her arms.

"Can't change the past." She breathed too quickly. "Can't change the past. Focus on what you're grateful for today." That was another pearl she had gleaned from Dr. Waters.

She drew in a deep breath and shifted into a more deliberate mental space, one she had had to practice. Her usual practice before she fell asleep, her grateful list. Her girls were at the top spot. Yes. God had clearly blessed her twice with those beautiful babies. She had a home for them, albeit a temporary one. Still, it was a roof over their head and a safe place to sleep at night.

There was a special place in heaven for Tom Watson.

They had healthy food to eat, she had a good nursing job. The next item on her grateful list: Asher was out of her life, and he was never coming back. She was glad he was dead.

She put his death on the list and it wasn't the last item, but in her mind she saw it in ALL CAPS. Because it was that good.

She had talked with Asher about a divorce several times over the years, the last time not long before he died. He'd refused each time and said he'd make sure she never got custody of the girls if they divorced.

He knew a little too much about her lucid dreaming, more than she wanted him to know. He said he'd tell everyone that she was mentally unstable, that she had been seeing a psychologist since she was a teenager, and that her vivid dreaming was probably a sign of psychosis.

She wasn't sure if he could get anyone to believe him.

But his threats were strong enough that they caused her to back away from pursuing the divorce. He had connections in town. He told her that for every mental health expert she found who said she was sane, he would find two who would testify that she wasn't. He wasn't about to be humiliated in public by having his wife leave him. That meant their custody battle would go to a jury trial, and she didn't want to gamble where her girls were concerned.

Sleep weighed heavy on her, and she floated in and out of sweet weightlessness. It felt so good to let go and be free.

Long shifts at the hospital, packing, the move, and this thick-walled quiet added up to one big, fat sleeping pill. She prayed she wouldn't dream, at least not in the way she had been taught. She couldn't—not at the manor.

Though sometimes, like a well-worn path, her mind just went in that direction without even trying. That worried her because—her children. She couldn't be off on some sleepy time adventure when it was her responsibility to care for her girls. What if one of them called for her and she didn't hear them? What if they tried to wake her and couldn't because she was too far gone into her own dream world?

There was little notice when she moved from the real world to her dream world. One minute she might be lying in bed trying to go to sleep, filling out her gratitude list, or maybe worrying whether she had done enough for her daughters that day. The next minute she opened her eyes and everything looked the same. There were those subtle signs, but sometimes she missed them. While she was at the manor and whenever it was time to sleep, she would keep a firm intent that she would not lucid dream. Not here.

That did it. She decided she wouldn't sleep at all right now. Instead, she would bring order to that kitchen. The cardboard boxes of glasses and plates and silverware were right where she left them. Peyton and the girls were still outside and that was fine. She didn't mind doing this work by herself, she preferred it. To her there was nothing worse than having someone else organize your kitchen. That made it impossible to find anything.

The freezer wrap ripped loud on the serrated edge, and she folded the cut sheet on the long edges to fit neatly inside the cabinet. Tacky as it was, this was less expensive than shelf liner, she rationalized, and she had to save every nickel. Tall glasses went in the back, short glasses in the front. She realized she would need a chair with a hard and sturdy seat. The girls would want to stand on it to get the glasses from the higher cabinets. She would get one tomorrow.

Mugs next. Her favorite coffee mugs were the only ones she took from the house. She slipped the first one from the funny papers she'd wrapped it in to keep it from breaking. She knew all her coffee mugs before she could see them because each shape was distinct and familiar.

This one was her *Nurses Call the Shots* mug, with a needle in place of the t. One of her patients' family had given it to her with chocolates inside of it when their dad had been discharged.

The next one had the prescription label across it with the word *Coffee* printed in bold letters. Her girls had given her that mug for her birthday. The last two mugs had happy girls drawn on it with their Mama in the middle. Her daughters had made those at school and brought them home for Mother's Day.

There was one mug left in the cardboard box, wrapped in newspaper.

She stared at it. There shouldn't be any others in the box. She had made certain that she threw out all of Asher's stupid college mugs, and she didn't bring any others with her.

She gritted her teeth tightly together. She pulled cool air in and out through her nose. With a steady hand, she reached for the mug. If she had mistakenly packed one of his tea cups, she would simply throw it out. *She* was in charge of her life now.

But she knew she hadn't made any mistakes. She had taken great pleasure in tossing the mugs into the trash can.

"Make me a tea, would you, Lay?"

Slowly, she unwrapped it and found what she knew as impossible: an ugly, brown, fat-bottomed mug with the words Born to Golf on the side.

She placed it on the counter. The pottery clinked against the surface.

She took one long step away from the counter and stared at mug, like she faced her former husband in the flesh. She remembered his loud, breathy sips and his slow smile at her over the thick molded rim. Like he had just won a tiny piece of her soul in return for arm-twisting her into making and serving him tea.

"Layla," she could hear him say. "What's for dinner?"

The memory of his voice made panic and heat rise within like she were about to be sick. Do whatever he asked, or else, that was the code she lived by.

With a deep breath, she pushed her shoulders back and lifted her chin. He was gone. So was *or else*. She stood tall in front of his memory, demanded her fear to be small, and without backing down she said, "You will never control me again."

A feeling of freedom surged through her and she remembered what it was like when she was young and strong with only choices ahead of her. Without obligation. Without Asher.

A husky snicker sounded behind her, one she hadn't heard in several months. Her newfound strength drained from her like the rushing of water through a pipe.

She swallowed quickly, her breath kicking up its pace. There was no one there, she knew. No one else in the room but her, and she would prove that. But she turned all the way around, and she found Asher posed casually inside the empty six foot frame she'd left propped against the wall. A shudder rumbled through her body and pushed a tiny whimper from her lips.

"Make me some tea, would you, Lay?"

He shouldn't be standing there smiling at her with his hands in his pockets. He was dead. In fact, she'd put his death on her gratitude list.

She'd seen the police photos of his lifeless body just below the grand stairway in Alcott Manor and how he had impaled himself on a sharp length of wood when he fell from the balcony. She identified his body at the morgue. She even planned his funeral, attended it with all of her family, and threw a handful of soil into his grave. She could still hear the soft thud from the dirt hitting the shiny wooden top of his coffin.

"Nice to see you, Lay.." His lips parted in a smile she'd seen him use too many times, and always when he wanted something. His teeth looked like yellow kernels of corn.

"This isn't happening."

He drew in a deep breath and walked around her, sizing her up, and too closely. "You're looking good. Real good. Lost a little more weight, I see." He touched his hand to her waist, and she slapped it away.

He clicked his tongue against the roof of his mouth five times and shook his head.

"You're not here. You're dead."

He shrugged. "Maybe."

She stepped backward.

"Give me a kiss, baby." His smile was dark and hungry and wide, and he ran his stubby pink tongue along the bottom edges of his top teeth.

LAYLA AWOKE with a start and half-expected to see Asher standing in front of her as he had been in her dream. She stood in her kitchen. Her breath was fast and shallow.

She drew in gasps of air. The room was empty, and even more importantly, she was alone.

A stress response.

That's all that dream was. She had indeed fallen asleep, dozed off without even realizing it. And she was sleep-walking again, not surprising considering the amount of stress she was dealing with right now.

Pressure, worry, strain, a strange dream was bound to happen.

Maybe this was even a little of her signature guilt messing with her, too. Because she was happy that Asher was dead—happy and damn near victorious now that she stood here in the little kitchen where he wasn't.

She splashed her face with water and listened for the smallest sound or movement, the tiniest evidence that she might not be alone. Nothing.

Thank God.

She slowed her breath and tried to think of normal things. Like how this kitchen would be filled with the scent of brown sugared oatmeal, toast, and coffee in the morning. There would also be the sound of arguing because Anna Kate would ask for a Pop-Tart and Layla would not give her one.

The box of mugs and glasses sat on the counter. She stared at it, wondering if Asher's mug was buried in the bottom of it as it had been in her dream.

"It's not there," she said aloud and only to herself.

She marched toward the box and unpacked the contents far more quickly than she had packed them, with sheets of newspaper flying into the air and drifting to the floor. She didn't line the shelves with freezer paper first, and she didn't place the big glasses behind the little glasses in the cabinet. But she did slam every glass and mug on the counter to make a point.

When the box was empty, she said, "There. Just a dream."

11

Mason waited on his takeout order at Sammi's-on-the-Sea. His mind was stuck on the image of Tom submerged from the waist up in a large bathtub full of blood-tinged water. His horror-filled eyes and mouth wide open. Like the last thing he saw literally scared him to death.

Tom was gone. Just like that. The man who had championed Alcott Manor's restoration had died, and in the home he had fought to save.

He ran his hand over his face. He couldn't believe there had been yet another death at Alcott Manor.

He and Layla hadn't talked about it yet, but the two of them would have to work closely together to finish the house. At least he hoped she would let him work with her. The house had come a long way, and there was a lot left to do. Frankly, he needed the money, and the credit to his reputation that finishing this job would bring. Taking over his father's business had been harder than he expected.

Layla Alcott.

His former best friend who never ceased to surprise

him. This time it was her appearance. She looked several shades different from when he last saw her.

"Hey, Mason." Frances, the cashier at Sammi's, smiled wide and tried too hard to be pleasing, as was her custom whenever he came in. Several times she had slipped him her number on the back of his receipt. He never called.

"Hey, Frances. That my to-go order?"

"Yep, got it right here." Frances flipped a pink-painted section of her otherwise brown hair behind her shoulder, peeked in the bag and moved things around. "They put two orders in here. Hang on, I'll fix it."

"No, two orders is right." He sifted through several bills in his black leather wallet and waited for her to give him the total.

"Oh." She stood uncomfortably corrected. "Alright. Then \$15.96 is your total."

He gave her a twenty and thought about what she would never know—that his mind was already made up. He'd made enough mistakes in his life, spent enough time dating the wrong girls. Essentially, he'd had enough of being on the wrong track for his life. From now on he was going with his gut to lead him to the right path for him. Dixie had been right when she told him that approach was probably his only option left. He'd tried everything else.

"Have a good night," he said to Frances.

He paused before turning onto the empty two lane highway, and he thought for probably the millionth time how different his life almost was. He wondered if he would have married Brooke Williams if she hadn't died. They'd dated through most of high school, she had been planning to attend the same college he went to. If she hadn't been killed, he might have been eating dinner with her tonight, along with a couple of their kids. Maybe they all would have walked the beach after dinner, then stopped by Dixie's so the kids could see their grandma. Brooke had their lives all planned out, and he might have rolled right along with those plans.

If she had lived. If Layla had refused him.

It was strange how even though ten years had passed, some part of his life was still unfinished. Because the night she died, all his plans with Layla snapped like a dried tree branch.

Maybe he would have married Layla. He'd kissed her after prom, as well as that day they'd shared at the lake. He'd really believed they were going somewhere. Maybe they still had a chance.

He'd gone to college, become a stockbroker. He'd dated other women. But he couldn't help but think now and then of Brooke and Layla and what might have been.

He was determined to find out who killed Brooke, and he would make them pay.. Not just for himself, not just for Brooke and her family, but for Layla, too. Her life had been nearly ruined that night.

Then he thought, also for probably the millionth time, about the kiss he and Layla had shared a few days before the campout. They had always been good friends, but something had changed between them that spring, a special closeness had developed. He was completely unguarded around her. He could be himself. He tell her anything.

There was a spark that lit him up from the inside whenever she was around, and it made him feel oddly invincible. He still wasn't entirely sure what that was, though he only experienced it with Layla. That one day on the pier, the feeling had been so strong, he just had to kiss her.

He pulled onto the highway. She looked beauty queen perfect when he saw her at the manor. Even with that giant cake crumb stuck to the side of her face, he thought she was one of the sexiest women he'd seen in a long time. With that straight blonde hair to the middle of her back and curves in all the right places, she turned his head even before he fully realized who she was.

She had a way of handling herself. Like she would be just as comfortable having tea in Buckingham Palace as she would be at the Friday shrimp and grits special down at Butts on the Creek. He liked that about her. She never judged and took people for who they were. She was the sort of person who found something positive about everybody.

She also had had a way with him. In school, he had been captain of the football team, president of the chess club, and one of the soloists in chorus. He was well-rounded, smart, not bad looking.

Layla never saw him as perfect like everyone else did. Pleased as he was with the mask he wore, he rather liked that she saw through his act. She showed up knowing where he needed to go next. That worked out just fine, because she was usually going in that direction herself. It was the easy rhythm of their friendship.

That is, until the awful night their senior year when they camped on the great lawn of Alcott Manor. Their church youth group had gathered for one final celebration together, before they would all go their separate ways. They built a bonfire on the beach and opened a time capsule that their group had put together when they were only eleven years old. Everyone shared their dreams for the future: their colleges of choice, career ideas, where they wanted to live.

He and Layla had plans. He was going to break up with Brooke the next day, because he had wanted to avoid her drama. Then he was going to take Layla out to dinner. That, he thought, was going to be their beginning. Too, they had shared that kiss. That one magnificent kiss that he couldn't have predicted, the one that grabbed him by the heart and soul, the one he couldn't forget.

That night everyone woke up in their sleeping bags under the full moon and the starry skies to find a living nightmare. Brooke had been attacked, the back of her skull smashed and bleeding. Her sister Jordan had also been attacked. Layla had been accused.

He should have come to Layla's defense right away, knowing she never would have hurt anyone. Though truth be known, at the time he did wonder if Layla had just had enough of Brooke. Like so many others. Finally, after several months and too much media attention, the police cleared her of all charges. They told everyone in a televised interview that Brooke's injuries couldn't have happened the way Brooke's friends said it did. Layla was innocent.

She didn't talk to him after that, because when everyone in town blamed Layla for what happened to Brooke, he didn't defend her. He had been her best friend and he didn't stand up for her.

Now, he was going to set this wrong to right. For Layla. For him. And for anything that they might have together. He just hoped it wasn't too late.

He drove onto the lightless curved road that would lead him to the manor. The tall pines on either side of the road were spiky fingers against a black sky. His truck leaned into the S curves and he glanced at his phone. It was usually now when Tom would call and they would go over the plans for the day. Layla and her family still needed him to finish the restoration. He needed her support with her family to make sure the rest of the job could get done without objection.

She had been an innocent victim so long ago and

because of him she paid a hefty price—publicly blamed and shamed and...

It was time he made that up to her, it was time she had an advocate, it was time she had someone to protect *her* for a change.

12

Getting the girls to bed on their first night in Alcott Manor wasn't as hard as Layla thought it would be. They weren't feeling terribly adventurous about the elegant but spooky space they were in; their new home was still intimidating. So it was a quick dinner of ravioli and salads, then bath and bed. They both insisted on sleeping in their mother's new bed, with their new dog, and made Layla promise that she would join them later. She promised she would.

When she was certain they were asleep, she searched for her cell phone then realized she must have left it in the car. She switched the button on the baby monitor base to the on position and carried the walkie-talkie shaped speaker with her. Layla had found the girls' baby monitor tucked in a box with their baby blankets and toys and teething rattles. Asher had told her to throw out the monitor years ago. Tonight it came in handy.

Tom had asked her to make a nightly round through the house. She hadn't yet done it. Now she could check on the rest of the house as she was supposed to and still listen for her girls.

She opened the door to the stairwell and flicked the light switch that looked like it hadn't been replaced since the early 1970s. It thunked loud when she pushed it up as if its job were heavy and cumbersome, and no light came on. Looking up where she knew the fixture to be, she turned the switch off and on again. Then again. No light appeared.

"Dang it," she whispered.

Was a trip upstairs and through the house was really necessary tonight? Tom's instructions had been direct but vague: "Go from room to room, turn the lights on, spend a few minutes in there. Make notes of anything that looks out of place or needs repairing. Visit every room to keep the energy moving."

She stared into the pitch black that was as dense as cement. She felt unnerved. Watched. She shook her head. Tired. That's all this was. She had faced so much in the last few months that she was just worn down. Now she was afraid of the dark.

She rubbed her eyes. Then, focusing hard toward the top of the stairs, she hoped to see a sliver of horizontal light at the bottom of the door, a target she could hone in on. Instead she thought she saw shadowy movement, like someone shifted their position.

She drew back from the stairs, looked away. Icy adrenaline rushed through her chest and down her arms.

Trick of the eye.

She toyed with the idea of walking outside and around to the front door, but she wasn't sure if the workers had set the security alarm. Maybe she wouldn't do the tour tonight at all.

Then she remembered the promise she had made Tom.

She had to walk the house three times a day. Guilt poked at her insides.

She glanced at the oversized frame where Asher had appeared in her dream. He was dead, she reminded herself. She looked toward the stairway. Being afraid to move forward was a sign that she was allowing a dead man to define her life. She set her jaw. *Enough.*

She searched the kitchen drawers for a flashlight but didn't find one. She decided she was being ridiculous. She walked through dark rooms all the time. Nothing bad ever happened before.

She studied the inky blackness and waited for the movement to repeat. It didn't. But the longer she stared, the more she could have sworn she saw the outline of someone sitting on a step. Staring back at her. A strange coldness swept across her body.

She forced herself to blink. The first step beneath her bare foot was not as cold as she expected. The wood was warped. Beaten down by the years. The analogy wasn't lost on her.

One by one the steps took her further into the darkness, and though she couldn't see what was ahead, she became too terrified to look back toward the light. She crept closer toward the top, two more steps, each one creaking from age.

The dark was a stygian depth, thick and secretive. It pressed against her skin. The walls in Alcott Manor were weighted with haunted history, full to their brim with her ancestors' suffering.

One…two more steps until some presence seemed to be in front of her. She paused with eyes wide and searching.

The cold made her body tremor.

She was determined to do this job. Determined to prove

that no one was there. Even if there were, she was determined not to be stopped.

Two more steps.

She felt someone in front of her.

His presence so real, staring her in the face. She knew if she reached out, she would touch him.

Dread rushed through her. That horrible feeling. She'd made a mistake. The odds were against her. There was no way out.

Her mouth went dry.

She squeezed her eyes shut.

13

Dixie Holloway sat straight and tall at her narrow pine desk and cautiously placed another tarot card in the tenth and final position of her Celtic cross layout.

She wasn't supposed to be doing card readings. Information through card readings could be faulty. Incomplete. Dark.

The card was a skeleton dressed in knight's armor, riding a white horse—the card of Death.

She left her finger on the card's white edge, dangerously keeping the connection open. Sometimes one or two more bits of information would come through. She needed to know.

Nothing else was coming through. She gathered the cards together, shuffled them and thought distractedly of how Layla lived at the manor. "If she were my daughter, I wouldn't let that happen." She put the cards in their black velvet bag and hid the bag in the drawer.

She rearranged several of the geodes and crystals and gemstones that she kept around the outer edges of her desk and selected her current favorite— a polished labradorite. This one was all about finding truth.

Her former husband Steele used to say, "Dix, you've got so many rocks in this place, I can't tell the difference between the outside and the inside anymore."

She glanced toward his recliner.

Sometimes he showed up in the evening when everything was quiet.

He wasn't there.

She ran her thumb over the stone. Tom had asked her to give him a reading on the house a few months earlier. He wanted to know if there were any ghosts in the manor, if they were safe to move ahead with the restoration, and most importantly, if Asher had moved on to the Other Side.

She'd sworn off readings a long time ago. For good reason. But Tom was a friend, and he was desperate.

Her reading had come back clean, so to speak. No, she couldn't find any ghosts, and no, she didn't see Asher. She had looked hard, too. But she wasn't sure she'd been right.

Crickets chirped from the back yard, and the pool lights cast an eerie glow across the lawn. Cherry tree branches dipped and swayed with the wind.

She and Steele put the pool in years ago to entertain their sons and their friends and to keep them close to home when they were teenagers. The gray privacy fence at the edge of the lawn stood tall and firm. It confined her.

At this age, she had planned to travel with her husband to see the pyramids, the northern lights, and the land down under. Instead, she was alone and anchored to a house that no longer breathed with the life it had when her family was young and loud and full of fun.

She grabbed the stack of photographs she had taken at the manor. Sometimes spirits left traces in photos.

She opened the French doors that led to the back yard and let the cool breeze wash over her. One by one she flipped through the pictures. Something was wrong with the manor, she could feel it. It was dangerous.

She reached the end of the pile of photos and started again. This time, she returned to her desk and used her lighted magnifying glass to examine the details of each photo up close. She looked for unexplainable shadows, orbs, transparent figures.

Nothing.

Just a few squiggly white lines that looked like dust or lint that had gotten on her camera lens.

She was missing something.

A chill drifted across her neck and she rubbed at it.

She laid the magnifying glass down, opened her laptop and the file of photos. Enlarged them to fill the screen. If she couldn't find anything this way, she was going to have Mason connect her laptop to her husband's big screen TV so she could see the photos even larger.

The house hid its secrets.

"Zoom out," a familiar voice said to her from across the too-dark den.

Her smile became the one-of-a-kind that only he could bring to her face. "You're late."

Her dead husband sat cross-legged in his former recliner as he often had, and tipped one side of his mouth in a sly grin. "I'm not late. You're impatient. Zoom out."

"What?"

He nodded to her computer "Zoom out. Not in."

She did as he suggested until she had a bird's-eye view of the great hall. "What am I looking at?"

"Pull back a little. Soften your focus," Steele said.

Dixie scooted away from the computer. "I'm going to need my glasses."

Her husband stood behind her and pointed to a place in the photo where curtains hung on the back wall. "Here. And then here. See?"

Dixie followed her husband's finger as it traced a glassy outline in the pattern of the fabric. "Is that a face?"

He still had the scent of pipe smoke about him and her heart ached to be close to him again. He pointed to another area. "That's his arm. And see that?"

"Why didn't I see this person when I was there? Why aren't they showing up like they normally do for me?"

"Not everything is visible at the manor."

A sick feeling rose up in her throat, she tried to swallow.

"You need to get Layla and her girls and Mason out of there," he said. Seriously.

She glanced at the watery reflection of a face. "Is that Asher?"

Her husband nodded. "Stay away from the manor. Promise me. He killed Tom. He'll kill you, too."

14

"Daddy?" Emma's voice called through the baby monitor that was still clasped in Layla's hand.

The presence in front of Layla shifted in a release of pressure and she dashed ahead in a frenzy, stumbling upward in the dark. Her knees banged against the rounded edges of the steps, her free hand hit everything in front of her in search of a way out.

She moved faster than she ever had, scrabbling, grasping and praying. And yet with the unseen presence close behind her she felt unbearably slow.

Her knuckles finally hit a door. She clamored up the final steps until she was upright, her hands fumbling the loose round doorknob that was cold in her hand. With a firm twist of the knob and a hard shove, the door flew open and Layla pitched forward, landing on the black and white marble flooring of the great hall.

She scuttled on all fours across the hallway, knowing that he was behind her, grabbing for one of her legs. When she reached the wainscoting on the opposite wall, she spun around and prepared to fight for her life.

The hallway was empty.

The open throat of the stairwell gaped wide in front her. Dark and quiet and waiting.

The sound of her breath bounced off the stone floors and walls and made her feel quite alone. The lights from other rooms shone bright, but the hallway lights barely flickered. She slid upward against the wall and eyed the dimmer, the one she knew controlled the gold and crystal sconces on the walls. Keeping her eye on the mouth of the stairway, she sidestepped to the light switch and pushed it up.

The light shone on the first few steps of the stairwell. She stretched upward to see the next few. She fully expected Asher's clown-like smile and dark eyes staring back at her. She walked closer, pushing the door wide with a squeak until the light from the hallway spilled downward.

The baby monitor crackled and she jumped.

"Daddy..."

Emma Catherine.

She was dreaming. Imagining that her father was still alive and nearby.

Layla stood on tiptoe and peered down the stairway: no one there. With light shining, the passage seemed unthreatening now.

The presence she had felt moments ago was gone. She tried to sense the danger, but it wasn't there. This was just an old staircase: old creaky wood and old electrical wiring in an old narrow passageway. Maybe she was reacting in old ways, too. The way she would have when Asher was still alive.

She waited for a noise, a movement, a feeling she couldn't explain, something to justify her reaction. But there was only warm light falling gently over an old nightmare. She drew in a deep and stuttered breath.

She walked down the long hallway and thought about what she looked like—scrambling up those stairs like a crazy woman. She chuckled nervously and sweat prickled under her arms. The air through the baby monitor breathed steady and quiet, like the ocean through a conch shell. Emma must have settled down.

Layla walked into the music room, her insides trembled from too much adrenaline. Too many memories. The oversized crystal chandelier glowed softly like hundreds of lit candles. The hard parquet floor, the antique Queen Anne's couch, and the robin's egg blue fabric—blurred. The historically accurate scene reminded her of the manor's dead zone. The strange place she'd been yanked into the week before, the unexplainable place between what used to be and the present day. Where young girls in hand-sewn dresses of yesteryear ran through the kitchen in flickering images and sounds. Where things happened that shouldn't.

If Tom were still around, she would have spoken to him about it. He was open-minded. He would understand. She backed out of the room.

She headed toward the kitchen. She couldn't have explained it, but there was another dimension to this house, a reality that couldn't be seen by most people. One that she couldn't see either, unless she shifted into a lucid dream and she had recently spent time at the manor. But she felt it.

Memories never died here, they continued to live on in some capacity, forgetting that their place was in the past. She wondered, and not for the first time, if that cake and the dog really did cross over from this other dimension.

She passed by arched doorways that were wide and tall enough to dwarf full grown men. Wall sconces cast more than enough light for her to see everything in her path. They also cast spindly, shifting shadows against the gold wallpaper. The grandfather clock on the second floor chimed. She stopped and looked back in the direction of the open doorway, still expecting Asher or someone to be cast forth.

The dream about the mug was a fluke. Stress. She and Emma were both dreaming about him as though he were alive.

Which he wasn't.

She passed the grand staircase, realizing that she was only steps away from where Asher had died. She wondered if she ought to leave a flower to help make peace. Then she decided what she really wanted to do was throw confetti.

She hovered at the doorway of the kitchen. She remembered Mason standing in this room, looking too handsome in his T-shirt and jeans. Seeing him again after all this time was such a strange thing. Odd and right out of the blue. There was a time in their friendship when she would have trusted him with her life. Funny how things changed, and not always for the better.

She remembered walking to the neighborhood pool with him on the weekends when they were about eleven. He was gangly then. His feet seemed to grow ahead of everything else, and it wasn't unusual for him to trip and fall for no reason. One minute they were having a conversation, and the next he was picking himself up off the grass while she was bent over in a fit of laughter. He had a way of tickling her funny bone, no matter what silly little thing he did.

Plain shelves along the kitchen walls stored plates and other dishes, and there was an austere but functional white sink that was standard for the day. The black iron range attached to a fireplace, and strangely she could almost feel the heat. The shadowy sense of kitchen work bustled around her like long gone experiences that couldn't settle.

A heavy wooden work table in the middle of the room had been sanded but not finished, and sheets of newspaper lay beneath it. She could almost see bowls of fruit and small barrels of sugar and flour. Maybe containers of spices, too.

When she turned, she saw the one thing she didn't expect: an ugly, brown fat-bottomed mug with the words Born to Golf printed on the side of it. Something loud and frightening jarred inside of her, an unwelcome awareness that once again she was not alone.

"Make me a tea, would you, Lay?"

Her breathing came fast and shallow, her heart raced to keep up, and a hatred for all things Asher fired in her chest. She felt bound and captive. Smothered and trapped.

She could almost smell it, that whiff of Asher she'd noticed on her first day here. Like a bad cologne, it drifted through the room and around her with a sense of ownership.

"No," she said aloud.

He was her past. She should not be afraid. Her body shivered, then she straightened her shoulders. She would not allow any sort of place for him

She cringed inwardly at the tiny squeaks her bare feet made against the hardwoods in the silence. She lifted the mug by the outside curve and smashed it on the floor. The commercial-grade pottery broke into thick shards that rocked on the floor.

If Asher had been alive, he would have raged about how this was his *favorite* mug, and he would have made her clean up the shattered mess. He would have made her replace it with a new mug, a replica. Then he might have slapped her.

Or twisted her arm. Or bent a few of her fingers just shy of the breaking point.

The metallic taste of panic flooded her mouth. She slid to the floor and leaned against a leg of the heavy work table. She strained to hear any evidence of his presence—footsteps, laughter, knocking. The silence didn't feel quiet. There was a vibe of movement even with no one around.

She willed herself to get up. She needed to walk outside or go downstairs. She couldn't move. The idea of a deep breath made her feel too vulnerable, though she desperately needed it.

The rap at the back door turned her inhale into a sharp gasp. A man's face pressed close to the glass on the back door.

Mason unlocked and slid through the opened door quickly. "Hey, Layla-pop. Everything okay?" His voice was tender and his use of her nickname was a sweet memory, not to mention a well-timed one.

She pressed her palm to her chest to calm her heart that pounded like a jackhammer. "What are you doing here?"

He placed a Sammi's-On-The-Sea to-go bag on the side table, sat next to her on the floor, and put his hand on her knee. "I thought you might need a hot meal on your first night. Joueat?"

She knew exactly what he asked. A good Southerner always combined those three words—did you eat—into one: joueat? She couldn't answer.

He studied her face then asked, "Everything alright?"

She nodded short and quick, keeping her secrets to herself.

He leaned toward her slowly, wrapping his arms around her and holding her close. Under normal circumstances, she would have pushed him away. But she had never felt more alone or frightened, so she allowed herself the momentary oasis of his strength. Her nerves were knocking together like they were surrounded by ice.

After a long moment he whispered, "Are you okay?"

The ice inside of her melted by half. She closed her eyes, let Mason hold her. He pulled away to look at her face.

"No." She caught her breath and fought a wave of embarrassment.

"What's wrong?"

"No, I mean, I haven't eaten. I'm fine."

The smell of food in the kitchen made her suddenly aware of how hungry she was. She had been so busy straightening up the kitchen, cooking and cleaning up that there hadn't been time for her to eat. "I'll put something together later."

"Well, now you won't have to." He gave her leg a little hug, as if to say I'm-here-for-you.

She was caught at the intersection of needing to create some distance and yet feeling a strange intimacy and comfort with him. Like time hadn't passed between them over the last ten years, like she'd never killed Brooke, and like Asher had never been a part of her life.

She pinched the skin on the back of her hand to make sure she was awake.

"Didn't like that mug?" His smile was the same. Easy, well-meaning and tipped in humor on one side.

She stared at the thick shards on the floor and decided to come clean for once. It had been a too-difficult week, and she didn't have the energy to configure politically correct answers anyway. "Asher used to have one just like it."

He nodded. "Reason enough."

She pushed the pieces away from her with the side of her foot.

"Here. I'll do that." He patted her knee twice as he got up. "You making your evening rounds?"

"Yeah. I was just on my way upstairs."

Mason's back was bodyguard broad, and the sheer size of him made her feel safe. She took that deep breath she needed, and the icy fear inside of her melted by yet another half.

He held the broken pieces in his open hand and showed them to her. "He's gone now," he said with such seriousness that she wondered if he knew about the way Asher had treated her.

Mason had never spoken positively of Asher. "I don't trust him," he'd said over and over.

She stared at the crumbled mess that he held in his large hands and felt comforted by what she saw.

"That's not a bad thing," she managed. "Wait, that wasn't *your* mug, was it?" She hoped it was, actually. Because that meant that Asher hadn't found a way to put it there.

"No." The pieces hit the bottom of the metal trash can with a clatter. "Wasn't mine. I don't know whose it was, but I wouldn't worry about it. Smashing a mug is cheaper than therapy." He wet a paper towel and wiped the floor where the mug had fallen.

She used the top of the long work table to lift herself upright. The table squeaked, showing its age.

"Do you like it?" He patted the table that was the center point of the kitchen. "We found her in the attic storage, I think she had been forgotten up there. Lots of nicks and damage, but I can bring her back. She'll be perfect again before long." He was changing the subject, taking the pressure off, giving her a minute to restore herself. They both knew he had walked in on her mid-falling apart.

His expression was reassuring, even interested. He

rested his hands on his hips and faced her, appearing as though he had nothing else to do in this world but talk with her. Just over his shoulder and through the window was a view of the great lawn, and a long-ago memory hit her like the sharp end of jagged lightning: Mason hovering over Brooke, her head bloodied and her sister Jordan screaming and pointing to Layla.

She blinked and refocused while he described the table's flaws—deep grooves from the cooks who used it as a cutting surface, an uneven slope and one leg shorter than the other. "But I'll bring her around. Before too long, she'll be all right angles with a smooth finish. No one will know what she used to be."

"Are you here to work?" she asked.

"No. I'm here because I brought you dinner." He pointed to the bag from Sammi's.

"Oh. You didn't have to do that."

"I wanted to." His smile offered compassion.

She knew she must look shaken, with little wonder as to why. With a glance to where the mug had been, she had a sudden urge to wake the girls, pack their bags, and leave the house. "Do you think there's any chance of moving up the deadline on the remaining repairs?"

He nodded hesitantly. "Ah, well. Tom and I laid out a schedule. Why don't we go over that tomorrow?"

"I want to get the tours going as fast as possible. He left us in a bad place," she said, referring to her former husband.

"Understand." His light brown eyes looked at her softly, warmly, and his gentle smile was quiet and patient. It was as though he waited for her to say something. If she had been her sister, she might have known the perfect thing to say.

As it was, their history coiled around her like a python,

so she just said, "Well. I guess I'd better get upstairs before the night gets away from me."

He gestured in the direction of the grand staircase. "Of course."

"I was actually going to take the back way. To avoid—" She didn't want to say his name, let alone stand anywhere near where he had died. Unless it was to throw confetti.

He frowned. Just as people did when they wished they hadn't missed the obvious. "Sorry about that." He extended an arm in the opposite direction. "This way, then."

She pushed her long hair over her shoulder and made a smile. "I'll be back in a few minutes."

"I'll go with you." His voice was cheery.

She stared at him for a moment and half-thought of telling him no.

Why was he really here at this time of night? Why was he giving her so much attention? When they parted ten years ago he never said as much as goodbye. She knew he hadn't forgotten.

He followed right behind her when they went up the spiral staircase to the second level. It felt good to climb so many steps and not be out of breath, not to have to pause because her knees or her back hurt and not to let someone pass because she was afraid of being judged from behind.

The first guest room they entered was framed with sunny yellow drapes and anchored with a gold-toned hand-hooked rug. The room ought to have been welcoming, but the period four poster bed, side table, and dresser were minimalistic at best, and more functional than gracious. The grand height of the room dwarfed the pieces, making them seem more suitable to a dollhouse.

Layla adjusted the yellow rose print quilt and fought a disconnected feeling, like she had fallen through the proverbial rabbit hole. The mug incident left her rattled. Each time she looked up, she half-expected to find Asher standing somewhere in the room.

"How's Jayne Ella these days?" Mason's voice was deep and clear and she jumped when it cut into the evening quiet in the room.

He leaned against the doorway. He flashed her an effortless grin, and she thought about how Asher would hate that Mason was here.

"She's a good grandmother, the girls love her." Layla turned out the light in the bathroom and passed Mason on her way to the next room.

"And Peyton? Is she living nearby?"

"She's in Boston, working in advertising. Not super happy with the big city. I think she's a little tired of the expense."

"That'll wear you out."

"And how about—

"Mason." Her tone was gentle, but she was firm. "I'm not sure why you're here tonight, and I sort of doubt that it's because you thought I needed a meal on moving day."

He looked at the floor and chuckled. "I know you've been through a lot lately. I thought you might want some dinner and company. That's all."

She shook her head, stepped across the hall to the next guest room, where the antique dolls on the shelves made her nervous. They all appeared to be staring at her through black eye sockets. She struggled with how to approach him. They'd known each other for too long to be strangers, and yet after all this time they were basically unknown to one another. So she spoke to him as she always had—directly and with a smile. "I don't believe you."

"Well. We're going to have to work together, now that

Tom's gone. I thought maybe we ought to get to know one another again."

A twinge of hope and disappointment tangled together in her gut, which she found annoying. There was no hope where Mason was concerned, and she wished her heart would grasp that simple fact. She gave him a gentle smile that said she still didn't quite believe what he was saying. Then she began to think of the tours that would begin soon enough. Mason would be a part of her past again by that point.

The bathroom light shone from across the room and she decided to leave it on for the night. The bedside lamp was also on and she turned that one off. Mason was now backlit by the hallway lights. When she tried to pass him, he stopped her with a gentle touch and she caught her breath.

"Okay. Truth. I've felt awful for ten years that our friendship ended the way it did. We're both here now. I'd like to make a fresh start."

An inadvertent laugh escaped from her. "Fresh start because of proximity? We don't have to do that."

"*I'd* like to have a fresh start."

She exhaled hard. Hands on her hips.

"Layla, look. Ten years ago—"

"I was really hoping we wouldn't rehash how our friendship ended. It was bad enough the first time around."

"I'm not looking to rehash anything." Mason's voice was soft.

When she reached the next bedroom, one of the masters that belonged to Anna Alcott, she heard him say, "I'm sorry, Layla."

She stopped mid-step and closed her eyes. She had longed to hear that apology for so many years. That it finally had arrived felt even better than she thought it would, and she had known it would feel pretty darn good.

He sighed heavily. "I should have believed you right away when you said you didn't lay a hand on Brooke. I don't know why the other girls were so insistent that you did."

A nauseating wave shifted through her.

She turned.

"I don't expect you to forgive me right away," he said." But I hope you can find a way. Regardless, I wanted to apologize. Finally." He took her hand in his and squeezed it twice to get her attention, until she looked him directly in the eye.

"I am...so sorry."

It wasn't his first apology tonight. But something about this one wrapped around her heart and gave it a heads-down hug. It was an apology filled with tenderness, regret, and full-on friendship.

"You and I had a lot of history together as friends. I should have known it wasn't in your nature to do something so violent."

"No, that wasn't my nature."

He slowly edged his way in front of her until they stood face to face.

"The way our friendship ended has always bothered me —like a train jumped the tracks. So, when I knew you were moving into the manor, I didn't want another day to go by without putting things right between us. And that's the real reason why I'm here tonight."

He looked at her like he hoped for a positive response, like he needed it from her. His mystical ginger brown eyes were full of regret and a softness she hadn't expected. She had missed this face, the way he looked at her, the way he could see into her, the way he cared. For so long, they had been like two puzzle pieces that fit together perfectly—the best of friends.

She looked for the walls she had constructed to keep him out but they were nowhere to be found. She indulged her heart. She placed her hand on the side of his face and ran her thumb over his cheek. "I've missed you."

He leaned into her caress with a long blink, like he breathed in her touch. When he opened his eyes again, they were full of longing. For a moment she thought he might kiss her. His lips parted slightly and she gazed at him, remembering how soft his lips had been in her dream.

Strands of crystal facets dangled from the overhead chandelier, they clinked against one another in the still room. She and Mason both looked up at it. A cold chill spread across Layla's back.

"It's probably just the air conditioning," Mason said.

The lights flickered.

"Look out!" Mason screamed.

The overhead chandelier crashed to the floor.

15

M ason and Layla picked themselves off the floor. The chandelier lay broken where they had been standing.

"Next time." Asher waited until they finally left the bedroom. He stared out the window. All that beachfront property. It had been his lifelong dream to develop the Alcott Manor land. That was why he'd married Layla Alcott. Though he would have married any stock-holding Alcott woman who was willing, who would have voted to tear down the house, and who would have voted to let his real estate company develop the land.

She hadn't really dated much. She was long overdue for Prince Charming. That meant every bit of attention he gave her made him look the hero.

What he hadn't predicted was that he wouldn't be able to persuade Layla to vote for the way he wanted. The vote had always been narrow between the two sides of the family — twenty-one of the shareholders wanted to restore, the other twenty wanted out and to sell the land to a developer.

Layla was easy to control on most things, but dang if she

didn't hold firm on this. Some malarky about how the house was special to her family. How it was an historical landmark that needed to be preserved.

He saw a hotel, maybe a mixed use land sale—residential and commercial. There were options, all of them profitable and enough to set him for life.

Mason put his arm around a badly shaken Layla. They walked down the hallway. How sweet. Reunited friends.

If she had voted the way he wanted, she wouldn't be a homeless mother of two. He would have given her a share of the proceeds before he divorced her. He didn't want to be unfair. He just didn't want to be married to her.

When he first decided to go after her, he thought the whole process would take less than a couple of years. Who couldn't sacrifice for a couple of years when there was a huge payoff?

Layla left the last bedroom door open before she and Mason began their return trip toward the kitchen for a quaint dinner together. Asher's temper burned somewhere close to where his chest used to be.

He rushed by them and slammed the door. The two of them jumped and spun around. Layla gripped Mason's arm. He patted her hand and said something about loose hinges and drafts. It wasn't right that she should have a second chance at life. Much less at love.

He had had her on his side of the Alcott Manor restoration dilemma for quite a while. The haunted house stories even worked in his favor. And the people who died there? Just brilliant. Helped his cause perfectly. Especially with her.

The house is literally killing people, Layla! It would be safer for the community, for everyone, if it weren't around anymore.

He could see her nodding even now. Oh, his little puppet.

Layla-pup. Not, Layla-pop. You could drag her anywhere.

He did what he could to keep her down. Anything to keep her tied to the house and the kids usually worked. By the end of the day, she was too tired and worn out to dream or hope or even think of wanting a better life.

Funny how that worked.

You would think that when someone was overworked, overtired and overloaded emotionally, they would dream of a better life all the time. Like Cinderella or characters in some Broadway musical.

But he found that she ran out of energy to dream. She forgot to hope. Guilt was effective in an evergreen sort of way, too. He never tired of using that one. Thanks to her Mom, she had so much guilt to work with.

He paced back and forth just yards from Layla and Mason while they sat in front of that magnificent ocean view. He was a gracious man. He could let his dream go. Sometimes things didn't work out in life. He had no use for that money now anyway.

What he couldn't tolerate, though, was that Layla might end up happy. Truly, madly happy.

He'd married her, made her feel loved, wanted and special. He gave her not just one, but two children, when she'd asked for them. He'd played his part perfectly. He'd played it so well, he should have won an award.

Now he was stuck in a house that should have been torn down a long damn time ago. A constant reminder that she'd failed him.

Unfair. Unjust.

Look at her—thin, pretty, blonde. A knockout. He shook

with anger at the very thought of her morphing into some beautiful butterfly while he was nonexistent. He might not be able to do anything about *his* life. That was over. But through a fortunate turn of events, he could place his finger on the scales of justice where *her* life was concerned. She was at Alcott Manor with him.

She would sleep.

She would dream.

And that was his way into her world.

For some reason Alcott Manor made her dream very special dreams. Powerful ones that left their mark on the world. One night when they were both asleep, and after an all-day family meeting on the back lawn of the manor, he found himself in one of her dreams. It wasn't his own dream. Strange as it was to say, he knew he was in *her* dream world. It was as if he were a guest in someone else's house. He was a visitor, along for the ride, while she drove the proverbial bus.

She dreamt they were on the back lawn at the manor again. The girls ran in and out of the water, letting the tide chase them. He grilled hamburgers and corn on the cob outside, and Layla approached him about a divorce.

"I told you..." he began, so emphatic when he spoke and shaking the tongs in her face. She wrestled his hand away and he burned the side of his hand on the grill. The next morning when he woke up, he had a burn mark in the exact same spot.

Now she was locked into Alcott Manor for a while. That meant her dreams would continue to come alive.

If he was going to spend an eternity here, she should have to as well. That would be payback enough.

All he would have to do was wait.

"Make me a tea, would you, Lay?"

16

"Jordan's back in Charleston."

Layla's knife poked through the bottom of her Styrofoam container and stabbed her leg. "Ouch —" She lifted the hem of her dress over her knee.

"You okay?" Mason examined the cut, a gesture he wouldn't have offered to anyone else.

A decade had passed without a word between them, though he had not forgotten what it was like to feel the simple warmth of her skin beneath his touch.

When he was younger, he wasn't sure how to handle the connection that sparked between them. Like she somehow reached unfamiliar depths inside of him, places within he hadn't yet explored. She wasn't someone to be treated casually, and what they shared was too important to experiment with. It had been a slow realization for him that she was someone unlike any other, someone reserved for the things that mattered most in life. He thought he had always known that on some level, and yet he wondered if perhaps it had taken him too long to figure that out. "I didn't think to pick up regular plates. Sorry about that."

When he walked in the manor earlier and found her smashing that mug, he figured that had something to do with Asher. Now his mentioning the name of Brooke's sister sent a knife into her skin. Would the two of them ever find peace, or would some part of their lives remain rooted in that night when everything fell apart?

"Again, I'm sorry about the chandelier. I'm going to have words with the electrician tomorrow."

"We're okay, and that's what's most important." Her smile was easy and familiar and reminded him of everything good, everything real, everything worthwhile.

"Have y'all spoken?" She lowered the hem of her dress.

He started to tell her that he and Jordan had dated when they both lived in New York. It was only for a short while and nothing serious, but he thought Layla ought to know. He didn't want her to think he was hiding anything. Charleston was a small town, and stories were shared more quickly than the common cold. And Jordan felt jilted when he called it off. Which meant that predicting her next move was impossible. Now didn't seem to be the right time to share that information.

"Here and there. Not much since she got back," he said. "We both lived in New York for a while, and I saw her more then. I think it bugged me too much that she lied about you killing Brooke. Lying is something I can't forgive."

Layla didn't look at him. She knew this about him already.

The lights from inside the manor cast a yellowish glow to the back veranda where Mason had set dinner for them. At the far end of the great lawn, the ocean crashed onto the packed sand in slow percussion, filling the occasional quiet with movement and sound. Warm breezes caressed and stroked, like nature nudged them to talk, to reunite, to move forward. But Layla was reserved. Resistant, even. He tilted his head to catch her eye, to get her attention.

She offered him a half-smile. "Long day. The chandelier falling really shook me." She quickly glanced over her shoulder at the manor as though someone called for her attention. Her face held the same expression he'd seen when he first walked into the kitchen tonight and found her sitting on the floor. It wasn't fatigue. It was fear.

Mentioning Jordan didn't help. He looked at the same windows along the back of the house and fought the unsettling feeling that they were being watched. The manor held a continual disquiet, an unrest, a lack of peace. Like a gathering took place within the walls and just beyond his sight. He wondered if Layla sensed it, too.

"I understand. Everything okay downstairs in the summer quarters?"

She nodded agreeably and talked about how grateful she was that Tom gave them the space. She was pleasant, friendly and even gracious. But something sat between them like an invisible wall, and he wasn't sure how to get through it. He thought about how strange it was to know you were meant to spend the rest of your life with someone, when the two of you hadn't even been on a first date.

His mother had taught him to lean into that internal voice of wisdom, the one that could guide you along the right path. Now he wondered if he had misunderstood, because Layla obviously didn't share the same sense of knowing that he did.

"What brought you back to Charleston?" Her question was direct, her voice soft and hesitant.

He finished his bite, put his container down, and wiped his mouth with his napkin. Then he looked her directly in the eye. He'd known this question was coming and not only was he ready, he hoped his answers would solve her resistance.

"Mostly a lot of soul searching," he said in earnest and waited for another question. When it didn't come, he kept going. In the way he had rehearsed. "When Daddy died—"

"I read about that in the paper. I'm so sorry. I wanted to come to the funeral, but I didn't know if that was the right thing—" She winced.

That was her polite way of saying that she didn't know if she would be welcome. "No, it's fine. I understand."

"He was so young."

"Fifty-four. Heart attack."

She shook her head. "So tragic. How is Dixie doing?"

"She's tough. Resilient. Amazes me every day how strong she is. She says she focuses on their time together and that gets her through." Something jarred inside of him when he repeated his mother's words.

"Sounds like her." Layla sighed. "I miss the talks she and I used to have. She was such a positive force in my life when I was growing up."

"She's always loved you." He poured wine into their glasses and the air filled with the scent of peaches and apples.

Layla's smile was sweet and misty, like previously forgotten memories warmed her heart. "Does she still do interior design? That game room she did at the country club was so exquisite. Like she brought the room over from a British castle."

Mason thought of his childhood home that hadn't been updated since he was in high school and right after the Reverend Milligan disaster. Between the too-dark shaggy carpet, the unfashionable kitchen cabinets, and curtains with sun-induced holes, it was obvious that Dixie had given up one of her brightest talents.

"I don't care about that stuff anymore, Mason," his mother said whenever he pushed her to restart her decorating. "I don't want to have anything to do with those women."

The women she referenced had shamed every client away from her. The country club, too. It was wrong. Unjust. Now her business was dead and her husband was gone. Mason sent her money each month to make her financial ends meet. He was happy to do it, but she should have been able to do what she was good at, she should have been able to earn a living, she should have been able to do both of those things without judgment.

"No. She helped Daddy a little bit with the houses he built. You know, staging some of the final homes so they would sell faster. She also helped him rearrange some of the floor plans, said she enjoyed giving him the woman's point of view."

"I'll bet she did." Layla raised both eyebrows in a Dixie-means-business kind of way and they both laughed.

"It was actually Dixie who got me thinking about coming home," he said to bring the conversation back to his point. "After Daddy died she said she noticed something about me, said she didn't think I was happy. That led to a lot of discussions about—"

"What is real? What is true?" Layla's lips broadened into a graceful smile at their shared memory.

"You remembered."

"Maybe not until this moment. But I well remember her advice. Wish I had held on to that through the years." Her eyes widened with too much to tell and Mason nodded in agreement. He wished he had held on to that advice through the years, too.

"I spent a bunch of time walking Central Park. Ultimately I realized that every answer to those two questions lead me back here—to the things I loved doing and the people I love most. Like carrying on Daddy's good name in the homebuilding business, working with my hands and spending my time with people I genuinely care about."

He wanted to add—people like you. But he knew saying that would make him sound psycho. It would bring the evening to an abrupt end, so he opted for a more gentle approach. He picked up their glasses of wine. "Let's walk."

She turned up the volume on the baby monitor so she could hear her daughters from a distance, and she took his hand when he offered it as an assist down the back stairs. They strolled next to the fragrant herbs and through the rose gardens, ignoring the area where they had camped over a decade ago, as if they could.

She told him about her girls, and her nursing career. They talked about old times, good times, and the best shared times, the last of which made them laugh uncontrollably.

He pointed to a gliding bench built for two, where they sat and watched the moonlight ripple over the waves. The seagulls and the whitewater serenaded their peaceful silence, accented only by the rhythmic squeak of the glider. When a briny breeze raced over the lawn, she closed her eyes and inhaled it deeply, her smile appearing as though she had finally found a safe place to let go, to trust, to be free. He thought he sensed an opening, a pathway forward. Like a gentle release, he thought he felt her carefully crafted walls relax, and he took the chance.

"I also came back to Charleston because I wanted to make things right with you," he said.

She turned to him, her sky blue eyes wide and soft. In a

flash, he thought he saw something sacred—a flicker of hope. Then she laughed gently, sipped her wine and adjusted her thin flowered dress that graced her ankles. "Well, you didn't have to move home to do that. You could have called. Or sent a letter. Email works."

A well-timed wave crashed loudly, like it objected. He turned and faced her more directly. "No. Making things right with you is important. It warranted a face-to-face conversation. At least. And—" He pressed his hands together and stared at them for a moment. This would either go really well or really badly. "I wanted—I hoped we might start our friendship again. When I found out you were single, I hoped we might try to pick up where we left off. Before everything fell apart."

Her eyes shifted toward him abruptly.

He ran his hand over his face, certain now that he was bungling this.

"What I'm trying to say is, the end of our friendship is one of the biggest regrets of my life. I realized, hopefully not too late, that a relationship with you was a once in a lifetime thing. I've really missed what we used to share with one another. I've missed *you*, Layla."

Her slightly open-mouthed stare made her appear as if he had stunned her into silence. He wasn't at all sure what she thought, so he just kept talking.

"It's why I took this job." He gestured to the manor behind them and was glad not to look at it.

She rubbed her arm slowly like she was brushing away a chill, and he hoped he hadn't given her the creeps. He hoped he didn't sound like a stalker. He hoped for the best. Oddly, he wondered if Dixie ever struggled with this, when she knew the truth before someone else did.

"You don't have to answer right away. Think about it." He

was completely tongue-tied around her and everything he said seemed to make it worse.

She stood and he figured she was about to say thanks and goodnight. The ocean breeze blew the bottom hem of her button front dress behind her and lifted the ends of her long, blonde hair.

He drew in a deep breath. He would give her time. All that she needed.

Finally, she sat next to him again. "What does that mean, exactly? Pick up where we left off?"

"I hoped we might try to go back—before everything fell apart," he said as plainly as he could and then realized he hadn't offered any clarity. "I'm hoping you would go out with me."

She scoffed. "You don't even know me anymore."

He exhaled and laid his heart and ego and feelings between them. She could do with them what she chose. All he had left was humility. He had spent a lot of time doing what Dixie coached him to do—following his heart, his happiness, his gut. It had led him here. It was all risk and vulnerability and trust, qualities he had only ever been able to embrace around Layla. But from the look on her face, he wasn't sure if that was enough.

"I'd like for us to get to know one another again. Take it slow. Enjoy the process."

She looked over the darkened lawn where it had happened. Two memories flashed in rapid fire in his mind, like they were stuck on a loop. Brooke lying on her blood-soaked pillow, Jordan screaming in the background that Layla had killed her. Then weeks later, the detective saying, "It's forensically impossible for Layla Alcott to have hurt Brooke. The facts are solid, and they just don't point to her."

An endless circle of mystery. The police never did figure out who attacked her.

"I haven't heard from you in ten years." She waved in the direction where Brooke had been killed.

"I'm sorry. I should have tried harder."

They stared at one another. She certainly didn't owe him anything. And although he knew it wouldn't be enough to bet on, he felt heat between them, simmering. The chemistry they once had was still there.

He could tell from the look in her eye that she wondered how much to trust. He knew he wasn't the only one to put that fear there, but he had played a role.

He held her hand in his. "When I came to see you, I hoped you'd let me apologize then and there and try to put things back together for us. When your mother told me you were with Asher and that you didn't want to see me, I understood. I mean, here I was—"

"What?" Layla's tone was scissor-sharp.

"I understood. You were moving on, beginning a new life. I screwed up."

"You came to see me?" She stood slowly, like something propelled her from the inside.

"I did. And then I also tried to find you at graduation, but you didn't go—"

"Because I'd gotten death threats from Jordan's and Brooke's friends. You came to see me?"

His chest tightened. He hadn't known about the death threats. He would have put a stop to that. "I did come to see you. Many times. Twice when Brooke was still in her coma. Several times after she died. I spoke with your mother each time."

She covered her mouth with her fingers. Her eyes shifted back and forth, like a horror movie played behind them.

He rubbed the outside of her arms to comfort her or steady himself, he wasn't sure. He could still see Jayne Ella's red-angry face scolding him for how he had hurt her daughter. "It was right after graduation. She told me to go away and stay away, that you never wanted to see me again."

Slowly, Layla backed away. Her gaze lifted toward the sky and she laughed, short and breathy. Not as though something were funny, but more like something was utterly unbelievable. "I never said that. And she never told me you came by."

Their eyes locked hard on one another. They said nothing for a moment. He stood and pushed his hands through his hair. "It never occurred to me that Jayne Ella was lying. You must have thought I blamed you just like everyone else. You must have thought I hated you. You must have thought—oh gosh, Layla. I even came by again before I left for school. She said the same thing, that you didn't want to have anything to do with me."

She kept her hand over her heart, like she tried to stem the hurt. "I didn't know."

He took a step toward her. "I tried calling you. Several times. But—"

"Jayne Ella had my phone number changed. The press kept calling, Brooke's friends and Jordan harassed me nonstop—"

It seemed there was a lot he didn't know about Jordan. Which surprised him, considering how much time they had spent together in New York. "I thought you were mad for how I acted that night. I thought you wanted me to move on."

Layla stared where the waves crashed. She finally turned to face him. "I—um. I wasn't mad. I was...distraught. Before that night, you had kissed me, and I thought it meant something. You said you were breaking up with Brooke and that you wanted to take me out. I thought we were heading someplace. And then...it was over and I thought..."

He stepped toward her until they were only inches apart. He felt nothing but gratitude that he could be this close to her again. "It did mean something," he said, remembering how her kiss made him feel. "Our friendship, that kiss. You. Us. This has never been over for me." He pressed his lips to hers and felt her body lean against his chest. Her kiss was even better than he had remembered—her soft lips pressing against his, awakening something inside of him. "This will never be over for me."

Her kiss lit a fire inside of him. It played upon the harmony of their friendship and made their connection nothing less than amazing. It stunned him and held him in the magic of it all, the magic he had only ever known with Layla.

LAYLA LEANED against one of the pillars. The evening ocean breeze was warm and playful and seemed to twirl around them like a playful child. Like it was happy for what they had managed to figure out.

Mason's eyes skimmed along the eaves of the manor. "The last decade could have been very different for the both of us if Jayne Ella hadn't interfered."

She remembered how her mother had pushed her into marrying Asher. "Story of my life." She wondered if he would have continued their relationship had Brooke lived. Or would he have chosen her instead? She wasn't ready to ask that question yet.

They stood beneath the portico, at the top of the stairs.

He held her hands in his. The great lawn and the ocean laid out in epic grace before them. "I know we can't erase the last ten years, but we could start fresh from today. There's no reason why not. Right?"

Except that all of the reasons *why not* quickly marched across Layla's brain, one by one, like a technicolor parade. Primary among them was that she was a murderer. She was the one who had killed Brooke and ruined their lives. She grinned like she agreed with him, while inwardly her heart dropped like a sinking ship.

"This weekend, I'd like to take you out on that date I promised you a long time ago."

She nodded, and he guided her into the kitchen.

"I'll plan something special," he said.

He must have noticed something in her expression, or maybe it was because she had become quiet, because he asked, "Are you uncomfortable staying here alone tonight?"

"I'll set the alarm, we'll be fine." A distant thought of Asher and the dead zone knocked at the outside of her mind.

"You sure? I could sleep on the couch. First nights in new places are always difficult."

Her throat tightened at the thought of having to walk down the dark stairwell again.

"Well, actually, the lights are out in the stairwell." She gestured in that direction with the baby monitor. "Maybe you could just fix that before you leave?"

His grin broadened in that all-American boyish style that made her knees do funny things. "I'll do better than that."

He closed the door behind him and locked it, then set the alarm.

"Mason, I'm not suggesting—"

"No, I'm just going to fix those lights for you. Then I'll sleep on the couch up here." He pointed down the main hallway. "In case y'all need anything. I'll leave early in the morning and come back with breakfast."

She found herself taking a deep breath. "Thank you."

"This house is a monster, too big, takes some getting used to. I have my phone on me, call if you need anything."

He gestured casually, in an adorable hunky-quarterback kind of way, a gracious smile on his lips said he was only too happy to help her. For a moment, it was as if the last ten years had never happened.

17

The stairwell lighting issue turned out to be a wiring problem. So they agreed to leave the door at the top of the stairs open to allow for plenty of light. They said their goodnights, but not their goodbyes. Her dress swished blithely against her bare legs when she went down the stairs. She didn't think about the dark stranger she had seen earlier in the stairwell, she didn't think about future living arrangements for her family, and she didn't think about anything financial. She didn't think because her heart was centered on all things Mason.

She pinched the delicate skin on the inside of her arm.

Ouch.

Definitely awake.

She tried to guard against hope because she knew, logically, it was futile. But step by pillowy step, her heart was still buoyed by everything she had discovered tonight. He had come by to see her back then, to continue on with what they had started. Wasn't that what he said? At the very least, he had said that what they had would never be over for him.

She remembered that.

She caught a glimpse of the great lawn that stretched from the manor to the ocean. Unusually so, her evergreen guilt about that night was at bay. It was covered by Mason's touch, his kiss, and his caress.

She glanced around the summer quarters, her makeshift home that was a far cry from the upstairs that was adorned with gold and crystal, marble and silk. Rough as the summer quarters were, she was glad that they weren't living with her mother.

Layla expected a surge of anger strong enough to make her eat cake. Chocolate cake. Maybe an entire cake.

To her surprise, there was no anger.

At least not tonight. Oh, she and her mother would have words. But tonight a wrong had been righted, an imbalance had been corrected, and past lies had shifted. Finally, to an honest track.

After Mason had left town, Jayne Ella kept saying that Asher was the only one who cared and the only one who ever would. Her mother said that Mason was gone, that Layla was a fool for caring about him, and girls like her didn't have many options.

As it turned out, Jayne Ella had been wrong on all counts.

She felt ten years' worth of rejection and anger fall away like chunks of rock from her heart.

Layla found her girls and their new dog sprawled across her inflated bed. Their arms and legs were stretched in every which direction, with no room left for their mother. She chuckled. So typical.

It didn't matter, she wouldn't be able to sleep anyway. She was blissfully-can't-feel-her-feet-on-the-ground-happy. Even though she knew it couldn't last, like the schoolgirl she once was, she pretended that it would. That it could.

She opened an old sheet on the couch, laid down, and stared at the bright moon that shone through the window. Though all she could see was Mason, his face close to hers. She closed her eyes and remembered his kiss. A blinding sense of hope surged within her like it was on a rescue mission.

In prompt response to such foolish hope, there came a parade of reasons why, even now, she and Mason could never be together.

Like following the groove of an old scar, her memory touched the events that led to that horrible night:

There weren't any tents at the campout, just sleeping bags and pillows under the stars. Jayne Ella had insisted on that so everyone could lie on their backs and study the various constellations and the Milky Way. But that meant that Layla had been able to see Brooke and Jordan and their friends looking at something on Brooke's phone, making faces with puffy cheeks and laughing themselves silly.

That was the day Brooke said she had accidentally taken pictures of Layla when she was changing. It was a brand new camera phone, and she was so sorry—all an innocent mistake. But not to worry, she said with a shoulder pat. She had deleted them. Brooke smiled, an evil tip of the lip smirk that told Layla nothing had been accidental, nothing had been deleted, and the worst was yet to come.

Once everyone settled into the quiet on that fateful night, Layla started her breathing. She planned to talk to her mother the next day about Brooke and the picture, and Mason as well, since both had been too busy to listen to her sooner. She also planned to talk to the school counselor on Monday.

That night, she did what she needed to do to deal with the stress and the worry and to keep herself from sleepwalking, because that, too, would have been humiliating. Not to mention that she probably would have ended up a mile or two down the darkened beach before she woke up.

In with the sparkling white light. Out with the dark smoke. It hadn't taken long before she woke up in her dream. She was well practiced with the process by that point. She had planned to dream about that day in the locker room, that would have been an exact recreation of the setting. And she was in that locker room for a minute. Though only a minute. Then a mysterious yank to her midsection landed her in the music room of Alcott Manor.

Not in bodily form, since the manor was locked up tight and no one could have gotten inside. Plus, she was still dreaming. She waved her hand in front of her and noticed the image trails the movement created. The air was thick and still, like she had been dropped into a glass jar and the lid sealed tight. No breeze, no movement, the environment had a strangely artificial feeling.

At that time, boards covered the lower half of the antebellum windows and vines of ivy crawled along the walls. Moonlight poured in above the boards and highlighted a fat snake slithering across the dirty floor. Dead leaves and trash crackled under its shifting belly.

The relative quiet was interrupted by a shock of piano music. Layla spun around to find a young girl with long dark curls playing Beethoven's Moonlight Sonata on a square grand piano. The girl was dressed for a concert performance with her bright blue smock and crisp white shirt with the frilled collar. A golden chandelier burned bright above her head with tiny gas-lit flames. Tuxedoed men and taffeta silk-clad women sat on furniture upholstered in robin's egg blue and nodded along to the beat of the music.

Layla walked toward them, unbelieving. It was a dream, yes. One of her lucid dreams, but this dream seemed to have its own agenda. Se reached toward them, the concert goers faded.

In their place were the four girls Layla had intended to

appear in her dream, and every muscle in her body tightened at the sight of them. Brooke looked exactly as she did that day at school—shoulder-length chestnut hair with highlights and a perky flip at the ends, brown eyes framed by dark liner and heavy mascara.

Jordan, Brooke's younger sister by a year, was taller and thinner and far more blonde. Prettier, too. Staci's too-short overly highlighted style was hair sprayed into its usual helmet that topped her perfect tan. Carmen was the shortest and most muscular and had the loudest laugh, which she used when Brooke showed everyone a photo on her phone.

All of the girls looked like variations of Brooke with their black cheerleader spirit uniforms—a cap-sleeved top and a very short straight skirt.

Her dream had gotten back on track, or so she assumed. She didn't know why the setting switched from the locker room to the interior of Alcott Manor and she didn't care.

"Did you really take pictures of me?" Layla asked. "When I was dressing?"

The girls ignored her.

"That's fat. Just plain fat," Jordan said to the other girls with a finger on the phone screen.

"It's diet," Brooke said and clicked to a new photo.

"Holy cow!" Carmen said and laughed so hard she snorted.

Staci's expression bloomed slowly into an open mouthed I-can't-believe-she-looks-like-that type.

"Excuse me," Layla said firmly. "Did you take pictures of me while I was undressed? Brooke?"

Brooke lifted only her gaze, and she nodded slightly. The slightest of smiles curved on her lips.

Layla marched toward her with hellfire and fury and with the never-back-down attitude she wished she had when Brooke had confronted her the first time that day.

"And you took those pictures on purpose, didn't you?" Layla shoved Brooke against her shoulders. "Didn't you?" she pushed Brooke again, and that time Brooke stumbled. Jordan stepped away and guided the other girls to do the same, leaving Brooke to face Layla alone.

Layla stood there, breathing hard. The anger inside of her boiling over at the unfairness of it all.

"Yes!" Brooke hissed and shoved her in return, her hands cold on Layla's shoulders. "Yes. I took the pictures of you on purpose." She leaned close to Layla. Her stale breath reeked of beer. "If you don't stay away from Mason, those pictures will go public." Brooke shoved Layla again, this time with her foot hooked behind Layla's left heel. She tumbled and landed flat on her back.

Layla got to her feet. In fact, she stood taller than she ever could in her waking life. She was tired of looking up at Brooke and the other girls, and she decided that she wouldn't. At least not tonight. She made herself several inches taller than Brooke.

Then she told Brooke what she had wanted to say for a very long time. Something she would need to say to Brooke in her waking life. "You have messed with me for the very last time. Enough is enough." For added emphasis, she stormed toward her, her arms outstretched at the last moment, and she shoved Brooke. Hard. When Brooke fell, it was through the rotted floor and head first onto the concrete floor several feet below.

Layla could still see Brooke's eyes, wide open with horror as a red circle of blood poured outward from beneath her head. Carmen, Staci, and Jordan screamed at the sight.

"You killed her!" Jordan yelled. She reached for Layla's neck, and Layla grabbed her hands. Layla shoved her as hard as she could and Jordan fell through the same open hole. Her sister broke most of her fall. The next thing Layla knew, they were all waking up in their sleeping bags at the campsite on the great lawn.

All except for Brooke.

She was dead with her head on her red-stained pillow, the same expression on her face as she had in the dream.

Jordan screamed. The back of her head was bloody, too.

Old guilt trailed Layla's recollection of that horrible night. Like a mythical monster, her guilt could be medicated with cake and other sweet treats, giving her at most a brief freedom. Though it always came back and with a vengeance, gnawing and nagging.

The swift happiness she'd felt earlier had ground to a full stop. What had happened ten years ago in her lucid dream at the manor was improbable, in fact, it was not at all possible. But when Jordan accused Layla of killing her sister, Layla knew, horrifyingly so, that Jordan had been right.

Somehow, lucid dreaming at the manor made things happen in Layla's waking world. Somehow, the manor had actually pulled Brooke into Layla's lucid dream, not a representation of her as it had always been before that night. All the girls had been pulled into that space in Alcott Manor that was neither here nor there. It was neither present nor past, but rather it was some place in between. Some magical place that made her dreams real.

Had Layla pushed Brooke in her waking world, she would have owned up to it, confessed to what she had done and paid the price. As it was, she couldn't confess to anything. Because there was no way it could have happened in reality. The police had proven that. There was no way into the manor. There were no weapons at the campsite. And so Layla's guilt raged on.

Now there were too many obstacles between her and Mason—Asher's leftover financial mess, her lucid dreaming that edged too close to his hatred of the paranormal, and the emotionally vulnerable place her dead husband had left her. But the biggest of all was the secret that she had been the one to kill Brooke.

If she told Mason, he would either turn tail and run, think she was crazy, or condemn her. Maybe all three.

If she tried to forge a relationship while keeping the secret from him, the weight of her guilt, or maybe the weight of the secret itself, would destroy them. Relationships didn't survive secrets. Not big secrets like murder. Regardless, they could never again have the once-innocent, hope-filled relationship of their adolescence.

She felt like that kitchen table that Mason rescued from the attic—deeply scarred, a little broken, and warped from years of too many hard times. He had said he could restore it to perfect, but that wasn't possible. For her or the table.

A soft knock at the stairwell door made her wonder if she were dreaming. Then she remembered that Mason was upstairs. Maybe he was checking on them? She also remembered she was in Alcott Manor, where strange things happened and so she called out, "Mason?"

He said, "Yeah, it's me."

She opened the door and found him standing there with his hands casually in his pockets.

"Everything alright?" she asked.

"Yes, fine. I just noticed that the evening security wasn't here tonight. Usually they park their patrol car out front as a deterrent and a cop walks the property. I don't know if they're running late or if there was some kind of screw up at the department. I wanted to make sure you had locked the doors and windows."

That was when she noticed it—the shadow of image trails that followed his arm when he waved toward the front of the manor. There was also a slight out of body sensation, a gentle otherworldly feeling. Her first instinct had been correct.

This was a dream.

"I see." She studied him carefully and wondered if some part of him was really in her dream as Brooke had been. Or was this just her creative imagination?

He tilted his head slightly. "Did I wake you?"

"No," she answered.

"Oh, good." He half-waved and turned to go. "Well, I guess I'll get back upstairs. Just check those windows before you go to sleep. The crew had them open while they were cleaning this area, and I doubt they locked them again."

Her heart cracked at the sight of him walking away. Tomorrow she would have to refuse his invitation to their long overdue date, she would have to tell him that it just wouldn't work out between the two of them. She wouldn't be able to tell him why, she would just have to leave him with the impression that she wasn't interested.

He took the first step and the old wood creaked, the second one did, too. She forced herself not to reach for him. He was a dream she would have to let go of.

He reached the third stair.

The weight of her disappointment and her need to share just one last kiss with him reminded her—this was a dream.

"Mason—"

He stopped. Slowly, he turned to face her.

She thought she might have caught a glimmer of hopefulness in his expression.

She whispered, "Don't go."

He held her gaze for a long moment. Like he was mesmerized and like those next few steps toward her would mean everything to him.

Never had anyone looked at her that way before.

When he met her, she noticed the stillness in the air, as though the house observed their every move.

A maid in a white apron came down the stairs behind him. She carried a tiny baby in her arms. She disappeared and Mason turned around. He shook his head. "Could have sworn I heard footsteps." He laughed at what he thought was his imagination.

She smiled with a shrug. With people from the past appearing and disappearing, and the terrarium-like quietude, she knew the manor had pulled her and Mason into its dead zone. For what purpose, she couldn't figure.

"Layla, I've missed you so much," he said. "You just don't know."

He lifted her hand to his mouth and kissed it gently. She noticed a tingly, electric feeling with the press to his lips.

Her heart beat hard against her chest, leaving her breathless.

He wouldn't have done that in their waking world, she didn't think. He had been cautious, respectful, proper.

Maybe this dead zone brought all kinds of dreams to life? His dreams as well as hers?

Just one last kiss with him, that's all she wanted. His hand trailed down her long hair. He kissed her, gently at first, and then with easy exploration. She told herself she would make him stop in just a moment, after just a little more.

He drew back.

A moment hung between them. Like the thick, wet heat of a Charleston summer.

She struggled to find the right words that would send him on his way. She had no intent to hurt him. The dead zone was a dangerous place.

At the very least, an unpredictable place.

He leaned in again. His hypnotic kisses made her think only of how happy she was to finally be with him, how he wanted to be with her, and how this would be their only chance to be together.

If she let this go much further, their memories tomorrow might prove confusing and out of sync with reality. Her internal compass suggested she usher him out the door.

But then he placed a line of kisses on the inside of her wrist.

And her words became...elusive.

Forgotten.

This was just a dream, she reminded herself.

A dream.

She wouldn't do this in her waking life.

But here, maybe she could live out this...fantasy.

This one last chance to live what might have been, what she had wanted for so long, and what would never happen in real life.

He lowered his lips to hers in another kiss. This one was so gentle, so loving, so perfect that it swept her right out of her gut-level guidance system and into a world where everything she had always wanted had finally come true.

For the first time in recent memory, maybe for the first time of her life, she would not play it safe.

She closed her eyes and visualized her dream according to how her life should have gone.

She opened her eyes. "I'll meet you there."

"Where?" he asked.

She opened the backdoor.

The dark night had been transformed into a beautiful sunny day.

A tall arch on the great lawn was laced with white flow-

ers. A minister waited for them on the other side of it. He
wore a black robe and held his open Bible in front of him.

Mason looked down and noticed he wore a tuxedo with
tails. He smoothed the front of it with his hand. "Right." He
smiled and kissed her on the cheek. "I'll be waiting for you."

Mason walked down the aisle first.

Layla followed in a simple and long white dress.

She joined Mason at the arch of flowers. They held
hands with one another.

They said their vows.

"I now pronounce you man and wife. You may kiss the
bride," the minister said.

Mason lifted and gathered her to him.

She poured herself into his kiss.

Wrapped in the pleasure of Mason's strong arms, she felt
every hard-weighted pound of her past dissolve into dust.

The financial landmines her ex left for her floated away,
and the sadness that long dragged heavy on her heart
melted into light. Every loss, every broken dream and every
unsatisfied need pushed her forward to what she really
wanted—something bright and brilliant and beautiful with
Mason.

They laughed and smiled and ran back into the summer
quarters together.

They drank champagne.

"Mrs. Holloway." Mason grinned and tapped his glass
against hers.

She smiled so broad her cheeks hurt.

He pulled her close to him.

He smelled like men's soap mixed with an ocean breeze.
Sort of a fresh, boozy, citrusy scent, and she drank it in. He
kissed her temples, her cheeks, her neck, all in slow
progression.

The intimacy between them dissolved her sense of control. What they ignited together was so new, so fragile. It was like Christmas morning. That unexplainable spirit of love that arrived uninvited and with perfect timing. Like a blessing. One that would vanish into a cherished memory the following day.

His hands had never before skimmed her body like this, but crossing this line together felt familiar to her. Wanted, even. Her heart raced and drove her soul closer to him, as though it knew on some cosmic level that being with Mason was where it should have been so long ago.

She thought for a quick minute about tomorrow, how he would bring her breakfast and how differently she would feel about him after such closeness. She fought the heartbreak she knew would come soon enough.

It would be hard.

Hard.

Hard limits!

She was supposed to be watching her time!

She searched the room for a clock and finally found an antique one on the wall. The slim gold pendulum ticktocked back and forth with a loud clicking noise. The nanny she had seen earlier sat in a rocking chair below the clock, her foot pushed against a wooden cradle that held a very small baby. They were oblivious to her, as the past always was in this place, then they faded from view.

If the clock told the correct time, then maybe she had been asleep for an hour and a half? She wasn't sure. She had gotten so caught up—

The sheer intensity of their togetherness created a stillness, a mark in time that she knew would echo through their relationship. Things would be different between them when she woke. Maybe that meant this wasn't right. But like a distant whisper, she could hear the once-very-real promise of their future together in each kiss, in the tightness of his embrace.

For as much as she cautioned herself to be wise and not to linger in this idea of something more, she couldn't help but lean into the flow of its forceful current. All that they could have shared grew with excitement from a murmur to a shout—an extreme fantasy that it could be once again.

The nanny reappeared and caught Layla's eye; the woman leaned over the cradle and patted the baby's chest. What must have been the original light fixture now hung from the medallion that no longer showed signs of age. White curtains that Layla had never seen before blew into the room with a breeze from the open window. The nanny lifted her chin and breathed deeply.

"What—" Mason asked.

Layla faced him. He stared at the area where the nanny and the baby had just been. "Did you see that?"

She shrugged with a smile. "You know how dreams are. Strange things happen."

He glanced across the room again and then back to her. "Why do you keep saying this is a dream?" He squinted at her neck.

"What is it?" Layla asked.

He traced a finger over a spot just above her collarbone. "I think I may have left a mark."

She touched the area.

"Might just be a shadow." He sealed the spot with a kiss. "You know my grandfather used to say that when you find the right woman, you'll just want to eat her up." His planted more kisses along her neck. "Apparently, he was right."

She giggled.

His smile brightened. "Of course, he also said that some days, you'll wish you had."

She tilted her head back and laughed aloud. A strange dizzying sensation flooded her, like her world shifted on its axis. The clock on the other side of the room tick-tocked, tick-tocked more loudly than before. She suddenly realized the time—two hours and fifteen minutes had passed.

She panicked. "I have to go! I have to wake up now!" She thought of her girls, how she needed to take care of them and how much they depended on her. She glanced at the clock again to make sure she got the time right. The baby was gone from the cradle and the nanny was fading.

She grabbed Mason by the shoulders and hoped she could scare him awake. "Wake up!!"

With a none-to-subtle yank to her mid-section, she was back in the summer quarters on the same couch where she had fallen asleep. It was the same couch where she and Mason had been, and the same couch where he wasn't anymore.

She leaned to the edge with her head in her hands. It ached like she'd been hit with a bat. Her body was weak, like she had left some essential part of herself behind. She'd stayed too long. Just as she had been warned not to do.

She glanced toward the second floor where, most likely, Mason was still sleeping. Or maybe he sat almost upright as she did, aching from the absence of what could have been between them.

Yes, staying so long had been a risk, and she might have crossed some sort of line. But, she decided, it was all worth it.

She lifted her head gingerly to check the clock on the wall.

It wasn't there.

18

Although the coastal sun shone bright at seven in the morning, Mason was focused on the way he had seen Layla the night before. Her cheeks flushed, her long hair tousled, and her lips bee stung and well kissed.

God help him. This dream wouldn't let him go.

He could still taste her sugary skin, and he could still smell the honeysuckle scent of her neck. He remembered the way she looked at him. The white dress.

The ending was abrupt and jarring and knocked him clean off the couch.

One minute she was in his arms, laughing and smiling. The next, she was gone.

He woke up alone.

He turned his truck onto the gravel and shell driveway that wound in front of Alcott Manor. The seatbelt was fastened across the coffee and breakfast he'd picked up at The Early Rooster Cafe. He placed a protective hand over it on the turn. He had promised Layla this breakfast.

"That's the sign of a good man," his father had always

said. "A promise kept." Of course, that was also a standard that got him into trouble now and then.

Ancient, curved oak tree branches swayed and dipped in the early morning breeze like long fingers that welcomed him toward the manor. Iced water poured over the inside of his stomach. It always did when he approached this property.

The project had been fraught with problems. He had to fight that not-alone feeling when he was inside. There were unexplainable breezes in empty, closed rooms, like someone passed by. Occasional thumps and bumps when no one else was around. Objects moving that shouldn't, like the chandelier that had nearly killed him and Layla.

These were ghosts, his mother had suggested.

He refused to agree.

Believing that sort of nonsense didn't get the house finished, it didn't help him meet his deadlines, and it didn't help him with Layla. However, each morning he did have to bear down before he went inside the house, like he braced himself to fight something ugly and hateful. He couldn't explain that. He decided that he didn't need to.

He would be glad when this job was done so he could get back to simple homebuilding. And away from the tragic history of Alcott Manor.

Working this job had served its purpose. It gave him an easy road into Layla's life and a way to restart his father's homebuilding business. But he liked a predictable order to his work, the kind that kept the chaos out of his life.

A black Porsche convertible came was parked in the driveway. His stomach soured.

He quickly focused his mind and guarded his thoughts of Layla, kept them in a secret place.

The owner of the car stood on the front porch. She

waved and broadened her princess-perfect smile. Jordan. She was a bombshell alright. Strangely, the older she got, the more she resembled her sister. Blonde and tan with red lips and narrow hips. Every boy's dream, every man's wish.

She was complex, and her moods shifted with the tides. Not that it was evident in the way she presented herself. Like the blouse she wore today, with its soft pink color and the ruffles at the ends of her sleeves. She wore it to fool men into thinking that she didn't have any sharp edges, that her personality was all rounded and gentle.

When they were in high school he had wanted her older sister, Brooke, more than he wanted to breathe. She would appear in the school hallway, in that short black cheerleader outfit, and the noise around him would just fall away. He might have been late for a class or on his way to football practice, but when she had looked at him with those brown eyes, his insides turned to mush. He had been pulled to her by a force he didn't entirely understand.

After Brooke died, he'd thought Jordan had something of the same effect on him. She leaned against the front pillar of Alcott Manor and waved to him like she had been waiting her entire life for him.

"Hey, Mason." Her voice was gentle and sweet in this early morning.

He scanned the area to see if Layla and the girls were around. He hoped he could get rid of Jordan before Layla and the girls appeared.

He tipped his head in a small nod of recognition.

Girls like Jordan Williams enjoyed the chase and the climb. But once she captured her prey, once she reached the pinnacle, she got restless. And that's when the problems began.

"What brings you out so early this morning?" He

rounded the back of his truck and unloaded the supplies he'd packed earlier. He ignored her slightly, like they didn't have a past.

"My water heater is acting up. Could you stop by tonight and take a look at it?"

She did this as a hook. She asked for his help to trigger some knight in shining armor gene embedded in his DNA. He was convinced it was some leftover response from the medieval period that, more often than not, just got him into trouble. Much like fight-or-flight from the cavemen days that didn't help as much as it stressed people out in modern times. He had taken care of this woman too much over the years. He honored promises he hadn't actually made.

He glanced at her without meeting her eyes. He turned and unloaded another box.

Her hair was freshly washed and curled into waves that fell around her shoulders. He wasn't close to her, but he could smell the scent of white soap, lotion, perfume. He didn't think she was a gal who tolerated a cold shower. He suspected there wasn't anything wrong with her water heater.

"Can't today. Have to help my mom with some house repairs after work." Which wasn't true. He hoped to spend time with Layla, maybe get to know her daughters.

Her bottom lip pouted, and he remembered how he'd once run his thumb over it.

He walked to the porch with a box under his right arm, a bag of breakfast items tucked in the crook of his other arm. A to-go box with two hot coffees in the other hand.

"I could really use the help." She squinted her eyes like she tried to focus. Her vision had been compromised. A result of her injury from the campout. She still had trouble recognizing some written words. These lasting injuries were the reason she didn't work much, and certainly why he had continued to take care of her for too long after she had been hurt.

She ran the nail of her middle finger over his chest, her head tilted just so. "I just thought maybe we could enjoy a late night snack and some wine? Why don't you come over after you visit with your mom? You look so stressed."

He moved away from her hand. It wasn't the first time she had extended this kind of invitation to him. Since she had returned to Charleston, she had asked him over several times—to take yet another whack at the (relationship) cat or just so she wouldn't feel alone, he wasn't sure.

"Can't tonight."

She expected him to ask for a rain check and to stroke her like a house cat until she didn't feel disappointed anymore. He didn't. He wouldn't.

"You sure? I'll wait up for you." She grabbed his arm, tugged him toward her and bit half of her lower lip.

"No, Jordan." He nudged her hand away with the box. "And knock that off, we're not that way anymore. Besides, my workers are here." He and Jordan had dated in New York. He realized soon enough that the both of them were just working out their grief over Brooke's murder.

"C'mon, don't be this way." She reached for his belt loop.

"Stop." He backed her off with his firm tone and a strong glare. "This is a professional environment."

"This is *not* a professional environment. Not like your first career where you wore those beautiful suits every day. All polished and pretty."

"Yeah, well. This *is* a professional environment, and those pretty suits about strangled the life out of me."

"You looked good in them."

"And that's what mattered most." Mason's arms ached

from the supplies he held. He managed to put the box and the breakfast items on the porch and decided he would walk Jordan to her car. He didn't think she would leave otherwise.

"Daddy won his mayoral race again and he wants to help you. He says that if your father's construction business is what you insist on doing, then he'll make sure you get first pick of the city's building contracts."

"Seriously?"

"Mm-hmm. He's already put your name in for several gigs. Says he wants to make sure that you're set in this town. You know the mayor can make or break a career, and I've told Daddy I want him to make yours."

"What strings are attached to these career-making gigs?"

"He wants you to walk away from Alcott Manor."

"What?"

"This is where Brooke died. It's where I almost died." She pointed to the manor. "He says this place shouldn't be memorialized into a tourist trap."

The thunder of footsteps along the wraparound porch caught his attention. He turned and saw Layla and her daughters hurrying toward their car.

A little girl with long, dark curls led the way. A taller and more blonde girl followed. Layla Alcott waved to him.

"Who is that?" Jordan asked.

"I need to get to work. Make sure you get that hot water heater fixed."

"You have children in the manor now?"

"It's the caretaker's daughter."

"You hired a caretaker?"

"Tom did." He knew this half-honesty would bite him in the rear sooner or later, but he was hoping for later. Much later.

"Mama, I forgot my lunch!" The little girl stopped on the front porch and was clearly panicked.

"I'll find it. You hop in the car," Layla said.

"I'm going to be laaaate!" the girl whined.

"I'll write you a note. Go on."

"She's...rather attractive for a caretaker." Jordan ogled Layla from afar. Mason knew she didn't recognize her.

"Jordan." If she mentioned that another woman was attractive, that was akin to hearing a tornado siren in the neighborhood.

"Do I know her?"

Mason gave her a don't-even cautionary glare. He gathered the bags full of egg and bacon and cheese biscuits and the to go box of coffees.

Layla walked out of the front door a few minutes later with a soft-sided pink lunchbox and a piece of paper in hand.

Mason handed everything to her. "Mornin', Layla."

He wanted to pull her into his arms, hold her close, and breathe in the flowery scent on her skin. "Sorry I'm late. I overslept."

"Mornin', Mason. Thank you." She accepted the coffee and took a sip. Her gaze never left his.

They walked down the front steps together. "There are egg and cheese biscuits in there, maybe you and the girls can enjoy them on the way to school."

"We will. Thanks again."

Jordan waved and marched in their direction. "Hey!" she sang in her friendliest, welcome-to-the-neighborhood tone.

Mason thought seriously about walking in the opposite direction and not coming back.

Layla placed the lunchbox and paper sacks in the front seat. Her shoulders squared off with Jordan. Mason knew

Layla recognized Jordan. He also knew Layla was confident that she was nearly unrecognizable herself.

She took a few steps toward the unwelcome welcome wagon heading her way, he thought perhaps to put a barrier between Jordan and her girls.

"I'm Jordan Williams. Mason's...friend." Her smile was coy and she emphasized the word 'friend', like that was code for something serious. Something illicit.

"Yes. I know."

"Have we met? I can't quite place—"

"Yes, Jordan. We've met."

Jordan's head tilted slightly. Like a small dog responding to a high-pitched noise.

Her upper lip lifted on one side. She gave a near-quiet grunt. It was a derisive noise she often made.

Mason wanted to caution her. He didn't. It wouldn't have done any good.

Jordan was a spoiled child.

Layla smoothed the front of her light blue scrubs. She rested both hands on her hips.

A pose.

A nervous laugh tickled the inside of Mason's chest. He ignored how Layala's hand shook when she ran it over her now-slim stomach. He just silently cheered her on and hoped on some level that she could feel his support.

"I'm Layla."

"Oh my gosh—" Jordan looked Layla over from stem to stern. When she finally seemed to realize that she'd stared long enough she said, "Well, congratulations. I'm sure it wasn't easy to lose all that weight."

She had shifted that quickly, that effortlessly from shock to mean girl mode.

Layla didn't grunt in return. But she did smile in Mason's

direction. A sweet, soft smile that highlighted his memories of his dream of her from the night before.

In a flirty move, she flipped her hair behind her shoulder, and that's when he saw it. Or about a quarter of it. A bruise just above her collarbone and at the bend of her neck.

His mouth went dry.

That mark hadn't been there last night when they had dinner. The flowered dress she'd worn had a wide neckline and wouldn't have hidden a bruise so prominent. But he remembered from his dream that he hadn't been able to leave her neck alone. The softness of her skin and her candy-sweet taste—

Jordan prattled on about something or other, and he barely heard her.

Layla didn't seem to be listening to her either. She caught him staring at her neck, and she adjusted her shirt. She brought her hair around to the front of her shoulder. When their eyes met, she appeared as alarmed as he felt. He tried to swallow.

"I need to talk with you," Mason said to Layla, though he wasn't sure what he would say. There couldn't possibly be a connection between what was on her neck and his dream. That was ridiculous. Stupid, even.

He felt the manor looming over the three of them. He wanted nothing more than to drive Layla and her daughters away. His heart stomped against the walls of his chest.

"I've got to run the girls to school, but I'll be back after work," she said softly.

Jordan stepped forward. Her glare shifted between Mason and Layla like she suddenly realized she was being ignored, like there was something going on between the two of them that didn't involve her.

"Layla—" he said.

"Well, I guess the weight loss wasn't the hardest thing you've been through lately, not from what I read in the papers anyway." Jordan gestured to the house. Then she leaned to the side to look at Layla's girls in the car. "How are y'all doing?"

Layla stepped in front of her and blocked her view. "We're fine."

"Enough. Let's go." Mason grabbed Jordan by the arm. He didn't know why the bruise on Layla's neck made him want to protect her, but it surely did.

Jordan jerked away from his grasp and moved toward Layla. "Good. I'm glad. Because I'd like to think you've come a long way since you killed my sister."

"Jordan!" Mason yelled.

"I still can't live a normal life, thanks to you."

"Mason, I'll see you later." Layla's voice was strong and confident.

She got into her car and drove away. He almost hear the ding of the gold bell that signified the end of the round. Layla had won that one. He knew that Jordan would make certain there was another.

"Why didn't you tell me you'd seen Layla and that she was living here?" Jordan rubbed the back of her head like her skull had just fractured, like she had an unsettled debt with Layla.

Mason took her by the arm and re-escorted her to her car with a renewed purpose. When they arrived at the driver's side door he gave her an answer he hoped she would listen to. "Because Layla and the manor and my life, for that matter, are none of your business. The police cleared Layla, that's over and done with. You and I don't see one another anymore and we both need to move on. At the very least, don't come to my place of work and her home and accuse her like that. Are we clear?"

She pouted again. This time there was a glare in her eyes. "You're making a mistake, Mason."

"For the first time in a long while, I'm not." He opened her car door for her and ushered her inside. When she was seated, he said to her, in part to reassure himself, "You and Brooke were drunk that night, Jordan. You and I both know that. There's no telling what really happened."

He hated talking about that night. It had been bad for everyone.

"What's gotten into you? We both lost someone we loved." She squinted at Mason, studying him. "Are you with *her*?" Jordan pointed in the direction where Layla had been.

"Who I'm with is none of your business."

She clicked her tongue on the roof of her mouth. "Wouldn't that be funny if the city inspectors never approved all that work on Alcott Manor? Might be hard to become the tourist attraction her family wants it to be."

He fought the crawl of obligation that had eaten its way through him for too many years. "You wouldn't do that."

"People who ruin other people's lives need to be punished."

"Don't do this," he said.

"Then stay away from her and this place and give us another chance."

Revenge was what she wanted.

"We can make a go of it this time."

"You're messing with people's lives here. Their liveli-hoods." He waved in the direction of the manor.

"And what did she do to me? I had a future as an attorney before I got hurt. That woman ruined my life. If she deserves anything at all, it's to be paid back in kind," she said.

"This is her property, and this is my job."

"I'd hate to see your business struggle with permit approvals and banks loans and such."

"Don't threaten me, Jordan."

She flashed him a your-choice smirk and hit the gas.

He jumped out of the way, watched her car leave the property. She meant what she said.

Jordan's car engine roared in the distance.

He was the only one who could talk her out of this. But she would want his loyalty in return, at the very least to stay away from Layla. He wouldn't do that, and she would make sure her father ruined him, his business and Alcott Manor.

He thought of Layla from the night before. With her flower print dress, and her hair falling behind her shoulders, she was the most beautiful woman he'd ever seen. He'd given up everything to be with her, to rekindle what had once been lost and to build something for the future.

He would not allow them to be over before they began.

ASHER CARDILL PACED BACK and forth behind the front windows of Alcott Manor, he wanted to know what was being said. From their body language, he could guess.

Layla had her defiant face on, the one she always wore when she felt the need to protect her girls. So he would assume that Jordan—dear Jordan—had been her usual passive aggressive or socially competitive self. Probably both if he remembered her correctly.

It had been Jordan and Brooke who opened the door for him to waltz into Layla's life. He was grateful to them, really, for beating Layla down so dutifully. In a very genuine way, Brooke and Jordan were just younger versions of Jayne Ella. Another woman who paved the way for Asher to have a place in Layla's life.

The triumvirate dispersed, leaving Mason to go to work on the manor. Asher followed him closely. Mason put his box of supplies on the floor and leaned on the old kitchen table.

He was clueless. He probably thought he had just had some run of the mill dream the night before. Little did he know.

Last night, Asher had been pacing the house when he heard Layla think of him. He didn't know what she had been thinking necessarily, but this bolus of energy hit him and he knew it was hers. It was sort of like hearing a unique telephone ring and you knew exactly who was calling.

He'd heard it before, felt it even, during her last dream. Layla thought of him, and that was his pathway into her dream world. When he heard her call this time, he followed it. Yes, if the traps he'd laid in the manor didn't pay off, this was how he would pay Mason back and keep Layla with him forever.

All in one fell swoop.

Dreams.

Layla's dreams.

19

L ayla stood just inside the entryway of the Alcott Manor summer quarters and strained to listen. Displaced footsteps, the echo of Asher's laughter, or an inexplicable thump—anything that might be a sign of his presence.

The ancient home's construction was so solid, it had survived the direct hit of a hurricane and years of neglect. The quiet on this lower level was different than in a modern-day structure. The silence was thick and palpable, as was the weight from the house above her.

It had been a short work shift this morning, only four hours because her kids had early release from school. She had hoped to relax with a cup of coffee and a book in these few minutes she had to herself, but now that she was alone she didn't like the feel of the quiet. Asher's mug, his appearance in her dream, her general sense that the house watched her—kept her unnerved.

What is real? What is true? She thought of the advice Dixie gave her long ago, questions she could ask herself to get a sense of grounding and direction.

He was dead. That was true. Also real.

Dead. Dead. Dead.

She said it over and over in her mind to give herself strength. Could he hurt her if his spirit were still here? The idea of him lurking in her unguarded private life was disturbing.

A knock made her drop her purse. Her keys hit the floor in a muffled *thunk*. She covered her mouth and nose with her hands.

She saw Mason lean in front of the side window and wave.

She opened the door, and he asked, "Did I startle you?"

Her heart jitterbugged inside her chest. "It's okay. Come in."

After the starring role he had played in her dream the night before, she wanted to give him a kiss and a hug hello. She caught herself.

That hadn't been real.

As predicted, imagined events from the night before led to a confusing day after. At least for her. Mason seemed perfectly at ease as usual.

He leaned in, kissed her on the cheek.

Heat simmered between them, and she wasn't sure where to rest her focus. The carpet, his shoes, his chest. Now she held two secrets from him. Still, she wouldn't have given up her dreamtime with him last night for anything. The closeness they had shared was well worth this embarrassment. She forced herself to maintain eye contact but couldn't keep her hand from fiddling with her gold earring.

Then he was the one who looked away, but not before he stole a glance at her neck and tried to make small talk. Did he see the mark? She adjusted her shirt to make sure the area above her collarbone was good and covered.

Once upon a time they had known each other so well they could have asked one another anything. No topic was too sacred. Now the sands of uncertainty shifted between them.

He hooked his thumbs into his jeans pockets. She noticed his neatly clipped nails and a flash memory of his touch from the night before flew like a shockwave across her mind. Her face flushed warm. She wished she could lean into him with the warmth of that memory. Tragically, today lacked the intimacy she had found with him in her dream, but that was part of the price she paid for choices.

The terrier that her daughters had named Winston ran into the room and jumped at their legs.

"A lot has gone on here, huh?" he gave Winston a scratch behind the ears.

Layla eyed the dog uneasily.

Winston licked Mason's hand several times, then hopped onto the couch and snuggled against the cushions.

"What?"

He gestured to the back lawn. "The campout."

"Oh. Yeah." A wave of guilt and regret nearly knocked her to her knees, and she wished she could be honest with him about everything that had happened ten years ago. She wished she could just pour it all forth and get it over with. Even if it meant he walked away, at least she wouldn't have to haul the weight of the secret with her any longer.

"Y'all doing okay here?" He was gorgeous in a classic way, with dark hair and light brown eyes. But it was his vulnerability that buckled her knees. She found herself wishing the night before hadn't been a dream and that circumstances allowed for something real with him.

"We're making it work, I guess. You know, you do what you have to do," she said, and then she had an idea. What if she just confessed? What if she just told him outright that she had had a dream that she had pushed Brooke, that Brooke fell and hit her head, then Layla woke up to find that Brooke had died from a serious head injury?

He'd never believe her, and what if that worked in her favor? Maybe they could laugh it off as a joke. Ha ha ha, how strange is that? Weird. Yeah. Weird.

She would say, Wow, I've felt really guilty about it for years.

And he would say, Well, you shouldn't. I mean, it was a dream, after all.

And that would be the end of that.

Maybe. At least she would have finally gotten the truth off her chest.

She drew in a deep breath and decided to just keep the confession simple. "Mason, there's something I need to tell you."

"I'm sorry about this morning with Jordan. I told her she couldn't come out here again. If I were you I'd be upset, too."

She gestured for Mason to take a seat on the couch. "That wasn't exactly what I was going to say. I probably should have mentioned this a long time ago, but I wasn't sure how to do that. It's an unusual problem. Complicated, really—"

He stared at the couch for a moment before he sat and then he said, "I'm sorry to interrupt. I just don't want there to be any rude surprises or secrets between us. I think Jordan is about to put something into motion that affects us both."

The seriousness of his tone and the mention of Jordan's name made her stop. She waved for him to continue. She expected him to say something about how Jordan still blamed her for Brooke's death and her brain injury. He did. But he also said she was jealous and was going to try to put a stop to Alcott Manor's plans for tourism.

"What?"

"Maybe I shouldn't have taken such a hard line with her. But I didn't think she would take no for an answer." He shook his head in disgust. "Jordan and I saw one another for a while. We were both living in New York at the time, and I think dating one another had more to do with some unresolved grief over Brooke's death than anything else. It wasn't serious."

Something in Layla's gut curdled at the thought of Mason and Jordan together. She looked away.

"I realized it before Jordan did. She wasn't all too happy when I called it off. I think that's the real reason why she's set Alcott Manor as her target."

"Can she *seriously* stop us from opening the house for tours? Or from finishing the restoration?"

"Her dad's the mayor. He's always been a little shady, I think. I wouldn't be surprised if he tried to shut things down for us."

"Us?"

He drew in a deep breath. "She said if I worked here—if you and I were together—she wants to make it difficult for me to get any more business done."

The room spun around and around. Like she was heading down the drain.

The income gone.

Mason gone.

She put her head in her hands. She had to have the money from the manor. She needed that income to pay off Asher's debt. To take care of her daughters.

He placed his hand on her back and she felt a rush of comfort from him.

"What did you tell her?"

"I told her not to do that. That she was messing with people's lives. Of course she thinks that this is—"

A chill rolled over her. "Payback."

His lips pulled tight in a grimace. "She still swears that you're the one who did it. I've put a call in to some of Tom's contacts to see what we can do about this. And I'll talk with her again."

"I'm so sorry, Mason."

He frowned slightly, like he didn't understand. "About what?"

"I—" She started to tell him that this was all her fault. Then she realized with a jolt she couldn't. Someone had to resolve things with Jordan.

If Tom were still alive he would have stepped in and handled everything. He would have brought Jordan to the manor for coffee, listened to her, reasoned with her. He would have charmed her right out of their way. Then he would have met with the mayor and found a way to get him to back down, too.

But Tom was gone. Jordan would never listen to Layla.

No matter how Layla tried to negotiate with her. Because she would always see Layla as the one who ruined her life, the one who was her sister's killer.

Which she was.

If she told him the truth about what she had done, he would leave.

She paced the floor and fought the urge to scream.

"I know." He stood and watched her, his expression lined with all the anger she felt.

"She probably left the manor and went straight to her father's office. Lord only knows what they've already done."

"I'm not going to let her ruin this for you and your family. I'll think of something to stop her," he said.

Layla didn't have any other options. "If you spoke with her, she'd listen to you, wouldn't she?"

His jaw muscles worked. "She's pretty angry at the idea that you and I might be seeing one another. But I'll think of something."

"You told her we were together?"

"She asked. All I said was that who I dated was none of her business."

Layla liked this side of Mason. The knight in shining armor who defended her honor and fought for what he wanted.

"I meant what I said last night. I would like to rekindle our friendship, I'd like to make things right. I'd really like to take you out."

The house wrapped its thick blanket of quiet around them. It felt like they were the only two people around for miles. She was torn between wanting what she had tasted the night before and backing away.

The closer he stepped toward her, the more she wanted him—for herself and to claim the future she believed they had lost so long ago.

"Is that what you want, too?"

"Very much," she answered honestly.

He flashed a smile that was fiercely confident. Then he lowered his lips to hers in a kiss. Soft and tender. Slow and promising.

The ring from Mason's phone interrupted. He asked the caller to hold for a moment. "This is one of Tom's friends in City Hall. Why don't you pack a bag with swimsuits for you and the girls? I'll pick y'all up in about an hour. We'll get out of here for a while."

She agreed.

The secret she had carried for more than ten years felt heavier than ever before.

20

Mason's red pickup truck hit every pothole on the dirt road, bouncing the girls into wide-smiling giggles in the back seat. Winston seemed to have a smile on his face. Layla didn't think a smile was possible for her, but her daughters' happiness was contagious.

"What did Tom's friend say?" she kept her voice low.

"He's reaching out to all of his contacts, letting them know what's coming. He said that Mayor Williams has a lot of influence. More than we would like." Mason shifted his glance between Layla and the road. She tried to ignore the frightened look in his eyes and tightened his lips into a line.

"Which means what, exactly?"

"It means that if the mayor does what his darling daughter wants, that we could be in real trouble."

The two cupcakes she had wolfed after Mason left the manor felt like bricks in her gut. She stared out the window and tried not to think how this fiasco was nothing more than what-goes-around-comes-around.

"I'm going to talk to her," he said and squeezed Layla's

hand. "I'll get her to stop. I won't let her get away with this. I won't." He squeezed her hand again.

"I'd like to say this isn't your problem. But the truth is that I really appreciate your help."

"I've already called her. Left her a message."

She nodded, not at all knowing how he would pull this off. His truck hummed a hypnotic melody. She remembered his father driving the same truck, she and Mason side by side in the front seat, the three of them singing along to the old Hank Williams song "Jambalaya" that played on cassette tape.

She glanced around the woodsy area. The ancient, craggy water oaks, the towering pines with the occasional eagle's nest at the top, and the rays of the lowering sun bursting now and then through the thicket.

The truck hugged a familiar S-curve in the dirt road.

"Are we going to old man Edmonton's lake house?" she asked.

"No."

She looked around the country road that was as familiar to her as the back of her hand. "We are. And we're about to come up on some overgrown blueberry bushes. Right next to that slate rock boulder—"

"Oh, this is definitely the road you remember. The one where we—"

"Shhh—" She smacked his arm with the back of her hand and nodded to the girls. She did not want them hearing what a wild child she had often been as a teenager. She didn't need her credibility ruined.

He leaned closer to her and whispered, "Where we skipped school so we could fish and swim."

She placed one finger over his lips and he gave it a kiss.

Her heart stuttered.

They pulled up to the hidden driveway and she recognized the two story home. It was a mix of natural stone, wood, and shingle, with large plate glass windows facing the lake. It had always been owned by a wealthy and reclusive CEO from up north who used it as his private winter getaway. So she and Mason used to come out to swim and fish in the other seasons, especially when they wanted to take a break from school.

"Welcome to my home." His grin was wide and full of secrets.

"*Your* home?"

The girls jumped from the truck. Emma tagged her sister and ran. Her dark brown ponytail swished back and forth. Anna Kate squealed and chased after her. Winston barked and ran between them like he was a part of the game.

"What do you mean *your* home?"

"I may not have enjoyed being a stockbroker, but it turns out that I have a knack for investing."

"And you bought this property?"

"Come on." He took her by the hand and walked her to the lake side of the home. She breathed deeply, happy to be away from the manor.

The giant oak extended over the water and a thick white rope swing hung from the longest branch. The girls ran up and down the dock, trying to figure out how to capture the rope and bring it to land.

"That is *not* the same rope swing—"

"I had a new one put in."

With just a few steps along the soft grass, his countenance relaxed. He breathed easier, like the land and the lake and the house were all a part of him. His secret hideaway.

This wasn't the first time they had held hands at this lake.

Like revisiting an old photograph, she had been over and over that scene in her mind.

They were on the deck near the original rope swing. It was years ago. He had just cracked a joke about what she didn't remember. But she did remember the look in his sweet ginger eyes and how he searched her face for just a flash of a moment before he took her hand.

"I can't believe you bought this place."

He shrugged. "This is where I spent many of the happiest days of my youth." His smile broadened into the confident one she'd always loved, the one that said he'd captured the flag, won the race, scored the winning touchdown. It was the smile that talked her into just about anything. She relaxed her guard. This was the friendship she and Mason used to share.

"We're going to work this out," he said.

She gave a heavy exhale.

He ran his hand through his hair and stared at the lake. "I really thought I had gotten rid of her for good."

"I thought I had as well." Jordan's presence felt the same way Brooke's always had—like she had tripped into some unexpected misfortune—a stomach virus, the flu or strep throat. She was the thing you didn't expect, and yet she managed to effectively knock you down for longer than you thought possible.

"Do your girls swim?" Mason pointed to her daughters who paced at the water's edge.

"Like fish."

"Then c'mon." He pulled off his shirt and headed toward the lake. He scooped Emma into his arms and jumped off the end of the pier. She squealed all the way, much to her sister's giggling delight.

Layla grabbed Anna's hand and together they took a running jump. Their laughter bounced off the water and the surrounding forest. It was their own private world.

The water was cool but not cold, and it washed away some of her stress. Watching the girls have fun with Mason took away more. They unofficially claimed him as their newest playmate and made him the center of their attention.

He had an easy way with them, matching their humor and their silliness with his own. She wasn't sure who enjoyed the day more, her girls or Mason. Tonight, she would add the lake trip and Mason to her gratitude list.

The girls took turns positioning themselves on Mason's shoulders. He lowered himself underwater. Then he rocketed upward, sending them into a dive or a flip. She hadn't seen her girls this happy in a very long time, and she knew he was everything Asher couldn't be. The edges of her heart crumpled when she reminded herself that these good times with Mason wouldn't last.

The girls asked for the rope swing. Layla was the first to demonstrate.

She flew through the air with her arms stretched wide like a pro. There were only two or so seconds before she landed in the water.

But she quickly realized why she reached for wings in her lucid dreams.

It was *this feeling* that she had tried to recapture.

"Mama!" Emma squealed from her perch on top of Mason's shoulders. "I didn't know you could do that!"

Layla bobbed weightless in the deep water, her smile felt

as natural as the warm sun on her skin. "Honey, I've been flying long before you were born."

The girls looked at one another with mouths open.

Layla swam to the center of the lake. Mason took the girls to the upper part of the grassy embankment, rope swing in hand. She tread water, swatted away nibbling fish and watched while Mason gave the girls instructions.

His voice was calm, his demeanor was sweet, and his humor was dry enough to keep their attention.

She didn't know if he was aware of it, but he had them in the palm of his hand. They finally swung out to where their mother waited for them. They were full of smiles and screams and laughter. They popped above water again with a light in their eyes.

They were confident and strong.

Mason had that direct effect on a person.

He'd always had that effect on her.

She'd long thought that her happiest, most carefree days were far behind her, but leave it to Mason to find a way to bring them back, at least for an afternoon.

By the time the sun set, the girls were finally spent. They cleaned up in the outdoor shower, dressed in dry clothes, and Layla combed through their long wet hair.

"Mama?" Emma had a particular tone when she asked a delicate question and Layla heard it. It was higher, with just a touch of false sweet.

"Yes, baby."

"Do you like Mr. Mason?"

Layla found herself nodding before she answered. "I do like Mr. Mason. Do you?"

"Yes," she said at once and turned to face her mother with a smile. "I like him a lot."

She bit the side of one hot pink fingernail and then asked, "Is that okay?"

She tilted her daughter's head back and kissed her on the forehead. "That's absolutely okay."

"Are you sure? Because I don't want to hurt Daddy's feelings or make him angry."

She noticed Anna listening closely to their conversation. "Daddy's gone, sweetheart. You can't hurt his feelings."

The girls exchanged a look.

Layla thought of the mug in the kitchen and Asher's brief appearance in one of her dreams. She felt ill. "What's going on? Girls?"

"I don't think Daddy likes Mr. Mason like we do."

"Why would you say that?"

Emma shook her head, indicating that she wasn't going to answer.

Anna Kate cleared her throat. "Because on that night when you slept on the couch, we heard Daddy yelling."

"You mean you were dreaming that he was yelling?" Layla didn't find that clarification any more comforting.

"We both heard him. He was really mad. He doesn't want you to like Mr. Mason and he told us not to like him either," Anna said. "He said he doesn't belong in our family."

Emma snuggled in close. Layla wrapped her arms around her. "Mama? Do you think God could find someone for Daddy to like in heaven so that he'll be happy?"

"That's a very good suggestion and I think we should pray for that. We all want Daddy to be happy in heaven."

Actually, Layla didn't really. But happy in heaven beat angry in Alcott Manor any day. He was her past, and Alcott Manor was a key part of her future. Her financial future. He didn't belong in either arena. She didn't want to believe that he could still be there, neither did she want to think about how he could intervene in her relationship with Mason, but the girls' stories were too coincidental.

She got the girls convinced that praying for him was all that was needed and that there was nothing to worry about. Mason took the girls to his outdoor ping pong table and got them involved in a tournament.

Layla made a phone call.

"WELL OF COURSE, honey. You know I'm always happy to have the girls with me."

Layla took the bone she was going to pick with her mother and placed it aside. Right now she needed her help. "I think they just need something familiar in their lives right now and spending the weekend with you would really help."

"Are you coming, too?"

She hadn't thought about herself or where she would sleep this weekend. Getting her girls out of the house and away from Asher had been her first priority.

"No, I've got to be at the manor." She would figure her sleeping arrangements out later. She wasn't sure how comfortable she felt about being at the manor alone. She could go to the manor, do her job, then maybe she would bunk with one of her friends from work.

"Are y'all there now?"

Layla slid the bone she would pick with her mother back to front and center. "No, actually we're at Mason's house."

"Oh."

"He bought the Edmonton place on the lake and we've been out here swimming."

"I see."

"Would you pick them up here? Mason brought us so I don't have my car."

Her mother agreed.

Layla couldn't wait to see her face when she pulled up to this glorious home to pick up her grandchildren.

"I have plenty of their pajamas and clothes at the house, and I'll feed them. Pizza tonight and pancakes for breakfast. After an early morning swim, of course," her mother said.

"Of course." Her mother could spoil them all she wanted.

Layla thought about Asher. How she couldn't let her girls live at the manor if he roamed the halls. *Her girls.* She would need her mother's help with that, too, and they would be happy to stay with her.

Asher was dead. But the memories of his anger made her shudder. She would have to be careful when she went back to the manor. If Asher had seen her and Mason in her dream, his temper would be beyond violent.

21

J ayne Ella put the girls in the car and slammed the door.

Layla and Mason waved from the front porch.

Mason slipped his arm around Layla's waist.

The look on her mother's face was nothing short of priceless.

Christmas came early this year.

Mason's winner's smile made a reappearance. They turned to go inside and he hugged Layla to him.

She'd never really known how warm and fuzzy revenge could feel until now.

"To be a fly on the wall when you finally talk with her about all the visits and phone calls she didn't tell you about..."

She imagined her mother's face—mouth open, no words coming out, a slow flush covering her skin. Jayne Ella hated to be caught off guard and she hated to be wrong. "That will be a very good day."

His phone buzzed and he peeked at the screen.

"Anything from Tom's contacts?" Adrenaline hit her chest in a long, panicky ache.

He shook his head. "It will be Monday before we hear anything, I would expect."

"Or Jordan?" She hated the idea of either one of them kowtowing to Jordan. Like she was some deranged queen who had to be talked out of ruining lives.

Mason walked them in the front door and she paused to take in the showroom quality of his home. The furnishings were pristine white, as were the walls and vaulted ceilings. Floor-to-ultra-high ceiling windows made the lake an extension of his home. His open air chef's kitchen could have housed a cooking staff and the outer deck looked like another living room. It was flawless and showed like the main feature from a design magazine.

"Can't say I ever thought I'd see the inside of this house. You've done an amazing job with it all."

They walked across the white shag carpet to the outside and she found herself feeling uneasy. Not just because she was concerned she might unintentionally leave a scuff mark on the ultra white room. But more so because with the girls gone, she had a hard time talking with Mason without thinking about the night before.

He described the various pieces and how Dixie helped him recreate the little bit of New York style he liked.

She thought of Mason in his tuxedo and her in her white dress. How they'd stood hand-in-hand on the great lawn, saying I do. Then afterward, a mini-honeymoon in the manor. She couldn't put her finger on it, but something wasn't right.

"What do you think?"

"Mmm? It's stunning."

"No." He laughed. "About dinner. Let me make you dinner tonight."

More time with him would only bring her closer to the inevitable train wreck of an ending that waited for them. "I should probably get back to the manor and make arrangements for tonight."

His phone rang and he reached into his back pocket. "Nonsense. I'll open a bottle of wine, grill a couple of steaks and we'll eat on the deck." He ushered her toward the deck. "Sit out here. I'm just going to take this real quick."

Mason walked out the front door and she sat on the deck to wait. She could hear him talking to someone out front, though she couldn't make out what they were saying. Probably something to do with his business. Maybe a delivery.

The lake held the echoes of their day together. She leaned against the railing and relived a few of the moments. The girls flying off the rope swing and doing dives and flips off Mason's shoulders. He was a natural with them. One day he would make an amazing father. She thought she felt her heart crack a little.

Several sheets of drawings were spread across the table, anchored by two large, water-smoothed stones. The papers looked like architectural drawings for different types of roofs and deck enclosures.

"I'm not leaving until I have your word." She heard a woman say from down below and she knew immediately who that voice belonged to.

"Jordan!" Mason yelled.

Jordan Williams stormed around the corner in a tank top and shorts like she was searching for something. As if on cue, she looked at Layla. Mason appeared two steps later.

"I knew it," Jordan said. She spun around, her ponytail

swished behind her. She marched up the hill to Mason. "You said she wasn't here. You said y'all weren't involved." She slapped him hard against the cheek. "Watch what happens next."

Layla stood stock still, listening to the two of them argue. A car door slammed and the car drove off. She waited.

Birds, frogs, and crickets chirped in the background. Water lapped at the shore.

The front door slammed. Mason appeared around the corner, hands on his hips and face red with fury. He grabbed a bottle of wine and two glasses on his way to the deck. He poured them each a glass.

"She's a piece of work, that one." He tapped his glass to hers, took a long drink and stared at the lake. "I can't tell you how many times I've wanted to get my hands on the sick bastard that attacked her that night. Whoever he is, he royally screwed up my life."

Slick and filthy regret slithered inside of her.

"You told her you wanted to see her again?" she finally asked.

He scoffed. "I called her earlier today. I thought I might be able to encourage her to give up her plan. It was a stupid idea, but I did tell her that if she dropped these crazy ideas, we could talk about going out again. For a minute I thought I might make progress with her. But apparently she came by the manor to see me and a worker told her they had seen you and the girls and I leaving together. You saw what happened next." He drank the last of his wine.

"Sorry. I thought I could turn this around for us."

She nodded and drank a long swallow. She seriously hoped that she didn't end up having to move into her mother's house with the girls.

"I'll figure out how to make it work. I will." He sighed.

They were quiet for a long moment.

"Are these for the house?" She ran her hands across the plans on the table.

"Yeah, that's something else I've been trying to figure out." He held his hand up to block the last of the setting sun. "The deck faces west and it gets too hot out here in the late afternoons. I thought about enclosing the area, adding air conditioning. But—"

"That's basically what the house is for, I guess."

"Yeah. Right now it's just not usable until the sun goes down. I could add a roof to it, but that blocks out the stars at night. So I'm still tinkering until it's perfect." He cursed Jordan's name and poured another glass of wine.

She knew he wasn't Asher and that he'd never hurt her, but his anger made her nervous. Sweaty palms and fast heartbeat kind of nervous.

A memory flashed through her mind—returning him from a party, Asher shoving her against the wall. "You humiliated me—ignored me in front of all those people! You should have been at my side!" She ran her hand over the underside of her jaw where the memory of his grip held firm.

"Aiming for perfection can be a block to your creativity. And your success." She quoted Dr. Waters, who had said this to her a long time ago. She tried to remember his words whenever perfect wasn't an option. Which was often.

"I come from a long line of perfectionists, you know," He chuckled. "My father, my grandfather—both builders, both perfectionists."

"I can't do perfect." She smiled sweetly, while her stomach churned with thorny fear. "I can't even aim for it, makes me, um. Anxious." Another memory revisited. This time of Asher complaining the tea was awful and throwing his teacup across the room. She had slept in the girls' room that night and intentionally dreamed that she and her daughters were free from Asher. "I try to dwell in possibility instead."

He stared at the plans, his eyes shifting from one object to the next.

"Possibility fuels creativity. Perfection steps on it. The idea of possibility drives confidence. Perfection drives insecurity." She said it for herself, mostly. And since nothing in her life was close to perfect. There was no sense hoping for it.

"You sound a lot like Dixie."

"I will take that as a compliment." She nodded.

"Possibility, huh?" He grinned with a sideways glance, the sun setting brightly behind him.

She felt the warmth of the sun and his smile.

"Come with me." He extended his hand to her and she accepted it.

They made their way to the lake and stopped at a hammock Mason had installed between two tall pines. He crawled into the wide rope netting and steadied it for her with his foot on the ground. At first she refused. But he insisted and she followed.

He held her close to him and pulled on the rope which kept them rocking back and forth. Mallards squawked and flapped. The lake sparkled with the final traces of the day's light.

"It's good to be here again. With you." She ran her hand over his chest, remembering what it was like to be so close to him in her dream. It was a strange and intimate secret they shared. From the way he had stared at the bruise on her neck, she wondered if he remembered putting it there. If he did, he would have thought himself completely crazy.

She flowed with what they had for the moment and hoped tomorrow would gift her a miracle. Hope is not a strategy, she could hear her mother say.

She sighed. Sometimes hope was all you had.

"I'm glad you're here." He tilted her chin. Then he kissed her the way he had kissed her in her dream, with warm sugary breath that made her want to taste him.

"Since I bought the house, this is the way I envisioned it."

"It's beautiful. Everything is just gorgeous."

"No, I mean, you here with me. When I came home I specifically bought *this* house on *this* land, where you and I had so many good times. I had Dixie decorate the interior to very detailed specifications because I wanted everything to be just so. And because I hoped that one day, if all went well, we might share this together. I've always seen *us* here." He stroked her cheek gently with his knuckles.

"You saw us here together?"

He nodded. His eyes were wide and revealing a shade of softness that she hadn't seen in him before. At least not before their night together and that was a dream, she reminded herself.

"Romantically?" As soon as the word left her lips she felt stupid for asking. But this wasn't her normal experience, so she wasn't certain.

"Preferably romantically." He smiled and ran his finger down the front of her neck with a delicate touch that made her toes curl. When his finger slipped inside the neckline of her top, she steadied his hand.

She had applied waterproof makeup to the bruise he had unwittingly left on her skin. While swimming she wore a swim shirt over her suit—for sun protection, she had been prepared to explain.

For her dry change of clothes she had selected a striped top with a narrow boatneck that covered the bruise nicely. But here in the light of day, if he tugged that neckline just an inch or two, he would see the bruise. She would have a hard time explaining that in a way that wouldn't freak him out.

"I'm sorry. I've made you feel uncomfortable. I didn't see any reason to keep that from you. We've known each other too long for that."

More than anything, she wanted to move into what he had envisioned, but she couldn't.

"We've only just reconnected. There might be things about me that you don't know."

"I'm looking forward to getting to know these new sides of you." He entwined his fingers with hers and gazed at them like he liked the sight of them together. "I've put in enough prayer time and soul searching to know that being here is right for me. You'll have to decide what's right for you. I'll respect your choice, whatever it is."

She held the depth of his gaze and met the sweetness of his kiss. If he cared about her this much, enough to see a future for the two of them together, then maybe he would understand. He'd said he was looking forward to getting to know these new sides of her.

After one last kiss he said, "I know you're generally opposed to perfect—though I would say that us, here together, is pretty perfect."

Layla rested her head on Mason's chest, and inhaled deeply. When she exhaled, the courage to share her secrets with him drifted away. Like a lost balloon.

∽

MASON WATCHED Layla doze in the late summer sun. There was something unsettled about her, something unfinished, something still waiting to be born. He'd seen it in her when they were younger. He always thought that one day, whatever this strength was would just burst forth and she would be a new person. Instead, it continued to build, just below the surface.

"We'll work this out," he had told her earlier. She had smiled, even cocked her head for two beats as Southern women did just before they blessed your heart.

Well bless your heart.

She didn't believe him. She didn't trust him.

She had that alone-in-the-world way about her and it wasn't hard to figure out why. Her mother made her way through life on the wheels of resentment. He'd never liked the way she wouldn't allow Layla to feel confident about anything, let alone herself.

Then there was Asher.

God really wasn't paying attention when he made that one. Dixie had said this about that man, and she was right.

Best thing that could have happened for Layla was for Asher to take that misstep off the second story balcony. Karma had her world class game on that day.

Asher hadn't even been a good provider for his family. Layla must have been supporting them on her salary. A foul metal taste brewed in his mouth.

The lake turned a darker shade of blue. The sky settled into warmer shades of pink and orange. Crickets and bullfrogs sang their evening song.

The hammock creaked when he pulled on the rope, and he hoped the rocking motion would give her a few more precious moments of rest. She'd been carrying a too-heavy load for too long, and it was time she had someone to watch over her for a while.

He thought of Jordan, how she wanted to destroy the Alcotts' plans for the manor and his home building business, too, for that matter. He thought of what Tom's friend said when they'd spoken earlier. That he would make a few calls and do what he could. But that, ultimately, Mayor Williams could keep the tourism plans for Alcott Manor in limbo for years. He might even be able to shut them down altogether.

22

Asher paced through Alcott Manor and listened intently for the sounds of his family arriving home. Laughing, jumping, running, and sometimes arguing. Layla usually brought the girls home right after school, but the sun was setting. They were nowhere to be found.

He slapped the fat handle of a screwdriver into the palm of his hand. One tap per slow step of his feet to mark the time. He'd been very busy.

Where were they? Her mother's? Mason's house? He didn't know where that was. Maybe she wouldn't even come home tonight. He'd seen parts of her dream. Herr sense of propriety had sunk to new depths.

Wherever she was, she would sleep eventually, and if she thought of him, he would hear that call. He was attuned to the sound of her dreams. Like the ringing of a doorbell, it was a signal, an alert. He had a way in. The door to her mind was unlocked and she was open for business. And then...it was payback time. Not just for Layla, but for Mason, too.

He hadn't been able to leave the manor since he died.

But wherever she was, her dream would be a bridge for him to get to her. A dreamy rainbow bridge full of bright colorful images that would drop him right where he wanted to be. He'd traveled it before, he knew the way.

He couldn't wait to show her what he had been up to in the manor. He had been such a busy boy today! So much of Mason's equipment had just been sitting around, waiting for an adjustment. The loosening of a screw here, the twirling of a bolt there, the fraying of cords everywhere...

He widened his eyes and called up the voice he used when the girls were younger and had begged him for story time: Mister Mason climbed up to the wall, Mister Mason had a great fall! All of Mama's horses and all of Mama's hospital men won't be able to put Mister Mason together again!

He clapped and wiggled. A feel-good shiver. He couldn't wait to tell her, to see Layla's face once she knew what he had planned.

After tonight, there would be no doubt in her mind.

Something horrible was about to befall Mason.

23

A glass of red wine balanced in his hand, Mason stood at the outdoor grill and cooked two thick filets and several vegetables. The sun had set. His profile was highlighted by the full moon that had only barely risen. She could see his jaw muscles flexing. With worry, she imagined.

He had checked his phone several times, but no calls had come from Jordan or Tom's contacts. Sharp pangs of fear shot through Layla's heart. She silently asked herself: What is real? What is true?

"You're awfully quiet." He managed a smile.

"Lots to think about."

He nodded and sipped his wine. He didn't press.

"I was asking myself your mother's questions."

He put the steaks and the vegetables on the plates and brought them over.

He raised his glass to hers and they clinked when they met.

She knew that he cared about her—that was true. But

was it real? Not really, because there were things he didn't know.

"Any luck?"

"No real answers, yet."

"The answers usually come eventually."

They talked about New York and how much he hated working there, how he had taken over his father's business, and how much he loved working it. The easy rhythm of the evening made her feel that their lives could always be this simple. She could see them spending every evening on the deck of the lake house, their cloistered haven that kept them safe from the world.

He stared at his empty plate for a moment. She knew he thought of Jordan and her threats. The fear was evident, like someone held a gun to his head.

"Do the girls often sleep over at your mother's house?"

She drew in a deep breath and let him change the subject. She didn't want to talk about Jordan or her threats, either. Plus the wine wrapped thick around her brain, like a fuzzy, comfortable sweater. She snuggled into that temporary carefree comfort. Their problems were too big to figure out tonight, anyway. "About once or twice a week, depends on my work schedule. She's slowly converting her home into an amusement park so the girls won't want to leave. She put in a pool with a slide and a trampoline on the other side of the yard. Next thing you know she'll build a merry-go-round." She sipped her wine. "And I'll let her. She can spoil them all she wants."

"Friday night is their usual night?" He pushed his empty plate forward an inch, leaned back and crossed his legs.

"No, typically it's Saturday. But the girls mentioned today that—" She stopped herself.

"Are they uncomfortable at the manor?"

She thought for a minute. Then decided to run with it. "They said they heard Asher in the house and that he was angry."

She watched his response carefully, saw his jaw muscles work and his lips press together more tightly.

"I wouldn't be surprised if Asher's spirit was still there," she said casually.

He shook his head and stared at the lake.

"I think some spirit was stuck at the manor for years," she said. "Then Tom brought in Dixie. One of my ancestors, I suppose. Maybe even Benjamin Alcott. You could feel that energy even from outside the house."

"Tell the girls not to share what they told you. That will come back to hurt them."

She realized just how much Mason held on to the hurt that had been inflicted on Dixie and their family over the Reverend Milligan mess. "A lot has changed since you were young. Mediums and psychics are on TV now."

"People are people. They judge. Especially in this town. The minute they find something that they can use against you, they will. Maybe the mystical is more accepted than it used to be, I'll give you that. But if you say someone is a psychic, that's not the same as saying they're a dentist."

"No. I guess not."

"People don't judge dentists. When the minister of your church finds out there's a dentist in the congregation, he doesn't stand in the pulpit and announce that the next four sermons are going to be on The Evils of Dentists. But when he finds out there's someone in the crowd who has gifts and she might know too much about the secrets you have stashed away— Well, we all know how that worked out." His face flushed slightly and his eyes hardened with old anger.

"That man had a lot to hide."

He reached out to her and she put her hand in his. "My whole family paid a huge price thanks to him. And while I don't blame Dixie, she couldn't have known how people would behave, I wouldn't want to see you or the girls go through anything like that. People judge. They talk. I feel protective of you, that's all."

"I understand," she said.

"I guess that's why I never much believed in it. Once you get burned, you just stay away from the source."

Layla wished her dream options had been as easy as simply not believing.

"You don't believe in those things, or you couldn't forgive those people for what they did?"

He paused for a moment and then he said, "Some people don't deserve forgiveness for what they've done."

She felt her hopes of endless lake house evenings fly off into the distance.

She made a smile and thought about how he and his brother ended up in her public school when all this happened. "You know, if the community hadn't been so narrow-minded toward Dixie, you never would have been kicked out of your private school and you and I might never have met."

He nodded slowly. "That is a silver lining on that dark cloud."

They cleaned up the dishes and went inside. It was dark and Layla felt the effects of work and several hours of sun and swimming. "I ought to get back to the manor. It's late. I'm beat." Adrenaline shot through her chest at the thought of being there alone or, even worse, with Asher. She decided she would do her job, then stay with a friend.

"I don't want you to be at the manor by yourself. I know we have police patrolling there, but—listen, why don't you just stay here tonight? It is late and the manor can do without you for one night."

She opened her mouth to object, even though she welcomed the invitation. "I don't—"

"I'm not suggesting anything. I have four bedrooms here. Two couches. You pick the spot you want and I'll choose from what's left. Make yourself at home."

"I feel like I'm invading your private space."

"I want you here for as long and as often as you want to be here. If the girls are uncomfortable at the manor, they're welcome as well. Come one, come all." He slipped his arms around her and snuggled her close.

She gently nuzzled her face against his neck and decided that being close to Mason at his home was far better than being close to Asher at the manor. "Maybe I will."

"Good. I know I'd feel better if you did." He winked as he walked away. "Relax here on the couch while I clean the grill. Then I'll show you around and you can pick the bedroom you want. I'll get you a T-shirt and I'm sure I have a new toothbrush stashed somewhere."

Layla sipped the last of her wine, even though she really didn't need any more, and took in her current circumstance. How often had she and Mason swam in that lake? And how many times did she dream she could live in this beautiful house? She was inside it now, but maybe further away from that dream than ever before.

Exhausted, she snuggled against one of the couch pillows and began to let go. The girls had had a great day at the lake. They were safe and happy at Jayne Ella's for the night. Maybe for the weekend. For as much of a pain in the neck as her mother had been in her life, she was a good sitter for the girls. It was the one break Layla had.

She wasn't at the manor tonight. Also good. Much as she was grateful for the money that the manor would bring her, she needed a night off from worry.

About the time she realized she was sliding down a gratitude list and into a deep pool of sleep, she woke to find Mason carrying her upstairs. He kissed her on the forehead and shortly thereafter she felt the cool sheets of a soft bed beneath her.

She would have thought it a guest room, but she quickly noticed that the bed smelled like Mason. He disappeared and she figured he was headed for the couch or a different room.

But then Mason slipped in behind her. He wrapped his arm around her belly and her eyes flew open in the dark.

As had become her first instinct for some time now, she pinched a small wedge of thin skin between her nails to see if she was awake. Tonight it was the skin from inside her forearm.

Yes, she was awake.

She ran her palm along his arm to make sure there were no tingles or other signs of her dream world. There weren't.

His kisses dragged along the side of her neck and brought her fully awake.

The years of being ignored by Asher, the slow build of affection between her and Mason, made her want to roll toward him. But she couldn't. She wouldn't.

Besides, he kept so many secrets from him. Once they finally came to light, he would hate her.

And then it hit her. He wouldn't be with her at all if he knew the truth.

Her heart crumpled.

She turned toward him.

In the dark, his lips brushed against hers, soft and teasing. She breathed in the subtle scents of skin, malt and honey. She dissolved into a mist of feelings, caught up in the storm of electricity.

Her head swam with this exquisite idea. This proof that life could begin again and in the most unexpected ways.

She shook her head slightly to clear it.

"We have to talk, Mason. There's something you need to know."

He pulled her close to him again. "Come here."

He snuggled her to him. The strong pillow of his chest and the warmth of his body comforted her. Their hands tangled together, sliding against one another and then falling into a perfect fit once again.

"We'll talk in the morning, okay?" He kissed the top of her head. "In the daylight. Right now I just want you close to me."

She sighed.

"We have plenty of time, I'm not going anywhere."

Too tired for coherent words, and knowing there was nothing she could have said to him that would have worked out well anyway, she relaxed her heart into his care. Just for one more night. She wrapped her arm around his midsection and anchored her hand beneath his upper back. His solid comfort beneath her was an intimate, sweet pleasure.

She didn't tilt her head to meet his lips, though she wanted to feel them with her own.

And even though she didn't deserve it, she felt vines of trust growing between her and Mason. Twisting and thickening, their roots pushing deep into the darkness. The trust gave way to hope and it nearly broke her heart to feel it. It was hope that tomorrow he would understand, hope that all would be forgiven and hope that what they had could last.

His breathing became more regular. He was drifting off.

The world around them dark and safe and comforting. The weightlessness moved over her quickly, and sleep pulled at her. She didn't have time to put together a gratitude list, but she did have one final thought when she nuzzled her head against his chest.

With any luck, tonight she would dream.

24

L ayla stood on the grassy banks of Mason's lake house where a shooting star flew overhead. Its image trail was as long as the sky was wide.

She knew immediately she was dreaming.

Under the bright glow of a full moon, she wiggled her bare toes in the soft, thin grass. It was spongey to her touch. She pinched herself, this time on the thigh. Her fingertips felt tingly and the pinch wasn't sharp. She could have taken a nighttime flight or skated across the water, she could have flown with that shooting star. But all she really wanted was to spend time with Mason.

A bevy of white swans honked from the other side of the lake and floated near an arched opening she'd never seen before. The lake rose to the halfway mark, and the upper arch held firm with its moss and braided tree root structure.

A pair of warm arms slid around her and she closed her eyes.

"I wondered where you were," she said. "I was about to come find you."

She turned around.

Mason looked just as he had when she fell asleep next to him. The tenderness in his cinnamon-colored gaze gave her that ticklish sensation in her heart. The one that urged her to move ahead.

"What are you doing out here?" he asked.

She wondered if he would remember parts of this dream, just as she suspected that he remembered snippets of the other one. She decided it might be best to keep things as real as possible.

"I wanted some fresh air. It's a nice night."

He glanced at the sky and then the lake, nodding slowly. "Something feels a little different, doesn't it?"

She startled at his recognition. "What do you mean?"

"I don't know. Everything feels a bit...dreamy. Maybe I'm tired."

She rubbed her palm against the warmth of his bare chest. "Do you want to go back to bed?"

An owl hooted in the distance and Mason tilted his head, like he listened. "No. You're right. It's a nice night."

He kissed her, and she wrapped her arms around him. Claiming him as her own.

"How about a swim?" He stepped away from her and headed for the lake. He motioned for her to join him.

She couldn't have him gallivanting unchaperoned in her dream; she would have to follow him.

"I knew you were still a wild child. Given the right conditions," he said when he saw her walking toward him.

They splashed their way through the lake, and she expected the swans to scatter. Instead, they bounced quietly on the small waves, like bath toys in a giant tub. She caught up with Mason, and she let him bring her close. She sealed their embrace by locking her arms around him, enjoying the feel of the warm water that slipped between them.

They floated across the lake like that, in each other's intimate embrace, until Layla realized they had reached the wooded arch she had seen earlier. An orangey glow emanated from inside the secret tunnel and the swans parted like they encouraged them to go inside.

"Did you know this was here?" She wondered if she had just missed it earlier in the day or if this was strictly a part of her dream.

He shrugged. "I've never seen it before."

They swam inside. The ceiling opened up like the inside of a cave. A small sandy beach sloped on the right, glittering and sparkling with hundreds of greenish blue gemstones.

"I think my imagination is working overtime," she whispered.

"I rather like this cave." Mason rested on the sand and floated with his toes peeking up from the water. "From now on, this will be our place and ours alone."

She felt like they were kids again, full of energy and wild imagination. It was like their whole lives were still laid out ahead of them. That it would always be like this—simple, safe, happy. Together.

Sifting dry sand through her fingers, she picked out three smooth stones. They glowed with an internal fire. She ran them over her palm, they clicked together, one large oval and two smaller roundish stones. He flicked a few drops of water in her direction and she laughed and dug her toes into the wet sand.

The cave was quiet except for the water lapping at the shore.

Curiosity bubbled up inside of her and suddenly she had to have that truth. "What were you going to tell me when you came to see me all those years ago? After Brooke's accident?" It was like the stones gave her the question to ask.

He rested on his elbows at the base of the short beach, the current sloshing against the sand and rocking his body. His expression became serious and thoughtful. She hoped she wasn't going to regret asking the question.

"I wanted to apologize for not standing up for you sooner."

She squeezed the three stones in her hand.

"I might have also been thinking about that kiss. That was something new in our relationship." His expression held the same questioning shadows he must have had over a decade ago.

She drew her knees close, nodded quietly, thinking of all the time that had passed since they were teenagers. And yet that time in her life still touched a wounded place in her heart.

"I'm so sorry," he said. "I screwed up both of our lives that night—I guess that's kind of an arrogant thing for me to say. But if I had believed you right away when you said you didn't hurt Brooke, if I had come to see you sooner—"

"Mason—none of what happened was your fault."

He searched her eyes, looking for something specific. Forgiveness, she suspected. From this expression, she could see the guilt—a heavy, worn out companion that he had carried for a decade. She could relate.

"Well. It's the fault of whoever attacked Brooke and Jordan. That's who screwed up our lives."

She closed her eyes for a long moment. "I'm so sorry, Mason."

"No, no, no. Don't do that." He kissed her again and again, like he could make the past go away, like he could erase her need to accept the blame, like he could make everything right. "I'm going to find out who did this. I'll make them pay."

She considered telling him right then. Right there. She even opened her mouth to say the words: I was the one who did it. But telling him in her dream was a cop-out. That was cheating, because he might not remember. She would have to tell him face to face when the time was right.

"I have the sense that you'll be able to do just that," she said.

"I guess all we can do now is look forward. What's happened is done."

He stroked the side of her cheek, soft and gentle. He was right. What's done was done, there was no changing it. Her signature guilt began to rise up, and she reached for Dixie's questions—What is real? What is true? This time she had a few answers.

What had happened to Brooke couldn't have been predicted. She was sorry that she had killed her. Deeply regretful. If there had been some way for her to make things right with her family, she would have. That was all real. And true.

His kisses were gentle, sending a shiver down her arms. The stones she held in her hand fell to the side.

"I thought I'd lost you," he said.

She looked at the top of the cave. She thought briefly about that orange-ish glow and how it didn't seem to originate from anywhere specific.

The tingling prickled more strongly in her chest, that meant-to-be feeling she had known long ago but couldn't place. The one she had learned the hard way to discount and reject because it could lead you astray.

It was a strong sensation tonight, and in the shadows of this earthly womb she thought maybe she could trust it. She thought she could let her hopes fly in this world that wasn't real, just like the night before.

Mason held her close and stroked her hair. "When I was away, when everything was supposed to be ideal and nothing was, you were the only one I thought of. Like you were calling me home."

She wondered if somehow she had, the simple result of his never being far from her own thoughts. Maybe that had been a beacon, a call from her heart to his.

She tried to remember that this was just a dream. She had forgotten for a while. "I don't want to let go of what we have."

"I hope you won't." He kissed her head.

"No, I just mean—" She couldn't say it aloud, but she didn't want to walk away from this dream. She knew she had to, though she hoped against all odds the possibility of it would become her reality.

"We'll have the rest of our lives together," he said, "if you'll have me."

They gazed at one another for a long moment, his eyes smiling with his own plan for the two of them.

She would have married him in their gem-laden, make-believe cave if a minister had been present. The only thing holding her back was how much she wanted this, how she knew that tomorrow it would be gone, and how dangerous it was to let her heart believe.

The walls of the cave were the dark underside of the thick wooded forest above them. Roots dangled from above with bits of black dirt clinging to the sides. The space had been hollowed just for them.

He smiled his winner's smile, the one that convinced her she could do anything, and he lifted something from the sand. "I love you, Layla."

A tiny breath escaped her, she'd been caught by surprise.

"I always have. I always will. So let this," he rested the largest of the three polished gemstones on her hand. "Be living proof of my love for you."

The fiery stone glowed with flashes of lightning yellow across the ocean of green-blue.

He raised his eyebrows in a question.

"What?"

"Will you have me for the rest of your life? Will you marry me, Layla?"

His proposition synced them with a cadence, like she and Mason had fallen in step with a pulse that emanated from the earth. For the first time she felt it deep in her bones, a true understanding of what *the right path* really was.

"You're serious?" She had to ask, even though he looked at her like she was the only other person in the world.

"Marry me, Layla. Make me the happiest man alive."

She stared deeply into those light ginger eyes that had shown her so much kindness and friendship over the years. The ones that saw beneath the surface.

"Yes," she finally said. Excitement bubbled from deep within. He pressed his lips softly to hers, she refused to believe this wasn't real.

"We will always be happy together, because our life will simply be a continuation of us." His breath was warm and whispering against her ear.

She placed the stone with the other two on the sand, regretting that she wouldn't be able to take them with her when they left.

She'd never taken herself for a daredevil before. But here she was, allowing her heart to dangle ahead of herself, dance with abandon, and live completely unprotected.

What a precious freedom and a priceless trust, like a leap from the rope swing with Mason nearby.

The thought of being married to him drove her deeper into her dream, where she was finally carefree. She imagined lazy Saturday mornings and bike rides as a family and beach trips and other plans for the future. Yes, she was all in for this life they would share. *All in.*

She struggled to remember something. The next thing on her never-ending to-do list. *What was it?* Make breakfast? Plan a wedding? The girls should have a role.

He ran his hands through his hair and she saw his watch.

The time.

No more than three hours.

"We should get back to the house." She gathered the three stones in her hand, even though she knew they would disappear.

"Let's wait until morning. I like this place. I'm not ready for reality yet," he said.

"Me either, but we should go." She wracked her brain for a reason that would motivate him. "I need to get back to a phone in case the girls need me."

He nodded in agreement and then spied her closed hand. "Do you have the stone?" Mason peeled open her fingers and three stones glowed in her palm like frozen fire.

She poured them into his hand and he moved them around.

"These are labradorite, you know. Stones of transformation and protection. If you believe in that sort of thing. Dixie keeps huge chunks of gemstones all over the house."

Layla backed into the water and swam toward the opening of the cave, anxious to get them out of the dream before it was too late and one of them ended up in a coma.

He didn't show any signs of wanting to wake up, so she weighed her options. She could scare him awake. That worked, but she hated to terrorize him like that. She wondered if she couldn't just get him back in his own bed where he might drift out of her dream. Then he wouldn't be startled.

He closed his fist around the stones and followed Layla into the open area of the lake.

They arrived at the grassy bank of Mason's lake house.

Dizziness curled through her and knocked her off balance. She was pushing the limits again, and there was no time to get upstairs. "Mason, we need to wake up now."

He cocked his head to the side. "What are you talking about?"

Slow clapping sounded from behind Mason and they turned to find Asher walking toward them. He wore the same black pants and shirt she had seen him in when he died. His eyes were darker, haunting. Terror pressed against her chest like a boulder.

Mason's lake house towered behind Asher. The idea of him intruding in their sacred space made her feel sick.

She jerked Mason's arm. "Mason, wake up!"

"Layla!"

Mason cocked his head at what was clearly impossible. "Asher?"

"Go away, Asher. You're dead." Guilt and fear and rage competed inside of her, but her first concern was Mason. She'd seen firsthand what could happen to someone in her dreams and she wasn't about to lose him. Let alone to Asher.

Asher leaned against a tree and examined his nails. "If only you had thought of me sooner, I could have joined you for a swim."

Mason took several steps in Asher's direction and Layla

scooted in front of him and focused his face on hers. "Mason. Mason! Wake up. Let it go, it's just a dream. He's nothing!"

"That's right, ole boy. Settle down." Asher patted the space in front of him like he told a dog to sit. "I'm nothing. In fact, I'm not even here. And I wouldn't be able to do anything with this." He pulled a long hunting knife from his sleeve.

Layla gasped and shook Mason. "Wake up, wake up!"

"Tell you what, Lay. Come with me and I'll leave him alone." Asher waved the knife.

"I'm not going anywhere with you." She said with every ounce of her strength.

"No? Not even to protect your boyfriend? The one who cast you over for the cheerleader in high school?"

Mason's hands clenched into fists. He stormed toward Asher.

Asher's eyes fired with malicious delight and he spun the knife in front of him.

He obviously knew that she and Mason were together. Layla knew Asher would kill Mason for that alone. So she did the one thing she knew she could do to save Mason, and possibly his life—she sprouted huge angel wings and flew in front of him, stopping him in his tracks.

"Wake up!" she screamed. She spread her wings wide and sudden.

Mason gasped and disappeared in an instant.

The night air around her was heavy and quiet. She quickly realized she had left a dream and entered a nightmare. If only she had woken up when Mason did, but her body must have been too tired.

Now she was alone with her abusive ex-husband, in a world where anything was possible.

Asher shuffled toward her slowly, casually.

Layla spread her wings and flew backward several feet, distancing herself from him.

"Those are a nice touch, Lay. I ought to get some of those for myself." He pointed to her wings.

"Knock yourself out, Ash." She had never called him Ash, no one did. And her tone carried a devil-may-care attitude. But beneath that cover, she was trying to think how she could defend herself.

How do you kill a ghost?

When he had been alive, he was protective of certain things: his business, his children. Even her to an extent because he needed a mother for his girls.

Her girls.

That gave him certain vulnerabilities. But now, he had nothing to lose. Not his reputation, not her, not even his life. If she had to kill him to protect herself, she wondered, how would she do it?

"Come to the manor with me, Lay. Our home sweet home. I want to show you a few things I've done." His tone was serious.

"What have you done?" She panicked at the thought that he might have destroyed the manor the way he did before he died.

"Just made some minor adjustments, that's all. Come with me and I'll show them to you." He extended his hand to her like they were friends.

She refused his gesture but decided that for as long as she was asleep, there was no way to get him away from her. She could fly away but if he'd already found a way into her dream, he'd just follow her. Whatever adjustments he had made to the manor were sure to be a disaster in the waiting. She decided it was better if she knew what they were.

"I'll meet you in the foyer of the manor. Keep your distance from me or you'll be sorry."

"Oh, my, look who finally gave birth to a spine. We should throw a party for the new arrival."

Every fiber of her being vibrated with hate. And though she knew it wouldn't do any good, she wished him dead. "Maybe you should try growing a new body part, too. Like a heart."

She didn't wait for his response, even though she knew one was coming. He opened his mouth and she dashed to the manor in a head start.

He arrived in the foyer a half second after she did.

"Touché," he said. "I'm going to have to get better at navigating this world."

She kept her distance from him and prepared herself to move or leave entirely. There was no telling what he was up to.

The workers had left the house dark and she hadn't been there to turn on any lights. The manor was as cool and silent as the historic graveyards that Layla and her sister roamed as teenagers. Beautiful and haunted, no signs of life.

"What is it that you want to show me? Unlike you, I'm going to be awake soon."

"Well, then by all means. On with the show." He manifested a black top hat and bowed slightly like a gentleman, a magician or ringmaster. His smile was slightly clown-like—insincere. Frightening.

She listened with every antenna for that shift in energy that took place before Asher struck. That subtle stillness that meant lightning was about to explode and she would end up nursing her own injuries.

A confusing mix of guilt and obligation smeared her insides and sucked at her strength. The same weakening emotions she'd fought whenever she was around her mother or Brooke.

"I get your jealousy, Asher. I might feel the same way if I no longer had a life to live or a body to live it in."

Asher clicked his tongue against the roof of his mouth and walked up the grand staircase to the second level. This was the same area where he'd fallen. "My how you've blossomed. Humor, wit, strength. I would even consider being married to you again."

"How flattering." A cold, nauseating sweat covered her.

A ladder leaned against the second floor railing and he jiggled it such that metal rattled against metal. "See this?" He held up a screwdriver like a magic wand and warped circus music began to play in the background, as if it came from an old crank organ. "I've figured out how to entertain myself around this place. Just enough weight toward the top of this thing and someone gets to experience what I did—a brilliant fall right into the afterlife.

"Seems like Mason likes to work with his hands, doesn't he? Wouldn't it be something if he died exactly the way that I did? Or any old way, really. I've been very busy around here. I may have even left a little something for you." He twirled the screwdriver around his fingers like a baton. "Of course, if he died first, you'd be considered something of a black widow. Especially after that whole Brooke thing years ago and then my death, of course."

She swallowed hard at the thought of Mason being hurt and at her being taken away from her girls. "You should go home, Asher. Cross over. Call it a night. You've had your chance at life."

"I've tried that, but oddly enough I can't seem to swing it. Something about the house just wants me here, I guess. Maybe it knows that I was its rightful owner."

She would tell Mason about the ladders, say that she saw someone fiddling with them and that they weren't safe. That would at least make him cautious enough to double check his equipment.

She checked her watch for the time. It was late. She tried to will herself to wake up, but nothing budged. She prayed her body was okay. She walked back toward the staircase; it was time to leave.

"Or maybe it wants you to pay a price for what you did."

Asher paused like she might have a point. Then a young woman in a navy bustled dress hurried down the stairs. A wide navy ribbon tied her dark hair at the nape of her neck, and her curled ponytail bounced with her every step.

Asher shook his head. "No, I think maybe it's just possessive. You know there's another party going on in here, like the house leads a double life. No one ever really leaves Alcott Manor."

She thought of the clock on the wall in the summer quarters. The one that appeared in her dream but wasn't there before or after. She also thought of the nanny and the baby and the dog. The house did lead a double life.

"But here's my point, Lay. In spite of everything you've done to me, I've decided to take you back. Permanently. So, you can join me the easy way. Or I can give you motivation."

"What would motivate me to spend eternity with you in Alcott Manor?"

"Mason." Asher gestured to the ladder he had altered. "You can come willingly, or Mason dies. Got it?"

Panic thrummed in Layla's chest. "No, Ash. I'm not coming with you. And neither is Mason."

"It's your choice. One way or the other, you will be with me. The question is, will you sacrifice Mason in the process or will you let him live?" He turned like he was going to leave and then shook his finger in the air. "Next time you dream, and there will be a next time, I won't announce myself." He pulled the same knife from his pocket that he had shown her earlier. "And then one of you will come with me. Hey, where did those glorious wings of yours go?" He pointed with the knife.

She checked over her shoulder and noticed that they were gone. Sometimes they did that, disappeared if she forgot about them.

When she turned forward, he had shifted close to her on that top step and she lost her balance trying to get away from him.

"Hey now." He grabbed the outside of her arm and his grip was cold and dead. "Don't go anywhere, Lay. I was hoping you might wear some teeny tiny lacy underwear and then we could pretend you're a magazine model. You could do it these days, you know." He traced her waistline with the tip of his screwdriver.

"Stop calling me that and let me go."

"Oh, by the way, do you think that old saying is true, Lay? You know, that old wives tale?"

She twisted inside of his tight grasp that felt like skeleton fingers. She thought her arm might break.

"The one that says if you see yourself die in a dream, you'll die in real life!" His voice pitched high on the last word and he threw confetti.

He let go of her arm with a shove and she screamed, tumbling backward in a free fall down the stairs.

25

L ayla, Mason, and Dixie waited several hours for the hospital to complete all of the tests the ER doctor ordered, including a CAT scan. Finally, the short, stout man with graying hair and half glasses near the end of his nose stood in the small sterile room with the three of them. He told Layla she was very lucky, that she only had a moderate concussion and ultimately she would be fine. There was no neurological damage.

She breathed deep with relief. Then she wondered how many times Asher had hurt her and her response had been something similar.

"You should carpet those stairs of yours," the doctor lectured Mason with a wave of his reading glasses. "That was a hard hit she took."

"Yeah," he said with a half-nod. "Thanks."

Layla and Dixie exchanged a glance. They both knew that Mason's stairs were already carpeted. Rail to wall.

"The nurse is preparing your discharge papers. It will be just a few minutes. Here are your aftercare instructions." He handed Mason a sheet of printed directions. "Ice, ibuprofen, and rest are the main items. The nurse will go over the rest of it with you." On his way out of the room, the doctor waved to Layla. "Take care, now."

After the heavy door shut, Mason rocked on his heels with his hands in his pockets and read from the handout. "Trauma consistent with fall on hardwood stairs." He raised an eyebrow in that sarcastic doctors-know-nothing kind of way. "I don't have any hardwood stairs in my house." He kissed her temple. "I don't know why you got back in bed after you fell. You should have woken me up right away."

The similarities between the way Brooke died and Layla's injury wasn't lost on her. She was just far luckier. She tried to find the words to tell him what happened. For his own safety.

"Mason—we have to talk about what happened last night. There's something you need to know."

He rubbed his hand over his face, tired from long hours from waiting and worrying. "Let's get out of here first. I'll bring the car around and I need to make some calls."

"Are people working at the manor today?" There was panic in her voice.

"A few crew members were going to do a walk-through and prepare a punch list."

"They wouldn't get on any ladders, would they?"

"Not a chance. That's my job."

"Stay off the ladders, Mason. I had a dream and...it means something, everyone needs to stay off the ladders."

"I'm not going to the manor today," he said in what she thought must be his most soothing tone. "Just going out to the parking lot to get the car. I'll be right back."

He didn't understand. He couldn't possibly, no one would. The singular idea that he could get hurt or worse played front and center in her mind. She had to figure out how to get rid of Asher.

Mason pointed a playful finger at his mother. "Don't talk about me while I'm gone."

Dixie tried to grab his finger and missed. When Mason was out of the room, her smile disappeared and she whispered to Layla with all seriousness, "What's happened, sweetheart?"

Layla thanked Dixie for coming to the ER, it had been her only request. Given the supernatural ilk of her problem, there wasn't anyone else she could trust.

She exhaled deeply.

Then she gave Dixie a quick download—her lucid dreaming and how that began, how being around the manor sometimes affected reality through these dreams, that Asher was still attached to the manor and somehow he had access to her through these dreams.

She left out the details where Mason was concerned. But she made sure to communicate that he had indeed made an appearance in her dreams and there was some evidence of that the next day.

"He shoved me down the stairs in my dream. That's how I ended up with this concussion. He's sabotaged the ladders. Maybe other equipment, too." She exhaled with some small relief that she had been able to tell at least one person, that she didn't have to explain anything, and that Dixie didn't judge.

Mason's mother covered her mouth with the tips of her fingers. "Explaining this to Mason will be like trying to convince a dog not to run outside of his fenced yard. He won't believe there are consequences. Has he seen Asher?"

Layla nodded. She pressed against the pain that throbbed in her head like a screaming red light. "Last night's dream. He wanted to go after him as soon as he saw him, but Asher had a knife. I got Mason to wake up before anything happened."

The air in the small sterile room was heavy.

"Did you bring them?" Layla asked.

Dixie's face tightened. Without looking down, she reached into her oversized slouchy purse and pulled out a black velvet pouch.

She shuffled a stack of rectangular tarot cards and Layla thought of Asher's parting words before he shoved her down the stairs. "Dixie, if you see yourself die in a dream, do you die in real life?"

She inhaled long and slow, like Layla had just asked the one question she wished she hadn't. She pointed to Layla's head. "In your case, with your dreams, I think we have to carefully assume that that might be true."

Layla swallowed a metallic taste of fear. She had hoped that since she knew she was dreaming, that might make a difference. Asher wouldn't care if he took their daughters' mother away from them. And she would never forgive herself if something happened to Mason. "I have to find a way to tell Mason."

Dixie shook her head. "He's always leaned into the luxury of not having to believe in this realm. Unlike me. I don't have a choice. And he's never gotten over what happened to our family when he was little. It was awful. Reverend Milligan probably still has a doll in my likeness with pins through the head."

Layla stood, the pain in her head worsening. She pulled on her jeans. Asher's warped smile flashed in her mind.

"How am I going to get him to believe me?"

Dixie stopped shuffling the cards. "I could try to talk to him for you—"

"He needs to hear it from me." Layla pulled on her T-shirt and thought about how Mason would react. He would think she was crazy.

Dixie spread a line of tarot cards on the over-the-bed hospital table. "Pick four with your left hand."

She did as she was told. She had pulled cards with Dixie before, but not for many years. She curled her hands into fists.

She pointed to the first card. "This one is the Tower card, that's you and Mason."

Layla leaned forward and frowned at the sight of a man and woman being tossed out of a burning tower.

"Chaos. Abrupt change. Difficult. Sudden."

It was repeating. She dreamed at Alcott Manor and now everything was falling apart.

Dixie stared at the card for a minute and then at Layla, as if she were getting some inside information she was hesitant to share. "You're keeping something from him. Whatever it is, you should talk with him about it. Sooner rather than later. For everyone's sake. And maybe it won't—" Dixie pointed to the next card, a man lying dead on the floor with ten swords piercing his body, and she frowned.

"Mason is about to face his worst nightmares: secrets, lies. He doesn't respond well to those, sees them as a personal betrayal. Also anything to do with ghosts or the paranormal. He likes for things to be logical. He likes his world at right angles. This isn't that." Her voice drifted off. "This is why I don't do readings anymore, we need to stop.

"Why?" Layla leaned forward and looked at the card.

It was entitled The Devil. A monstrous beast stood in-between a naked man and woman, holding chain leashes that connected to the iron collars they wore.

Dixie pointed at it. "Because of that."

Layla forced a swallow.

"Not all information that comes through is of the Light. I learned that lesson the hard way. "That's Asher. He's between you and Mason. Neither one of you knows how to get away from him." Her eyes moved back and forth like she was reading something. "He wants to even the score, honey. He wants revenge. He blames you for what happened to him." The color drained from her face, her lips were drew into a thin line. "He wants you dead. And with him." Dixie gathered the cards together and threw them in the trash.

Dixie returned to her seat. "Trust me. Best to be done with those."

"I just have one question."

"Okay," Dixie said.

"How do I get rid of my dead ex-husband?" Layla asked.

Dixie lifted her eyes to the upper part of the room, her focus somewhere within. "What's Asher's unfinished business?"

"His work was flat when he died, nothing to wrap up there. I never thought he was particularly attached to the girls. Alcott Manor, though. He always wanted to own that property. It was the reason he married me."

"So he's finally occupying the property he always wanted. He has no interest in moving on."

"He said he tried and the house wouldn't let him go. Something about it being possessive and there was a party going on that he could hear but not see."

"There is something about the energy in the manor, nothing moves on too easily from that property. There's always a piece of that home in the past, like a root or an anchor. Like anyone with a difficult beginning, I suppose, it clings to what it can. Maybe it's hanging on to Asher."

"And me, possibly. He was very controlling when he was

alive." She thought for the millionth time to tell someone how Asher had abused her, how he had punched and hit. But she couldn't bear the shame. "Probably because I was his link to owning the manor and I never came through on that. I always voted for restoration. It was one of the few places I stood my ground, and he hated that." She told Dixie briefly about his insurance policy and hers and how she thought he planned to kill her for money and her stock.

"Oh, Layla." Dixie rubbed her hand along her knee. A mother's concern shadowed her face.

Layla tried to conjure the courage she needed. "How do I kill a ghost?"

Dixie gripped her own hands tightly in front of her. She leaned forward. "I don't know. I think you should just stay away from the manor altogether. Mason should, as well."

"I need the income that place is going to generate and I'm the family representative. Although Jordan is trying to shut that down."

Dixie didn't seem to hear her. "The Other Side wants him, honey. They don't like it when people stay behind—it leaves things out of order. His dying in that house kept him from the magnetic pull that most people just flow with when they die. Normally, that would have carried him over."

"Maybe I need to do something to him in my dream."

Dixie bit the side of her lip. "I think he has more freedom and more control in your dreams than he does otherwise. And you're more vulnerable there." The two women sat in silence for a while. Neither one came up with a good solution.

"Alright, sweetheart. Do this. Think about what is true. Think about what is real. Do you remember these questions? I always posed them to myself in times of trouble and I've found that it can help guide you toward a solution.

Anchor yourself in the truth. Stay away from what is false and not important. We may not have the final answer right now, but one thing is for sure, the answer is always in the truth."

"Jordan?"

Layla and Dixie spun toward the sound of Mason's voice.

"What are you doing here?" Layla and Dixie leaned into the hallway in time to see Mason escorting Jordan around the corner. Jordan looked over her shoulder and when she spied the two women she smiled and slid her hand into Mason's.

Layla's throat promptly went dry. Her heart began a fast-paced jog.

Dixie pulled her back inside the exam room and patted her arm. "Riffraff has to be escorted off the property. That's all that is."

It was too late to be calmed. "Just the sight of her sends me into a panic. It's like junior high and high school all over again." She thought she might throw up. Had she heard their conversation?

"Mason doesn't care about her. Not anymore. I can promise you that, darlin'. If he has any contact with her whatsoever, it's to move her on. Okay?" Dixie said like she read Layla's mind.

Layla was embarrassed for Dixie to see her like this. Which was funny because Jordan was the one who ought to feel embarrassed for her behavior, and Layla was certain she didn't.

"Don't you worry about this. Anyone in their right mind feels ill when they see Jordan. It's just good common sense to feel panicked when you come into contact with a crazy person."

When the nurse arrived with the aftercare instructions,

Layla told her, "I'm a nurse, you don't have to go through these with me."

"Actually, I'm required to. And I'm going to need a signature from you at the bottom of the page here, agreeing that I went over everything with you."

"We'll honor this delay as a part of the law of perfect timing," Dixie whispered.

Layla wasn't sure what the law of perfect timing was, but she couldn't shake the dread that had cemented itself in her gut. Jordan and Mason together was not something she ever wanted to see.

After the nurse had collected Layla's signature and payment, she wheeled her out to the patient pick up area. Jordan and Mason were talking near his truck and Layla didn't like the sparkle in her eye.

26

"What did Jordan want?"

Mason held her hand in his until she asked this question. Then he pulled away, shook his head, and exhaled hard. "Jordan."

"Why was she at the hospital?"

"She went to the manor this morning and one of the refinishers told her I was at the hospital. I guess she thought I was sick or something."

Layla fumed at the idea of Jordan dashing to Mason's side. "Were you able to talk her into calming down about the manor?"

He returned his hand to hers, rubbed his thumb over it. He gave her a reassuring glance, but she could see that something was troubling him.

"Not really. She said tat a few city building inspectors were going to visit the manor next week and that we might find them hard to please. She reminded me that the city won't allow the manor to open for tours until it's passed all of its inspections."

The pain in Layla's head throbbed harder. "What did

you say to that?"

"It wasn't possible to tell her much. I asked her to have lunch on Monday and I'll see what I can do then."

Just before they arrived at his lake house, she called the girls again to see what they were up to. She also gave her mother an update on her condition. Jayne Ella told her to rest, and that the girls were hers to manage. She was sure that her mother was now trying to push her into Mason's arms as much as possible.

To her mother's knowledge, Asher was out of the picture, so onward and upward. Her mother might even play dumb when she finally cornered her on how she kept Mason away from her that summer. Brand new day, brand new plan. No memory of yesterday. She would have made a great politician.

Once at his house, Mason fluffed pillows and brought her tea and tried to get her to relax on the couch.

"Mason. Sit down. There's something you need to know."

He sat on the edge of the couch and stared distractedly at the floor.

"I'm sure you remember—" she began.

He raised his finger and shook it as if he'd just thought of something he needed to voice and right away. "Just one quick thing—what did you and Dixie discuss while I was getting the car and talking with Jordan?"

With a jolt, she realized that Jordan must have overhead part of her conversation with Dixie. Jordan probably knew Mason well enough to know what he thought of the mystical world and couldn't wait to use this information against her.

"I know better than to believe anything Jordan says, especially if she's saying it to me, because she always has an ulterior motive. But I found her outside your hospital room, apparently listening to your conversation with my mother. According to her, you told Dixie that whatever you dream comes to pass and Asher is still alive in the manor and..." He exhaled hard as though he couldn't believe what he was about to say. "That he's trying to kill us?"

She didn't think she had ever hated Jordan more than she did in this moment. Mason waited for her to refute what he said and to call Jordan ridiculous. He had the *please* in his wide-eyed expression.

"Okay, this is part of what I wanted to talk with you about. Not everything that happens in my dreams shows up in my life. But when I'm around the manor, some things do."

He didn't move, but something drained from him. It took the color from his face.

"Mason. The manor has some sort of effect on me, something I would never have deliberately chosen. My dreams and the manor have created some kind of bridge that Asher has used to get in touch with me. He's sabotaged the equipment at the manor with the hope that that will hurt you or worse." She went into patient detail about how Brooke and Jordan endlessly humiliated her at school, the resulting sleepwalking and sleep eating, seeing Dr. Waters and his recommendation that she do lucid dreaming.

She had mentally rehearsed this speech a hundred times, much of that in the last hour. But when the words came out, she knew they fell short of his understanding. He barely looked at her when she told her story, frowning toward the lake like he struggled to hear what she was saying.

"When I moved into the manor with the girls, I thought —I thought everything would be okay. I guess because I needed that arrangement to work out."

"So you dream something at the manor and it happens in your real life...like some premonition thing?"

She squeezed her eyes shut for a moment. "Not exactly like a premonition. But yes, a few times. If I'm at the manor or if I've spent a lot of time at the manor, then there is a real life carryover from my dreams."

"Okay," he answered in his not-believing tone.

"We moved in and a dream happened—I can't control when they happen—and Asher was in it. I wrote it off as a stress dream and tried to ignore it. But then last night I dreamed you were there."

She eyed him cautiously, wondering if he would remember what they had shared. She wanted to bring up the proposal and hoped he would say, "I thought that was real! Yes! Let's!" With his hands folded, he stared at the ground, his eyes in narrowed, his lips pressed tightly together.

"We swam in the lake and there was this cave." She pointed toward the opposite bank.

Mason sprang from his chair, then walked to the other side of the room with his hand over his mouth. "Not possible," he mumbled. "Not happening."

She wondered how it felt when someone told you they had made an appearance in your dreams. That they knew things about your most private, unguarded moments.

"When we came out, Asher was there."

He stared at the lake. "Wings," he finally said.

Her heart thumped hard.

"You had these wings." He motioned with his hands. He scoffed like he couldn't believe what he was saying. "How do you know what I dream? Coincidence, I guess. Or maybe we've spent a lot of time with one another lately and it's just one of those weird things. But you can't expect me to believe that you made my dreams happen. Or that my life is in danger because your dead ex-husband's spirit rigged some equipment and he told you that through a dream."

"I know this is hard to believe. But we're talking about your safety. Please have an open mind."

"Layla. Are you sure you feel okay?"

"I'm fine. Mason, I wouldn't share any of this with you if it weren't important. I know how you feel about these things." And that was true. Because he had chosen to come back to her, knowing she was who he loved and who he wanted. To save his life, she was eliminating herself from his world, sentence by sentence.

They stared at one another quietly. Her head pounded with so much pain that she squinted to see straight. Mason's nostrils flared slightly, as if he had been challenged and had no intent to back down.

She went into the kitchen and put soap and water on a paper towel. She scrubbed at the lower part of her neck, the spot where she had been diligent about keeping the water-proof makeup. In a rectangular wall mirror, she checked the area on her neck, then turned and showed the small bruise to Mason.

His line of sight fixed at her neck and his chest rose up and down more quickly than usual. She knew what he must have felt. She'd experienced that same terror several times where her dreams were concerned. Like seeing Brooke's dead body or Jordan's bloody head or Asher's spirit, this was another one of those moments when proof showed up in the midst of the impossible.

He finally reached out cautiously, running two fingers along the mark he'd left on her. He shook his head almost imperceptibly and said, "Can't be."

"You can't go back into the manor, no one can. Not until

Dixie and I figure out how to get rid of Asher," she whispered.

He paced across the floor and shoved his hands through his hair. "Layla. I don't know what's going on here. I really don't. But this work is my father's business, *my* business, and the job's not yet done. Plus, do you know how many workers I have on my payroll right now? Just for the Alcott Manor project? They're expecting to have their jobs next week, they're expecting to get paid. As am I, frankly. I can't just tell them not to come in or that I won't be there because there's a ghost in the house. I'll lose my workers, I'll lose—"

He scoffed and paced again. "If I shut down that job, even for a little while, that will ruin my reputation—with workers and future clients. What's the rest of the Alcott family going to say about the work coming to a halt? They won't be happy, I'm sure they'll be vocal, and that will trash my reputation, too, especially in light of what Jordan and her father are trying to do to my future opportunities."

"Going back to the manor could end your life."

He shook his head, his mouth moving without sound until he finally said, "I don't know what to say." He waved toward her neck. "But it was a dream, and— I—I can't tank my father's business. The job at the manor is big for us and I can't screw this up."

She rested her head against her fingertips and dreaded the one card left that she had to play. For his sake, because she hoped it would save his life.

Her heart twisted.

"When Brooke was killed..."

He slowly cocked his head to the side.

She tried to speak, but her throat had gone dry and her voice broke off. She sipped her tea. She reminded herself that nearly everything they shared had been in her dreams, none of the meaningful experiences of late had been real. Only dreams. So she wasn't really losing anything, not really. However, her heart couldn't quite get on board.

"I had been lucid dreaming for a few months by then, it was really helping me. But that night we were here at the manor and Brooke had been particularly awful that week. This was right after you took me to the prom. At our lockers that day at school, she called out to me in a way that got nearly everyone's attention in that crowded hallway. Then Jordan said that her mother had lost weight on some diet and maybe she could get the name of it for me. That I couldn't possibly feel good about myself at my size. She said she was just trying to help.

"But then she started humming that old song, 'Big Girls Don't Cry.' Her friends joined in and soon they were all singing it at the top of their lungs. I was so humiliated. I just walked away without saying anything."

"I never knew." Mason sat lik3 something pulled him down from the inside. "I wish I had."

Layla lowered herself to the couch, her insides shaky. She told him how Brooke had taken pictures of her with her phone while Layla had been changing in the locker room.

Mason swallowed visibly.

She described to him how Brooke, Jordan, Carmen and Staci were all gathered around Brooke's phone that night, looking at photos, making fat jokes and laughing. How they must have been looking at the photos of her, and how she thought Brooke would email the photos around. How she knew if she slept at all that night that she was going to sleep-walk or sleep eat and how that would have been humiliating. She told him she coped how she could, by crafting a lucid dream.

Layla went on to tell him about the entire dream: how

Brooke had admitted to taking the pictures and threatened to send them out. How they had pushed one another and how on the last hard shove, Layla was quite a bit taller than she was in her real world. And, finally, how Brooke had toppled backward and fell through the rotted hardwood to the cement floor below.

A hardness solidified in his expression. "*You're* the one who killed Brooke?"

The anger in his eyes was more than she could bear and she looked away. When she finally found the courage to look at him again, she said, "Yes."

Something left her when she finally admitted to what she'd done—a heaviness, that rock of a secret that had been lodged inside of her for ten years. She inhaled deeply and exhaled more fully than she thought she ever had. But the condemning look in Mason's eyes almost stopped her from breathing altogether.

"I was following doctor's orders on how to use the lucid dreaming and how to handle her bullying. I—didn't want to be a victim anymore."

"This is why Jordan and Carmen kept saying that you were the one who killed Brooke. You said you never touched her. You lied to me?"

"I didn't—I mean, I didn't physically touch her. At least not— It was a dream. You heard the detectives, she was three inches taller than me, there was no concrete floor outside, and as the detectives said, it couldn't have happened the way Jordan and Staci and Carmen had said it did. Not in real life. Only in my lucid dream. So how would I have proven anything, even if I had admitted to it?"

Mason paced around the room, his dark hair disheveled and lines deep across his forehead.

"I would have said something to you, but at the time I wasn't even sure what to tell you."

He stiffened into a hard wall of resistance and the soft memories of what she found with him, the bright hope she had dared to play with was disappearing fast.

He focused on something on her arm. When he moved her sleeve, he revealed four fingerprint bruises on her skin. "What is this?"

She exhaled hard. "Asher's fingerprints. When he grabbed me in my dream last night."

His mouth fell open. He was speechless.

"I'm sorry, Mason. I'm more sorry than you'll probably ever know. She just went on and on that day about you and her and marriage and wasn't I lucky not to have a boyfriend. I always had a crush on you, she knew that, and she was taunting me. And I—I thought—" She ran her hand across her forehead. "Look, please, just don't go back to the manor. Not yet."

"I'm not screwing up this job. I'm restarting my life here and my company's reputation is important." He stepped away then turned toward her again, quickly. "I guess as long as you don't dream anything else about me, I'll be fine."

She felt his comments as a punch to the stomach and took a moment to catch her breath. "Mason, he wants me with him. If I don't go willingly, he's going to take you, as motivation for me. He'll kill you."

He looked down. "I can't do this. I can't." His words were definite, resolute, and final. She wiped the tears from her cheeks.

A hardness flavored the way he looked at her. "Jordan was right all along. You're the one who attacked her and killed Brooke."

"Yes," she repeated. "Yes, I am."

SHE MADE her way to Mason's bedroom where she picked up her bag that held her swimsuit and a few other items. She fought the heavy sense of sad satisfaction that she had been right.

She made a quick call to a car service and headed to the front porch to wait for them to arrive.

Mason stood near the front door, his eyes focused and fierce.

She swallowed the nausea that rolled within her. "I'm sorry, Mason. I really am. I wish things were different for us. I wish Brooke and Jordan had never been hurt. And I wish —" She started to say that she wished she never dreamed. But she thought of the dreams she had shared with him and said, "I wish for a lot of things right now."

He shifted his stare and seemed to search for something to say. His mouth opened and closed, but nothing came out. When he looked at her again, he shook his head. Their more recent memories floated between them, they were utterly real and yet completely unexplainable. She remembered his proposal and that mystical rock on her finger and decided that dreaming about the possibility of love was akin to playing with fire. She had gotten burned.

She decided she should have stayed within the imaginary walls she had built around herself not that long ago. Because she had been right the first time, she wasn't ready for a relationship. She wasn't ready to trust. After all she had been through and all she had done, maybe she never would trust again.

"I don't know what to say," he finally said.

"That's fine," she said, even though nothing was. "But I'm not wrong about Asher or what he's done to the ladders and the other equipment in the house. So please, be careful. Because you may not like what I've told you, but it's the truth and you could get hurt. Or worse."

"Where are you going?"

"I called a car service." She couldn't bear to say her mother's name or to say that she was going home.

He nodded reluctantly.

She shut the door behind her, knowing that was the final note to the song she and Mason had begun a long time ago. Half of her hoped that he would open the door and apologize, say that he understood everything now and he had made a crazy mistake. The other half of her just wanted to leave and be done with it. She had to start putting herself back together.

She wouldn't go back to the manor, not with Asher there. She would text Mason in the morning and let him know that she wouldn't be able to fulfill the caretaker job.

She waited for her car. Nausea finally got the best of her and she threw up in the flower bed just outside Mason's front door. When the nurse had gone over the nearly-endless aftercare instructions, she had said that nausea and vomiting were possible side effects.

"Final parting gift," she thought with a cough. "I killed the girl you wanted to marry, then I lied to you about it, then I threw up in your front yard. Can't wait to see what I do next."

Her car arrived, she climbed into the back seat and never looked back. She couldn't bear the heartbreak.

She dialed her mother and told her she was coming home.

27

Asher watched Mason storm through Alcott Manor in a quiet, lumbering rage. He picked up every ladder from the property and tossed them into a dumpster parked in the front drive. He also threw in any piece of equipment that had a motor or a screw.

He hadn't expected this, but it seemed that Layla-pup must have let his cat out of her bag. She must have told Mason the equipment had been sabotaged. Not before one of his workers died, though. Early this morning, Mr. Sandy Hernandez died from a fall. Seems that the scaffolding that Sandy worked from wasn't as sturdy as he thought. Horribly bloody accident. Sandy fell on a circular saw that had been left below the scaffolding. No one ever really thought about just how much blood was in the human body until it started to pour out.

Pity it hadn't been Mason who fell. He had worked from that same scaffolding for the better part of two days at the beginning of the week. It had taken Asher a long time to turn those screws and loosen the bolts.

These days he had plenty of that. Nothing but time, really.

He had spent a bunch of it waiting in the old nursery upstairs, rocking in the antique chair and listening for her call. A simple thought was all it would take for him to have an open door into her world. But her mind must be on other things right now. Troubling things, maybe.

Another ladder clanged. Mason tossed it into the dumpster and Asher felt a sense of pride. Not just because Mason was irritated that his equipment was destroyed, but more so because he looked awful. Whatever was wrong with him, he had lost his GQ appearance. He looked more like he had been on a three-day bender.

The bloom must have fallen from the relationship vine.

Asher patted his fingertips together in a tiny clap and cheered in a whisper. Mason didn't like to be humiliated, that was his soft spot.

Which gave Asher an idea. When he finally did kill him, he would do it slowly, with an audience and in such a way that cut Mason down to size.

Before Tom died, Asher heard him telling Mason that they would throw a party to commemorate the end of their very long road of restoration and announce their plans for how and when they would open the manor for tours.

Mason would be there, as would Layla and the rest the family. That would be the most perfect occasion for something violent.

LAYLA CURLED onto her side in her old double bed and listened to the birds sing their morning songs. She had done this every morning for the last month. Gotten her girls ready, drove them to school. Crawled back under the covers.

She worked out an arrangement with the hospital to take the three weeks of paid vacation she had accrued over the years, as well as a week of sick leave. HR accessed the ER reports and gave her time off to heal.

Each morning her mother offered to make her scrambled eggs. Layla refused, saying she would make toast later. The smell was sickening and usually sent her running to the bathroom.

"You need to see a doctor, honey," her mother said from the other side of the bathroom door. "This just isn't normal, it's going on too long."

"I did. Yesterday. It's just a virus, it will pass."

What Layla didn't share was that she had known almost from the first sign. In the same way she had known twice before, because there was a subtle difference in this kind of nausea. The tide had a deeper roll to it. A sense of ownership, a possession she would have to flow with for several months.

She had taken a test. When that one came back positive, she went to a different store and bought two more tests. Different brands. Because surely that one was wrong. When she took those, she decided all the tests must have been from a faulty batch and she went to her doctor.

"That can't be!" she said when her doctor presented her with the confirmation of her blood test results.

"Apparently it can. Because you're pregnant. Congratulations."

Layla must have appeared shell-shocked because her doctor raised an eyebrow and said, "Let me guess. Y'all used a condom. Or he had a vasectomy. You were on the pill? I've heard it all. If you're having sex, this can happen. As a mother of two I guess I don't have to tell you that." The doctor crossed her arms over her folder and raised her eyebrows.

Layla chose not to tell her doctor that the only time she had had sex in the last several years was once in a dream with Mason. She didn't mention it was a make-believe honeymoon. A fantasy. But she did schedule her first ultrasound and prenatal visit, then went home and cried.

She had gotten sick on the morning she left Mason's house. That was exactly the way it went when she carried her two girls. She had been nauseated and vomiting from almost the moment of conception.

She pressed her hand to her stomach.

Mason would never believe her.

At least not until the baby was born and they could do blood tests that would prove this baby was his. Ultimately, though, wouldn't a baby be just the thing that would push him away forever? Not that he wasn't already gone. Since she left his house that day, he hadn't called or texted or emailed. She had killed Brooke and kept that from him. He would never get over that.

She turned her face to her pillow and hid the sobs that rose up and out. They poured day and night. She kept thinking that at some point surely, she would be empty and they would stop.

Today wasn't that day.

He had never recovered from the way the community outed and ousted his family when he was a kid. Now he was the hometown-boy-makes-good, starting fresh, rebuilding his father's business, starting a new career, and her dreams gave life to his old nightmares.

She understood why he hadn't called. She couldn't blame him. He had probably spent ten years hating whoever had killed Brooke. Only to discover that person was her.

She pushed herself upright and headed to the bathroom. Whichever mastermind learned to bottle morning sickness could use it as a war weapon and rule the world, because it would drop men to their knees.

Her phone rang and she didn't recognize the number on her Caller ID, but she answered, figuring it was someone from work. Probably someone from human resources checking on her. If she didn't answer, they would just keep calling.

After wavering for a moment between the phone and the bathroom, she decided she had another two to three minutes before she lost it. Fortunately, or unfortunately, her stomach gave early warnings.

"Hello?" Her voice was scratchy from being sick and her throat was clogged from crying. At least she didn't have to pretend to have a sick voice.

"Hey, darlin'. It's Dixie."

28

Before Layla could get the car into park, Dixie was crossing her front porch and heading straight for her. Her arms outstretched. When she'd invited her over, Layla thought she should decline. Mason wouldn't want the two of them to spend time together and she didn't need another conflict.

But aside from the debt, her lucid dreaming, and the appearance of Asher, there was now the breakup with Mason and the pregnancy. She needed to talk with someone who could understand.

Layla wouldn't tell her about the baby, not before she had a chance to tell Mason. He was the father. She did want to talk with her about the breakup, though. Not because she expected advice on how to fix it, but it would just be helpful to get everything off her chest.

Dixie was about ten steps away from her when she stopped short and gasped. Layla quickly looked down at her body. Except for a slight straightening of her waistline, she wasn't showing yet. If anything, all the morning sickness had caused her to lose a few pounds. She had been upset to distraction lately and thought maybe she had done something stupid, like left the house in her pajama bottoms.

But no, she only saw her normal jeans. Her favorite skinny pair, in fact, and ones she wouldn't be able to wear again for about a year.

"What's the matter?" Layla asked.

Dixie's softened focus trailed a few feet from Layla's midsection and then it finally stopped. "Oh, my. Oh, honey." She pressed her hand to her heart. "Do you know that you're —I mean, are you aware that—"

The tears came too fast for her to stop and she covered her face with her hand. She should have known she couldn't hide her secret from her child's intuitive grandmother. Dixie rushed to Layla and held her as tight and secure as any mother would hold a child. She hadn't realized it until just then, but Layla had been drifting like a leaf on the wind.

LAYLA RELAXED into the burnt red fabric recliner that she remembered Mason's daddy sat in when she had often visited in her youth. Tired from a long day of work, he would hold a bottle of beer in one hand and something to eat in the other. But he'd always get up when she came in, saying, "Lay-la-pop! Aren't you the most beautiful girl I've seen today!"

He always reminded her of a lumberjack, with his broad shoulders, straight dark hair, and affinity for darkly colored plaids.

"When did you find out, darlin'?" Dixie asked from the kitchen.

"Yesterday for sure from my doctor. It's early yet."

Dixie served Layla chamomile tea in an antique cup and

saucer covered in pink roses. A tiny hairline crack ran diagonally across the largest rose.

"And I guess our boy Mason doesn't know since I've not heard anything about this?" She curled into the matching recliner and rested her chin in her hand.

"No, he doesn't know. And he wouldn't have any reason to suspect either."

Dixie narrowed her focus, like Layla just offered a riddle.

Layla drank a long sip of her tea. "We weren't—I mean —I wasn't interested in—"

"Wise choice—" Dixie nodded as only a mother could when referencing wisdom and hard won lessons: lips together, eyes closed, deep nod.

"But then he showed up in my dream, and—I didn't think—" Layla put her face in her hands, partly from embarrassment and partly from disbelief. "I thought it was just a dream, and I—we—"

"It's okay," Dixie interrupted with a soft voice. "You don't have to explain. I was young once, too. So no, of course he wouldn't suspect. Oh, boy."

"Never in a million years did I think this would happen. Never. I mean, never."

"Well of course you wouldn't. Why would you?" Dixie patted Layla's knee.

Layla exhaled hard. "Because events in my Alcott Manor-influenced dreams have left their mark before, though not always, and I certainly didn't think pregnancy was a possibility."

"No one would have." Dixie pushed a few soft brown curls away from her face. "Wait. What do you mean your dreams have left their mark?"

Layla put her tea cup on the side table and told Dixie in detail about the dead zone and what happened with Brooke and Jordan at the campout. "It was me. I killed Brooke. And Jordan's injuries have wrecked her life. Or at least her plans for her life. I suppose Jordan could have done something besides be a lawyer if she put her mind to it. It's still my fault."

"Oh, honey. Tragic for everyone. Good heavens, the guilt." Dixie put her fingertips on Layla's leg. "So, this dead zone. It's like an alternate reality of some kind. And whatever happens there, the effect shows up in the waking world?"

"In a nutshell," Layla said. "And not always."

Dixie nodded, trying to put all the pieces together. "And you see people from the past there?"

"Yes, all sorts. A child playing a piano for a small group of adults, a nanny and a baby, some children, a dog—oh my gosh. I almost forgot about the dog—he's ours now, we named him Winston. And the cake!" Layla stood and pressed a hand to her forehead.

"What cake? What do you mean?"

"Just before I moved into the manor, I was off property, went into a lucid dream, and the manor pulled me into its dead zone. There were children running through the kitchen with their puppy. He had a red collar with a jingle bell on it and a red ball in his mouth. Then there was this chocolate-iced cake on an antique stand on one of the tables. I ate some of it, again thinking it was just a dream. I woke up, I went to the manor. There was the same chocolate-iced cake on the same stand on the same table and piece of cake sat to the side with a bite taken out of it. A bite that *I* had taken."

Dixie tipped her head back, her mouth slightly open in an a-ha kind of way.

"A little while later, I found Tom and Mason with the

exact same puppy I saw in my dream—golden terrier, red collar with a jingle bell. And a red ball. He's our dog now, he goes everywhere with us."

"Oh, my," Dixie whispered. She closed her eyes and frowned slightly, like she was reading the situation, getting a feed of information and not liking what she was seeing.

When she opened her eyes, they were glassy and unfocused, like she had just returned from some other realm. "The past is overlapping the present at the manor, like two realities or two eras trying to exist in the same place at the same time. The energetic trajectory at that intersection is pulling the past to the present. When you're in the dead zone, you're caught up in that pull. So whatever you do in the dead zone, you might as well be doing it in the real world, your waking world. Because the manor makes it real."

Layla lowered herself to the edge of the recliner. "They were dreams. I never meant for any of those things to really happen. I never meant to kill Brooke."

"No, you didn't," Dixie said. "But the manor is drawing things and experiences from that space between here and what used to be, into the real of this world. Like the dog and the cake and—"

"Brooke's death, Jordan's injuries and my pregnancy." She placed her hand protectively over her belly. "It doesn't discern anymore between what's happening in my lucid dreams and what happened in its past."

"You're right." Dixie looked away, her focus softened again like she listened to another voice. "The manor's history must be unresolved in some way. It's reliving its experiences, trying to work something out, trying to remove something from its past. Right a wrong."

"In one—"

Dixie shook her head and raised her hand to quiet Layla, so she could listen to something Layla couldn't hear. "This dead zone has a hold on you, Layla. It knows you, it has your name. Wherever you are, if you dream, the manor will pull you in. And whatever you dream in that space will become real in your life. Don't go in the manor anymore. And for heaven's sake, don't dream."

She lifted her teacup to her lips for a sip, her hands shaking. "My last dream with Mason, I wasn't even at the manor. We were at his house. I had a dream that we were swimming in the lake, and then we were in this cave. I thought of Asher on our way back to the house and he showed up shortly thereafter. It's like my thinking of him made him aware of where I was. That dream is how he got to us."

Dixie nodded. "I think the manor could pull you in from wherever you are. Since you've been in its dead zone, it claims you as one of its own, as if you and your dreams are a part of its past."

"Sometimes the dreams just happen. I can't always control it."

"You have to. Don't dream. Asher will get to you that way, as well as whoever else is in that dream with you."

They looked at one another for a minute. Then Layla said, "Okay."

"So that was what you had to tell Mason."

Layla told her about their conversation and how she'd left. "He's beyond angry. I doubt he'll ever speak to me again."

Dixie muttered her son's name. "You know he's an adult and I try to stay out of his business. But it's hard. I told him he had to stay away from the manor, that Asher was there.

He told me not to get involved. Have you dreamed at all since you saw him?"

"No. I think I've been too tired and too sick." She leaned forward and put her head in her hands. "I've got to have the money from the tours. Asher left us with so much debt, I can't breathe."

Dixie patted her on the back. "Oh, sweetheart."

"How am I going to get rid of him? He's dead and he's still ruining my life."

"I don't know. He's not a normal ghost in a normal house."

Layla popped her head up. "Please don't tell Mason that I'm pregnant."

"No, sweetheart. That's your news, not mine."

"I need to get stronger first. I need time to prepare myself emotionally for everything he's going to say. You know, that the baby isn't his and so forth." The tears continued to fall.

"I wish I could shake some sense into him for you. Of course you and the baby are welcome here any time. Anytime at all. I won't intrude, but I want you to call me to help whenever you need it. Babysitting, errand running, sleep time, you name it. I'm here for you and him."

You and him? Did Dixie say that because she was accustomed to having boys? Layla wanted to ask, even though she tried not to get too attached to her babies until after twelve weeks and the risk of miscarriage had lowered. That never worked for her; she had been attached from the beginning twice before, and she was attached now. "I'm going to need that help. I have no idea how I'm going to manage three children on my own."

"You won't be on your own. You'll have me. And I'll bet that Jayne Ella will help more now that Asher isn't around."

Layla thought that might be right. This baby would be raised by women: sisters, mother, grandmothers.

Layla finished her tea, and when Dixie offered her a BLT with extra bacon, she accepted. She hadn't known she was hungry until Dixie's cooking was an option. Even though it was just a sandwich, Mason's mother did it extra well.

After the first bite Layla said, "There's just something about grease that's comforting when you're pregnant."

"When I was pregnant with Mason. I walked around with a small container of shoe polish."

"Shoe polish?" Layla caught sight of several green-blue stones on a desk by the window. They were the same stones from her dream with Mason. A chill covered her upper back.

"Something about the scent calmed my morning sickness. I think I have an old tin in Steele's shoe polish kit. Let's give it a try." Dixie headed toward her bedroom.

Layla turned the smooth stones in her hand, the fire of the yellow bursting through the varying shades of green blue, like the color reached for her.

"That's labradorite," Dixie said from behind her. "Do you like it?"

"Very much. It looks like it comes from another planet."

"It's a very mystical, protective stone because its vibration is about truth and the coming forward of that truth." Dixie put the shoe polish on a nearby table and folded Layla's hand around the stone. "You keep it."

Maybe that's why the stone had been a fit for her: the coming forward of truth. If nothing else, her slate was clean. She had finally told the truth. And though she wasn't eating much these days, neither was she craving cake.

"I'm here for you. Know that. No matter what." Dixie's brown eyes held a fierce protectiveness and Layla let it rule her. One day soon her typical mama bear fierce side would reemerge and this baby would be under that protection. For the time being all Layla felt was sick and overwhelmed. She appreciated the strength that Dixie loaned her.

Dixie hugged her as she used to and for a moment Layla felt like a teenager again—at Mason's house, wrapping up a meaningful discussion with his mother and feeling better about life. She could even hear the memory of the front door slam, keys hitting the porcelain bowl in the foyer and the clunking of work boots. She waited to hear Dixie's husband yell, *Where is everybody?*

When another wave of nausea hit, she picked up the shoe polish and gave it a long sniff.

"Oh, darlin', I wish I could make that go away for you. I do remember how awful that can be."

Layla drew in another long sniff. "It does kind of work. Am I killing off brain cells by doing this?"

Dixie laughed. "Maybe so. But Mason turned out alright."

"I wonder if I can just make a necklace out of this. You know, to keep it handy." Layla positioned the tin of shoe polish like a medallion that would hang on the end of a chain. Dixie laughed again until something caught her eye across the room.

"Hi, Mama." Mason stood in the doorway. He looked at Layla. "I thought that was your car out front."

Mason wore a dark gray shirt with the words Holloway Construction scripted in white across the front over a single line drawing of a house.

Layla's heart banged against her chest like it needed a way out. She wasn't prepared to talk with him.

"Why are you sniffing shoe polish?"

Dixie never missed a beat. She crossed the room and

gave her son a hug and kiss. "You look terrible. Do you want some soup? How about a BLT?" She placed her palm on his forehead and he moved it away.

"I'm fine, Mama. Can we talk?" he said to Layla.

He did look ill. Maybe about as bad as she felt. She entertained the idea of walking out the back door, right on through the grass until she reached her car.

Telling him she was pregnant was going to be a humiliating discussion. Particularly when he asked who else she had slept with because he couldn't possibly be the father.

"Please, Layla?"

She realized the day of feeling calm and capable was never going to come, so she said, "Fine."

She sniffed the shoe polish and headed outside.

MASON WAVED Dixie off and followed Layla. He knew what he looked like. He hadn't slept or eaten much since Layla left his house a month ago.. Everything she told him flew in the face of what he knew was real.

Layla sat on the edge of the pool and dangled her feet in the water, looking like a page from a magazine. He had always thought she was a beautiful girl, with a peach-perfect complexion, voluptuous figure and gorgeous hair. For a while he thought the simple life he wanted with her was finally happening.

Until she started talking about dreams that came to life and how she had been the one who killed Brooke. He sat next to her and wondered if seeing her today was a bad idea. If it was too soon.

"Hey." He heard his mood filter into that one clipped word.

She barely looked at him and that was about the response he expected.

He sat next to her. "I'm sorry I haven't been in touch."

She glanced at him. The watery sadness in her eyes hit his heart like a knife.

"I can't seem to get my head around what you told me."

"Yeah, I know how you feel."

"I just—I don't understand."

She placed her hand on her stomach. "About Brooke—I really would have told you sooner, there just wasn't a way. It was hard for me to understand. Harder to talk about. You never would have believed me anyway."

He winced. "You killed Brooke?"

"Not intentionally. I didn't even imagine killing her. Not even—" She sighed. "We were in the same sort of dream you and I experienced. It can leave its mark on reality, apparently." She shook her head, turned away from him, and sniffed the open tin of shoe polish.

He couldn't imagine what she was doing. He didn't remember any of Dixie's home remedies being shoe polish. Neither could he figure out these dreams of his that she knew about.

"I've spoken to Jordan twice about the manor, and unfortunately, she's still set on making things difficult for us. City inspectors come out next week."

Layla lifted the metal tin to her nose again.

"Is that my dad's old shoe polish? Why do you keep sniffing that?"

She closed her eyes for a long moment. When she opened them again, they were full of tears. "Because strangely, it helps calm the morning sickness."

"You're sick?"

"No. Mason, I'm pregnant. With your child, in case you

were going to go there." She sat on the edge of a lounge chair and wiped a tear from her cheek.

"That's not possible." But something about the way she looked at him hit him square in the gut. He kneeled on the ground to be close to her. "We've never—"

"In my dream, actually. Just once at the manor on our honeymoon." She rolled her eyes, shook her head. She touched her neck where the mark had been. "I know you remember at least part of that dream."

He sank onto his heels. "That's just not— I mean—a baby? Are you sure?" From the look on her face, he knew she would throw the shoe polish at his head if he asked her if he was the father.

"Several drugstore pregnancy tests. One blood test from my OB/GYN. If you want to do a paternity test after the baby is born, we can do that. And I'm not asking you for anything. So you don't need to worry."

"She says she's pregnant." Mason knew his mother was in the room somewhere, though he had only a distant awareness of her. He stared at the dark brown shag carpet beneath his work boots and, for the first time in years, he didn't think about how she needed to switch it out for something new. Instead, he replayed his discussion with Layla in his mind. He tried to find a shred of logic.

"Without going into any details, we haven't...we haven't had that kind of relationship." He had had rather vivid dreams about her. But guys did that all the time and no one got pregnant. She wasn't the type to sleep around or cheat or lie. She wasn't crazy. If this had been Brooke or Jordan, he would have suspected them of all four of those possibilities.

With Layla, those options were off the table.

Strangely, she knew about those dreams. She could recite them verbatim, and they left their proof on her lower neck. He couldn't explain that.

He finally looked up.

Dixie sipped from a brown bottle of beer and eyed him steadily.

"Well, she is pregnant," she said. "I saw the baby when she pulled up today. Do you want to know its gender?"

"No," he said quickly. There was no gender because there couldn't be a baby. "How did she end up here?"

"I called her. I hadn't heard from her since I saw her at the hospital and I wanted to see how she was doing."

He pushed his fingers along the tension that gathered at the back of his neck. "None of this makes any sense."

"Sometimes you have to use prayer and intuition to find the real logic in things, as well as your right next steps. I've taught you that."

"This is medical science. What she's saying isn't possible. And it's awkward because I'd made it clear that I cared about her. That I had come back for her."

"It is possible. And I'll tell you why." Dixie described how the manor was pulling its past through something called the dead zone and into the present. "It appears that whatever happens in that dead zone has its effect in reality. Objects and living things can even travel from the dead zone to our side of reality."

He could barely hear his mother's voice. He was stuck in this mystery that Layla had laid at his feet. He was circling around and around it. Not finding any good answers.

A baby.

"She mentioned that y'all weren't seeing one another much since the hospital."

"She, um…" He lowered himself to a straight back chair. A familiar feeling of terror crept up behind him with fangs and claws. "She was the one who killed Brooke."

Dixie pressed her lips together. "I know. She told me. She may have hated her the moment she pushed her, but I don't think she really thought Brooke would die, sweetheart."

He could still see Brooke's blood-red pillow and the horrified expression on her face when he'd found her. "She's still the one who killed her."

"Yes. I think she probably is."

"That changed all of our lives forever." He paced the floor. "I almost married Brooke! Jordan was going to be an attorney! Their parents have never gotten over—"

"I know." Dixie stayed seated with her legs casually crossed, as if she had expected everything he said. "I know. The house may have done you a favor on that one."

"Mama!"

She examined her fingernails and pushed at one of her cuticles. "You know, the problem with losing someone when they're young like Brooke is that we have a tendency to forever see them with blurry edges and a glossy lens. With so much taken away from us, we lose perspective. We romanticize who they were and how perfect everything would have been if they had lived. In reality, we don't know what that would have looked like. People change. We change. Maybe we change in ways we were supposed to all along. That's all I'm saying."

Dixie glanced to the outside yard and Mason wondered if she not only referred to Brooke but also to his father.

"The truth is that the manor played the biggest role in Brooke's death. Being at the manor is what changed everyone's lives forever."

He exhaled hard, trying to get rid of the grief that rolled inside of him nonstop. Whether it was grief from losing Layla or from learning she had killed Brooke, he really wasn't sure. "This is all just too farfetched."

Dixie pressed her hands together like she was going to

plead with him or say something that she really needed him to hear.

"Do you remember when you were in high school and we would talk about some of your friends? I could tell you all about them, how y'all interacted with one another, things that they thought or did—"

"Yeah, I didn't like that."

"Why do you think that was? Honestly."

"Honestly?" He struggled whether to hold his tongue or just to let the truth out.

"Honestly."

He went with the latter. "Because I saw that kind of thing destroy our lives once before. It's not about needing to fit in or needing someone else's approval, it's more than this stuff just not making sense to me. I didn't want to be a part of it then, and I don't want to be a part of it now. It's just—look, no offense, but I can't be a part of Layla's paranormal stuff. That's not the life for me."

"Son, I adore you, you know that. But you and I also know that you don't like anything that leaves you feeling out of control. You're just like your father was in that way. You like a strong sense of order, everything going according to plan and knowing what to expect."

"What's wrong with that?"

Dixie leaned forward and clasped her hands. "Nothing. Except that life rarely goes according to plan. So you need a strong gut to understand what the real battle is."

He plopped down in his father's recliner and felt an odd resemblance to the man that used to sit there.

"For our struggle is not against flesh and blood, but against the rulers, against the authorities, against the powers of this dark world and against the spiritual forces of evil in the heavenly realms. Ephesians chapter six. Verse twelve."

He didn't look at her. This type of discussion is where they parted ways.

"You may not want to talk about evil in this world, or the evil in the manor, but it exists. And it's affected your life. It's still affecting your life," she said.

He still didn't look at her.

"You came back here because you love working with your hands, you love Charleston, you love being near your family, and you love Layla in a way you can't explain. You gave up New York and all that money to do what makes *you* happy for a change. Now you've got that within your reach, and you're going to let this get in your way?"

"An unexplained pregnancy and ghosts and murder are big things— Look, I get that there is something unique about her dreams, but I don't get the rest of it. I don't get how she killed Brooke or got pregnant—"

"The manor has a place within it that—"

"No, I am not going there. I just don't—" He waved her off.

"Okay. Well. Suffice it to say that the manor will take whatever happens in her dreams and make them real. She didn't choose any of those things. She's just trying to deal with it as best she can. If you were smart, you would forgive her. You would help her." His mother stood and pointed her finger at him. He knew something serious was coming. "Fears are to be faced, Mason. You're running from yours."

His mother's words took the wind out of his sails. As only she could do. He had to admit, he felt like he was running hard from something. To his mind, running from some things was just good sense.

They squared off with one another across the den that hadn't changed since he was in high school. He wondered which side his father would have taken if he were still here. His, probably.

"You are going to have to decide which is more important to you—Layla or your stubborn need to control."

"This is not about control."

"While you're at it, you need to forgive Reverend Milligan and everyone else in that community who nearly ran us out of town."

"This is not about forgiveness either," Mason said.

"It is, actually. It always has been. You need to pray for them while you're at it."

"Some people don't deserve forgiveness or prayer. What they've done is too heinous."

"Forgiveness is about your attitude, not their actions." She narrowed her eyes. "And some people do deserve forgiveness, Mason."

She left the room.

He stared outside. He'd made a bad decision by following his gut and coming home to Layla. It boxed him in, made him unhappy, and led him to yet another dead end.

30

Layla held tight to the interior door handle of her mother's car. In part because her mother drove too fast. Also so she wouldn't reach over and smack her.

"You had no business going through my trash can. That's invasive," she scream whispered. She didn't think her daughters could hear her since they were in the back seat with their earbuds in, but she wasn't sure.

"I was taking out the trash—like I always do—and ten positive pregnancy tests is hard to ignore." Jayne Ella shook her head like she tried to move hair away from her face. But her hair was styled too tight for that, and she just looked ridiculous.

"Glad you took the opportunity to count. Sounds like you did more than just glance into my trash can. Sounds like you were digging."

"Matters not. You have really gotten yourself into a situation here, missy. And with two girls who you're supposed to be setting an example for, no less."

Layla felt her cheeks grow hot. "Nice judgment. First of

all, I have nothing to be ashamed of, and when my girls are old enough, I will happily tell them my story. I'm proud of the role model that I am for them."

Her mother turned on to the familiar pebble drive.

Layla glared at the facade of Alcott Manor.

This was the week when the restorations were supposed to be completed and celebrated by the entire Alcott family. A party had been planned weeks in advance, heralded by Tom before his death. Nothing fancy, the catering was potluck, although Jayne Ella had hired a band. With everything on pause yet again, Layla had requested that they postpone the festivities. After all, there really wasn't anything to celebrate. Thanks to Jordan, city inspectors were in and out looking for problems, and after yet another death, Mason's team had stopped their work.

But the family chose not to call off the gathering. The general consensus was that since there were things they needed to discuss, they would turn this evening into a family meeting. They decided to show their support and make it known in every way that they would overcome these challenges, too. They even ordered wrist bands for everyone, imprinted with the words Alcott Strong. Layla didn't wear hers. Jayne Ella wore three.

Jayne Ella parked the car beneath one of the majestic oak trees and reapplied her lipstick. Layla kept staring at the manor. She wouldn't step foot inside. In fact, she hadn't wanted to come to this stupid party at all, except Jayne Ella insisted they bring the girls. She had gotten them all excited behind Layla's back such that it was impossible to talk them out of coming. And she surely wasn't going to allow her daughters to come here without her.

Asher was in there somewhere, probably watching her. A burning sensation lit in her chest.

She couldn't help but think that if they had never camped on the back lawn of Alcott Manor that everyone's lives would have been completely different. Her dreams would never have gotten mixed up with reality, Brooke would never have been killed, and maybe she and Mason might have spent the last ten years together.

She looked at her girls in the back seat, giggling and singing along with whatever was playing on their tablet. Of course in this alternate reality, that didn't happen where she was with Mason, she wouldn't have Anna or Emma. She didn't think she could bear that. They were her life.

"Disgrace," her mother whispered and dropped her lipstick into her make-up case.

"Yes. It is," Layla said. Though she knew she and her mother were referring to two different things. She placed her hand just below her belly button, where her newest baby resided. Dixie had slipped and said *him* when they last spoke about the baby. She didn't know if she meant that generically or if she had an unguarded moment and shared the baby's gender.

A boy. A son.

She envisioned her life with a boy—lots of blue in the nursery, baseball games, playing catch in the back yard. She wouldn't be able to reuse any of those girl clothes she had saved. Anna Kate and Emma Cath would spoil him silly and insist on carrying him everywhere like one of their dolls. With a mother, two sisters, and two grandmothers around, the child's feet wouldn't touch the floor for the first five years of his life.

"Girls, run on around back. I hear the band playing already, so y'all can dance. I'll be there in a minute. No cake, Emma Cath! Do you hear me?"

Her girls bounced out of the car with smiles and giggles,

completely unaware of their mother's state of mind. She was grateful for that, at least. "Do not leave the great lawn, and do *not* go into the house, do you understand?"

Their "Yes, ma'am'"s overlapped, and they skipped and hopped their way around the manor.

When Layla was sure they were out of earshot, she stepped close to her mother. "Mason told me that he called me and came to see me after Brooke was killed."

Her mother brushed imaginary dirt from her pink and black flower print dress. "I don't remember that."

"I think you do, Jayne Ella. I think you deliberately kept that information from me so I wouldn't have any hope to be with Mason. And so I would marry Asher."

Her mother shook her head and shrugged as if she had no idea what she was talking about.

Layla leaned closer to her mother. "Mason said that he called and came by numerous times before he left for school and you never told me.

Jayne Ella stopped brushing her dress. She licked her lips and met Layla eye to eye. "Fine. He came by, and he called. Are you happy? I didn't tell you because I didn't want you to get your hopes up. You loved that boy, and he only had eyes for someone else."

"Didn't want me to get my hopes up?" All at once, she realized how she had dutifully followed her mother's orders. *Don't get your hopes up.* Hadn't her mother said that at every turn of her life?

She remembered that horrible, hot, blustery day when her mother told her and Peyton that she and their dad were divorcing. He had met someone else. Someone younger, prettier. Jayne Ella made a point to emphasize that on that day and many, many times over the years. Like younger and prettier was some sorcery that held sway over their weak father. He had succumbed to the siren's call. "What a fool," she often said.

It might have been that day when Layla learned not to get her hopes up, and it became a preprogrammed response.

"You mean you wanted to control my life because you didn't think I could manage it well enough on my own. Or maybe it was that *you* didn't think *you* could manage *your* life well enough on *your* own."

"What? You never had a chance with Mason and I didn't want him leading you on. Asher was interested. You didn't have any other options. I was trying to help you," her mother scolded.

"I think this is called projection."

"What are you talking about?"

Layla thought her mother's self-awareness might not completely fill a thimble. "I had options. Mason was interested in *me*. We had a chance. You kept us apart. Your arrogant interfering kept me from the man I was supposed to spend my life with." Her voice was scratchy from yelling without raising her voice.

"I didn't know why he kept coming around that summer with his tail between his legs. But I wasn't going to let him ruin what you had started with Asher. I didn't want you to spend your life lonely." Tears clogged her throat.

"Things could have worked out for us if you had just stayed out of the way."

"Mason always tried for some kind of perfectness ever since his family got knocked off their social standing all those years ago. You could see it in his eyes with that the football scholarship, the job in New York, Brooke. He wasn't for you."

She wanted to say that he wasn't that way anymore. That he had grown up. That the better side of him, the more meaningful side of him she had known through the years had won out. But she wasn't sure. She wasn't even entirely certain now that her mother had been wrong all those years ago.

But the way her mother's words implied that Layla wasn't good enough made her feel competitive, so she said, "You know, whenever Asher felt threatened, he had this way of keeping me in line. He would curl his hand into a fist like this, then he would punch me here." Layla pointed to the center of her stomach. "Or here." She pointed to her ribs. "Sometimes he aimed for my back, but it was most often on my torso. So no one would see the bruises."

Jayne Ella's freshly pinked lips parted.

"So you'll understand if I'm not pleased with what you did."

Her mother's usually tall stature deflated.

Layla got out of the car to let her mother sit with that news for a while, but to her surprise, her mother got out as well. Jayne Ella adjusted her dress, hooked her purse on her arm, and started toward the manor. Layla stood in her way.

"Mason and I shared a kiss years ago, before Brooke got hurt. I realize that may sound like nothing, but it meant something and not just to me."

She expected her mother to apologize or to at least cry, but something hardened in her eyes.

"We had a chance. He was going to break up with Brooke, he said he was going to ask me out. He came back to Charleston in part for me. That's what he told me."

"Then where is he now?" Jayne Ella finally said quietly. "When you need him most? I would guess this wasn't in his plan?" Jayne Ella gestured to her daughter's midsection.

She knew her mother's way of making her feel cheap

and rejected had more to do with the emotional pain from her own divorce than anything else. But it stung. Every time.

"Ladies! Join us!" Her mother's two sisters appeared on the wide front porch of Alcott Manor, looking tan and relaxed and holding mint julep cups. "Alcott Strong!" they sang.

"Hey, girls!" Jayne Ella broadcasted her ever ready smile and party-happy voice. She wrapped her arm around Layla's shoulders and whispered, "You'll have to move on without him. Find a way to pick up the pieces. Make a life for yourself with this new baby. I'll be there with you every step of the way, of course."

Layla dropped back. Jayne Ella plowed ahead. This was exactly what Layla was afraid of, her mother's continued and controlling presence in her life. And the absence of Mason.

She glanced at the newly painted pillars of Alcott Manor. When she had first arrived several weeks ago, she thought things were finally changing for her. Now it seemed she had gone from the frying pan to the fire.

Asher would enjoy this turn of events. Nothing made him happier than when her freedom was just beyond her reach.

MASON DRANK a glass of beer and watched all ages of Alcott family members dance on the wide green lawn under endless strands of sparkling white lights. Tonight's gathering was supposed to mark the end of a long, hard era for Alcott Manor. It was supposed to launch the beginning of a far more prosperous one. At least that's how Tom had it planned.

Instead, Mason had had to make a presentation to the family members about the fact that the restoration was still ongoing. He explained to them that it would have to continue on for a few more months. Might be a year. Much of it depended on what the inspectors found. And yes, some of the repairs were being challenged. Yes, another person had died at the manor. He fell from the scaffolding. Accidents happened. Mason left out the part where the scaffolding had literally fallen apart beneath him and that he might have fallen onto a circular saw.

He had tried talking with Jordan again, but she wasn't taking his calls.

Jayne Ella came through the house with her sisters over an hour ago. He'd waved to her, but she managed to look right through him as if he didn't exist. Layla must have told her that she was pregnant, that he was the father, and that he had broken up with her.

Layla's girls danced with each other on the back lawn to the loud band music and dashed among the other guests in an occasional game of tag. Whenever they needed something they went to their grandmother or another relative. There was no sign of their mother, and he assumed she stayed away because of him.

He drained the glass and placed it on the kitchen work table he had completed in time for tonight. The wood was finally smooth and its original stain restored thanks to his hours upon hours of hand sanding and finishing.

His fingers moved along the smoothly polished grooves. When he chose to work on this table, he had plans for it that involved Layla. Simple dreams—toasting with a glass of wine by candlelight, making plans for the future.

He had made good in life. He had come a long way from being the kid no one wanted to have anything to do with, the one who parents kept their kids from, the one who ended up with his brother as his only birthday party guest.

His years as a football player who dated the cheerleading captain and prom queen had given him the silent revenge he'd wanted. Even going to New York and making scads of money had continued the trend. No one could poke a hole in success, that was solid. If he were going to be completely honest, he didn't want that payback to end. If only he could have been happy living that life, he would have stuck with it.

Strange that he left what didn't work to move to what he was sure would work, only to find that nightmares from the past reared their ugly head.

More than anything else in the world, he just wanted to share a simple life with Layla. His best friend, the one with whom he had shared all his dreams and secrets. But these dreams of hers, the ones that couldn't possibly be real, wrecked everything. He slammed his fist on the table and the glass crashed on the floor.

He cleaned up the broken glass and searched for a trash can, but they had all been taken outside before the party began. He couldn't leave it in the sink, someone would cut themselves. He opened a small drawer to put the pieces in and saw the crayons and paper and scissors he had gotten for the girls some time ago. When he bought those items, he'd thought they might make paper dolls together. His heart slipped a couple of notches in his chest. He put the broken glass into the drawer and swept it to the side. He'd give Layla's daughters the materials tonight before they left.

He pushed the screen door open and nearly ran into someone.

"Layla."

Her face was calm. Not happy. Not angry, which was

good. Though it might have been worse than that. Her demeanor was more along the lines of...*disappointed.*

He hated disappointed.

Disappointed made him shrink in his shoes.

She was all soft and Southern-girl-attractive in a hot pink blouse that bared her shoulders and clung to her curves. If she was pregnant, there were no signs of it in this outfit. His mind drifted back to the time before things got complicated. Before there were discussions of a ghost that threatened his life and before he knew that her dreams could leave a mark in the world.

He kissed her on the cheek and her perfume wafted around him in a subtle gardenia scent.

"I wasn't sure you were coming," he said.

"I needed to be here for the meeting."

"Maybe we ought to talk," he said.

Her watchful eye combed the outside of the manor as though someone were spying through the walls.

She placed a finger over her lips and pointed to the screen door that led to the inside and he wondered if someone was standing there.

Mason and Layla walked along the outer fringe of the celebratory crowd and toward the quiet beach. Away from the manor. On the way, they passed a small marker his mother had insisted they construct. It read: In Memory of Anna Alcott. That spot was known to be the place on the property where Anna had died. Several antique rose bushes had been moved from the main garden to form a frame behind the marker.

"Do not let the girls go into the house," he heard Layla say to her mother, who left the gathering when she saw her daughter. "They can have fifteen more minutes, then y'all need to head home."

"How are you going to get home?" Jayne Ella shifted her gaze to Mason and her eyes hardened. Her lips flattened with an air of disgust.

"I'll get a cab."

"Call me if you need me," her mother said.

Mason and Layla walked to where the grass met the beach. The music was distant and they could hear one another more easily.

Layla had a compromising for-the-sake-of-the-baby attitude with him. As if she wouldn't be around him otherwise. She had sent him a text offering him the opportunity to attend an ultrasound appointment. But he couldn't figure out how to respond, because she couldn't be pregnant.

He was certain that they would get to this appointment and the doctor would say, "I'm sorry, honey, but there's no baby." Then Layla would get counseling.

The band played a slower song, a sign the evening was winding down. The tide, too, had calmed and cast forth only tired waves that sloshed onto the wet sand. Like it had given up its strength for the night.

"Layla, I wish I could understand your dreams and the manor and what happened to Brooke." Actually, what he really hoped was that she would say the ghost-dream-stuff was all a joke. That she hadn't really killed Brooke. He tried one last time to lean toward everything he had hoped for with Layla, but he was met with a wall. This was the same feeling he'd long recognized as a dire warning, the one that said he was in danger, the one that said he should turn back.

"I just can't. I've been over and over this in my head and —I can't work it out. I don't know how you see what I dream, maybe you have some of the same gifts as Dixie." He looked at the ground and kicked a shell with the toe of his boot.

"Isn't it possible that there's a more reasonable explanation for everything?"

She stared at him like she carefully weighed what he had said. Then she glanced at the stars in the night sky, the moon's reflection on the dark ocean, then back to his eyes and said, "What about the baby, Mason?"

A shot of panic hit him in the chest and he searched for the right thing to say. All he could find was that wall of anger. "I don't know what to tell you about that."

"I can wait until this baby is born and we can do a paternity test and maybe then you'll believe me. I've already spent a big part of my life with someone I couldn't trust, someone I couldn't talk to and who didn't believe in me. So I understand why this is hard for you. I really do. It would be hard for most people. But I just can't do this."

"Layla—" He reached for her and she stepped away. "Layla, please."

She did an about face and her skirt twirled outward with a flair. "I've made this mistake before. When I married Asher, it didn't feel right. I went with him because my mother had me convinced that I didn't have any other options.

"Well, I don't care if I don't have any other options. I'll have this baby on my own. Because if I were ever going to be with anyone again—and honestly, at this point, I don't know that I would—that person would have to be someone who loved me for who I am. Not because I own a huge chunk of Alcott Manor. Or because you've built me into the image of an ideal wife. But because you think the whole big flawed and scary package of me is where you want to be. And if that's not what you want? Then forget it. Because all I am is all I have to offer and I'm not settling for less than someone who wants the whole of it." She exhaled hard. A final note. "Not again. Not ever."

"Where are you going?"

"Leave me alone."

He watched her storm to the beach, knowing with a knot in his gut that they were finished.

31

L ayla stretched on the sand and stared at the half-moon that hung over the ocean. With bright stars pinned so clearly around the crescent, she would normally have thought it a gorgeous night. However, the warm breezes, the soft waves, and the cool sand were some distant ideal that didn't reach her.

She thought about the white cake with white icing she had seen when she and Mason walked outside. If she could get just one thick slice, that would go a long way to numbing every emotion she didn't want to feel right now.

She heard the murmurs of family cleaning up on the great lawn. She hoped her mother got the girls home and off to bed like she told her to. Emma had been munching on sweets and junk food, and Layla knew she would feel ill if she didn't get to bed on time.

People moved in and around Alcott Manor tonight, completely unaware that Asher Cardill haunted its rooms. She had to figure out a way to get rid of him before he struck again. He and Jordan were well on their way to stopping the tours.

She hadn't slept well at her mother's, but she knew better than to doze off near the manor. And she knew better than to think of Asher when she was close to sleep, close to dreaming. That combination would put her in contact with him, and she wasn't going to do that. Not again.

So even though the rhythmic waves did their best to lull her to sleep, she turned her energy in the other direction, just like navigating a car. One spin of the wheel and she was moving on another course. She thought of her daughters and how often they had played on this beach as a family. She worked to get herself fully awake. Then she heard Anna Kate's laughter, round and robust and leading-the-way-infectious.

Was this a memory?

The girls occupied so much of her brain space that sometimes she heard their voices when they weren't even around. Occasionally, just as she was falling asleep at night, she even thought they called her. She'd go to their rooms and find them sound asleep.

Anna's laugh sounded again, louder this time. Definitely real.

Why hadn't her mother taken the girls home?

Layla didn't know the exact time, but it felt late and she *had* told Jayne Ella… That was when she noticed Anna Kate's laugh had an echo to it, like a trail, but with sound.

No.

Had she inadvertently pulled them into a dream? An almost dream?

She wiggled her fingers in the sand to remind herself where she was, like a tether to the real world. Then she headed over the empty lawn, floating as she often did in dreams, toward the manor.

Through the back window, she saw Asher and the girls

just beyond the kitchen hand-in-hand in ring around the rosey style.

"No!"

She grabbed a handful of sand and mashed the grains between her fingers and under her nails. The hard tug at her midsection yanked her back to her body and awake with a gasp.

She ran toward the manor at top speed, hoping against hope that what she had seen wasn't real. Surely her mother had taken the girls home as she had instructed. Surely they weren't inside sleeping where they would be susceptible to one of her Alcott-induced dreams. Surely.

When she arrived in the living room, she saw Emma asleep on one couch with a washcloth on her forehead and Anna curled onto her side and fast asleep on the other couch.

"There you are. I've been calling you, where have you been?" Jayne Ella turned the corner with her phone in her hand.

"Is she sick?" Layla placed the back of her hand against her daughter's cheek and was relieved when it was cool.

"Oh, she's fine. Just ate too much cake is all, I think. We spent about forty-five minutes in the bathroom, but she never got sick. Too much party and too many sweets. Where were you?"

"Down at the beach. I thought I told you to take them home and not to let them into the house?"

Layla tried to wake her daughters with a gentle shake and by calling their names, but they didn't budge.

"I got to talking with everyone and lost track of time. Not by much. I decided to just let them rest here for a little bit. I thought about taking them downstairs to their own beds, but I didn't want to miss you in case you came through. They are completely knocked out."

"I see that." Layla knew where her daughters were. Their bodies were on these couches, but their spirits were out and about and dancing with their father. "How long have they been asleep?"

"Eh, not long. Fifteen or twenty minutes, maybe a little less."

"There you are." Mason stood in the hallway. "I didn't want to leave until I knew that Jayne Ella had found you."

At the sound of Mason's voice, tiny butterfly wings flickered in her belly.

She opened her mouth to speak and her jaw clicked.

"Do you want me to help you move the girls to the car?" Layla's mother spoke in a low voice to her daughter and ignored Mason.

"No," she answered quickly. She didn't want their bodies and their spirits to be too far away from one another. Neither did she want her mother to notice how impossible it would be to wake them. That would worry her and she might call a doctor. "I'll stay here with them, you go on home. I'll call you in the morning."

"Are you sure?"

"I'm sure." Layla guided her mother toward the front door.

"I'll come back in the morning to pick y'all up."

"We'll probably sleep in. I'll call you." Layla shut and locked the heavy door. She ran to her sleeping girls.

Mason stood nearby while she tried to wake Emma.

Layla moved between the two couches, shaking one girl, calling her name, and then doing the same with the next. "Wake up, Anna Kate. This is your mama, wake up!"

"Are they okay? What's going on?"

"You wouldn't believe me if I told you and I'm not going to waste my time explaining." She shook her daughter by the shoulders and her body wobbled, lifeless and empty. Her baby wasn't at home. "Emma Cath! Listen to my voice, sweet girl. Wake up!"

"What's wrong with them?" Mason took their pulse.

She sat on her heels and sighed hard. "They're with Asher."

"They're dead?"

She shook her head. "No. But they'll be in a coma soon enough if I don't get them back into their bodies. They only have about two hours left."

"ASHER WAS PROBABLY WATCHING and waiting to pounce," Layla said. "I must have picked them up in a light dream without even realizing it."

He tapped the backs of the girls' hands and called their names. "We have to call 911, Layla. This looks serious."

She positioned herself on the couch, put Emma's feet over her lap and held them close. "No. They're trapped in this house, Mason! I have to go get them." She breathed deeply, trying to descend into a relaxed state, one where her lucid dreaming would kick in.

He scooped Anna into his arms, her head lolled back and her arms hung loose. "I'm taking her to the ER—"

"Put her down!" Layla shouted, her mama bear side fierce and ready to attack.

Slowly, Mason returned Anna Kate to the couch. He placed her arms on her stomach and moved her hair out of her face.

"You're scaring me, Layla."

She held her hands out in front of her as if she could calm him or keep him still. She could not have him taking her girls away, let alone running off to the hospital with them. "It's the manor and my dreaming. I understand if this is too much for you, but right now you need to let me do my thing so I can get my girls."

"You're serious."

"I am serious. Now I can handle this, just—you need to let me get to it." She didn't actually know if she could handle it. Standing up to Asher wasn't something she had had much success with. And Asher as a ghost wasn't someone she knew how to overcome. For her girls, though, she had to figure it out.

"They're not sick?"

He glanced at the girls and ran the back of his fingers down the side of Anna Kate's face. For as much as she believed Asher to care about her girls, he had never touched them as gently.

"I would call an ambulance if I thought they needed a doctor's help, but they don't. I woke up before they did. Asher has their spirits in this house."

He laughed once and shook his head. "Layla, you just— you've got to—first you say you're—" He waved to her midsection.

"Shhhh!" She raced to him and put her fingertips over his lips. "Don't." She gestured to the walls to indicate that Asher was listening.

They stared at one another in the night shadows of the manor. Her heart begged for him to believe her. She turned toward her girls.

"What do you need for me to do?"

She spun around, faced him. Not at all knowing how he would respond to what she was about to ask. But she needed his help. She had no idea how to kill a ghost. "Will you help me get the girls back home?"

They stared at one another for a long moment.

Finally, Mason nodded.

She breathed a heavy sigh. She explained how this trip would be like the last two times he became a part of her dreams.

Only Asher would be waiting for them this time.

To kill them both.

32

L ayla sat on one couch with Emma's feet in her lap. Mason stretched out on the floor with a pillow beneath his head, acting as though he had just been selected to perform onstage in a magic trick.

She lowered the lights. She coached Mason on deep and steady breathing. "Sometimes, if I'm meditating deeply enough, the lucid dreaming will just kick in for me. I don't have to be asleep," she whispered. "So, fall asleep if you can, but don't stress about it. I might be able to pick you up even if you're not completely out."

Her thumb stroked the delicate arch of Emma Cath's foot.

Still warm. Good.

She checked her watch—two hours left. In that remaining time, she and Mason would somehow have to get the girls convinced that reuniting with their father was a bad idea, that this was all just a dream and they needed to wake up.

Don't stress. Just breathe.

The deeper you relax, the closer you get to your babies.

Babies.

There were three now. One far smaller than the rest.

She heard the antique and elongated pace of the tick-tock and opened her eyes to find a grandfather clock against the wall that hadn't been there before. The gold base of the pendulum swung left, then right. It took its time to move from one side of the chamber to the other.

The dead zone.

Emma's feet were no longer in her lap. Anna Kate wasn't on the other couch anymore. Though her children were here, in her dream, in this bridge of time that Alcott Manor occupied, Mason was not.

She thought of him as vividly as possible, remembering the light in his eyes and the feel of his straight dark hair through her fingers. She prayed he had been able to drift off, or at least drop into a deep enough meditation, so she could pull him in.

Asher had the home court advantage. She wanted Mason's support.

"Can we go swimming later?" Emma's voice came from the direction of the kitchen.

"Maybe," Asher said. "Did you bring your swimsuit?"

"Ohh. I think it's still at Grandma's house. Can we go get it tomorrow and swim in the ocean?"

"Probably. We'll have to let your mom work that out when she gets here."

"Mama's coming?" Anna Kate asked. Her voice was upbeat but tired. Like it was Christmas morning and she hadn't gotten nearly enough sleep the night before.

Layla followed her daughters' voices with the same focus as if they had screamed for help. They were in danger —not only because their dad was a ghost and he didn't have any restrictions in Layla's dreams, but also because the clock was ticking on their bodies' life. If she got them back, but not soon enough, they would fall into a coma.

She arrived in the kitchen to a familiar scene—both of her daughters and Asher playing cards around the table and drinking hot tea. Emma sat in her father's lap and he coached her on sneaky ways to win.

"Mama! Look! It's Daddy!" Anna Kate said.

"He's alive! See? I told you he wasn't dead!" Emma Cath spun around and hugged Asher's neck.

Below table level and off to the side, Asher made the blade of a knife slip from his sleeve and the silver metal glinted in the kitchen light.

"Make me a tea, would you, Lay?"

Her soul cringed. Like he fastened a collar around her neck with those few words. "Just like old times, right?"

"Exactly like old times."

Asher gathered the knife inside his sleeve, got up, and put his youngest daughter in his chair.

"I've missed you." He kissed her on the cheek and every part of Layla leaned away from him. "Listen, I know it must have been a shock to find the girls with me. To tell you the truth, it was just one of those spur of the moment decisions. I felt your dream—like the opening of a door, like a passage, like an invitation from my long-lost love. Then the girls were there, and I just thought—what a great opportunity to get the family back together. I knew if the girls were with me, you would soon follow."

"Why don't we let the girls get some rest and you and I can catch up." She made an accommodating smile and stepped toward her daughters. She was going to whisper a secret to each of them, that they were dreaming. She knew she would have to tell them several times and encourage them to wake up.

Just try.

She had to plant the seed, create a little doubt.

"Why are you looking at your watch? We have all the time in the world." He stood behind Emma, his hands on her shoulders. Like he owned them.

Layla stood next to Anna. "I'll stay here with you, Asher. But it's time for the girls to go to bed."

Emma pointed across the room. "Mama, it's Mr. Mason."

Layla turned to find Mason just outside the kitchen doorway, drawing back, wide-eyed and obviously not yet ready to be seen.

Thin black wings spread behind Asher in an instant and a single flap put him behind Mason. The knife he had hidden up his sleeve pressed to the front of Mason's neck.

The girls screamed and Layla gathered them close.

"No one invited you, *Mister* Mason," Asher said.

"It's my fault, Asher. I must have thought about him. Let him go, he doesn't even know what's going on. I'll get him to go home."

"Daddy!" the girls yelled. "Don't hurt him!"

"It's okay, it's okay. Daddy's not going to hurt Mr. Mason. I'm just going to send him home."

"And how are you going to do that, Layla-pup?" A distant bud of evil formed in Asher's eyes.

"I'm not here to hurt anyone. I just needed to clean up after the celebration. Asher? What's going on?" Mason played it beautifully, no sign of any nerves.

Layla was proud of him.

But Asher wasn't buying it and that gave her cause for more concern.

"Mason, this is a dream. You can leave any time you want by just waking up. Right, girls?" she asked.

"What are you taking about, Mama?" Both girls turned their worried faces to her.

"Shhhh, it's a dream. Just a bad dream. Wake up, girls, wake up!"

"Wait just a second!" Asher wrestled Mason into one of the straight back kitchen chairs. "Hand me that rope from the supply box there, would you, Emma Cath?"

Emma reached into the box of spare tools and removed a few lengths of rope and handed it to her father. Asher tied Mason's wrists behind the chair back.

Mason was far more athletic than Asher and, under normal circumstances, he would have flattened him with a punch. But her dead husband had a stronger sense of himself in this world. If he had figured out how to create wings, he apparently figured out how to have strength as well.

Layla and the girls stared at the blood that dripped from Mason's neck and wrists. "Wake up, Mason," she whispered. It had been a mistake to bring him here.

"Everybody wake up!" she screamed.

"Mama, what's going on?!" the girls cried and clung tightly to her.

"Wait, wait, wait," Asher said calmly as though everyone was overreacting. "Girls. My sweet, sweet girls. If this is just a dream, and you wake up from it, then you won't have your Daddy back, will you?"

Emma and Anna shifted their glances between Mason and Asher.

The girls hiccupped teary breaths.

"That's not right, Asher." Layla thought to lie and tell them not to worry. That when they woke up, their dad would still be there with them and they would be a family again. She'd put them into therapy for recovery.

"But it's true, isn't it? They wake up? I'm gone from their lives forever. Is that what you want, girls?"

They both shook their heads and hugged their father like they held the key to his life.

Asher beamed with poisonous pride. "Then it's not a dream and there's no reason to try to wake up." He waved his hands and said *wake up* as though that were the craziest suggestion. Like *jump off a cliff!* "It's just that easy, then. Hang on to me, my babies. Hang on to me."

"Oh, Daddy," the girls cried. Literally cried.

Thanks to Asher, anything she suggested to them would be refuted with "but we don't want Daddy to die!"

"What about the rest of us, Asher?" Mason struggled against the ropes that bound his arms behind his back and to the chair.

Asher sat the girls at the table again, wiped their tears, and kissed their cheeks as if he cared.

Emma Cath peeked at Mason, a dark shadow of worry flitted across her angelic face.

Yes, baby. Something is wrong. Terribly wrong. Follow that scent.

Layla willed her youngest to hear her thoughts. Her sweet, street-smart baby, who was having her sharp-needled compass dulled and confused by her own father.

"What's the matter, Emma Cath?" Layla asked.

"Um. I think Mr. Mason is hurt. Daddy, why did you tie him up?"

Asher stroked her hair as though he owned her. "I think he just needs a Band-Aid. Don't you worry."

"Why *did* you tie him up?" Layla asked.

Asher kept his eyes on his girls and the cards that Anna Kate dealt. But Mason shifted his stare to her.

"Wake. Up," Layla mouthed to him. One of them ought

to get out of this mess and he wasn't much help anyway, tied up as he was.

Mason only shook his head.

"When a stranger walks into my house uninvited, I tend to think they're here to hurt us."

"He's not a stranger, Daddy," Anna Kate said. "He and Mama are old friends."

"I'm not here to hurt anyone," Mason said.

"Oh, Mister Mason," Asher sighed. "Now you two girls play the game I just taught you while I talk to Mommy. The grown-ups will work this out. Okay?"

"Gin?" Anna Kate asked.

"That's right, darlin'. And when you win you say..."

"Sa-weeet Ginger Brown," the girls said together.

"Daddy will take care of everything."

Asher's eyes had gone flat and dark. Layla wondered if maybe something were missing. His soul, perhaps? Or maybe something had infected him, like a dark spirit. Dixie had said something about how darkness could come through. Or was this his true color making itself known? Perhaps in this dream world, he couldn't hide this part of himself as well as he did when he had a body.

"Come with me, Layla-pup. Let's have a chat."

Asher put his arm around her and she pushed it away.

Mason squirmed in the wooden chair and it rattled against the floor.

Asher clicked his tongue against the roof of his mouth. "Girls, don't get too close to him, okay?"

They nodded and Asher escorted Layla into the main hallway. Her feet were spongey against the carpeted floor, a subtle reminder that this wasn't real. And yet reality was far too close to her dreams than she would have liked.

"Let's make a deal, shall we?"

"And what deal would that be, my dead husband?"

He shook a scolding finger at her then dragged it along the outer curve of her face. "This strength, such spunk. I'm going to have a good time with this."

She smacked his hand away.

"Oh, oh, oh—" he sang. "Careful there little mama. I do hold all the cards here."

She wished she had spent more time doing more physical things in her dreams. Swimming underwater and flying to Paris with her own wings didn't help her much now.

"You want your daughters to live a long and happy life. And I would guess that right about now you regret bringing Mason into our home."

"I didn't bring him here."

"Actually, I think you probably did. But never the mind." Asher waved his hand three times and turned in a circle. He was playing the part—the man of the house.

"Point is that I think we can reach a compromise. I'll let the girls go home and Mason, too, if you'll agree to stay here with me. All I ever wanted was to own this property. Not the house, really. But since I can't do much about that, I might as well enjoy what I can.

"Of course I never planned to spend the rest of my life with you either. But looking the way you do these days— well, I hate to let *that* go to waste. Plus I'm due."

Due.

The word reminded her of the baby she carried. Not here. But there, where her body was. She needed to get back to it, soon. The baby wouldn't survive without her.

"What exactly are you *due*, Asher?"

"A reward! Remember I'm the only one who loved you when you were fat."

She cringed at the word, that tiny word that was more like a weapon.

"You never loved me, Asher."

"Okay. Got me there. But I was the only one to marry you, and the only one to sleep with you. I deserve a reward for that."

A laugh slipped out before she could catch it. "I'm not sure the sacrifice was yours, Asher."

He shook his head and pointed his cigar at her as though he were impressed. "I am going to have so much fun with this! Taming you the first time took consistent effort. But this—*this* is going to be a challenge. Can't wait."

She charged him with the speed she had seen him use earlier in the night. If he could do it, she could do it, she thought just before she took flight. In an instant, her wings were outstretched and her hands landed tight on his throat.

He tumbled backward and onto the thick, patterned rug, surprised and angry.

She'd never wanted to kill someone before, not really, not like now. She pressed her thumbs against his throat. He gagged and she felt the thrill of success.

His face turned red but his joker's smile slowly bloomed and his hands circled her wrists, lifting them away from his neck with strength he had never shown in life. He pressed his hips against her and said with a whisper, "Make love to me, Layla. Right now, just like you did with him." He nodded in the direction of the kitchen.

"Argh!" she screamed and flew away from him.

He brought himself upright, laughing as though they had just been roughhousing. Innocent play. "You'll come around, my girl. And you're looking surprisingly good these days."

"I'd rather—"

"Die first?" he interrupted.

"That's not what I was going to say." Though it was and they both knew it.

He paced back and forth, eyeing her.

"I'm not leaving without my children."

"Yes, I see that. And Mason? You're going to wait for him, too?"

"Mason can take care of himself."

"Mmm. Maybe. Doesn't seem to be doing so well right at this moment—but tell me. This protective hand thing you keep doing." Asher placed his hand across his abdomen. Then he took it away and put it there again.

She looked down. The gesture had been instinctual, to protect. She kept her gaze steady. Her mama bear side rose up quick and fierce.

"I've only seen you do that twice in your life. Both times you were pregnant." His eyes locked with hers. "Could it be that Mason is about to be a daddy?"

"You're an idiot, Asher." She no longer thought about a way to convince the girls to wake up, she only tried to figure out how to kill her dead husband.

"No. I think I'm right. You're not that hard to figure out, Layla-pup. Never have been. This little development must be why you're so driven to get home, why you won't trade places with them."

"Maybe I just don't want to spend eternity in a hundred-year-old property with a deranged ghost."

He cocked his head from side to side. "Maybe. Or you want to get back to your body so you can give birth to that baby. A boy this time, maybe. Right? Then Mason would be yours. Wow, you finally roped him in, eh?"

"Mason and I are done." She willed herself not to put her hand over her belly.

"Mason is in the kitchen, tied to a wooden chair. So y'all aren't quite *done*. And actually, I usually do know what I'm talking about."

An old, familiar feeling came to life inside of her, like a cobra rising out of a basket. The snake-like guilt and fear danced with one another while Asher paced in front of her. He stroked his chin in the way he always had, the way he did just before he reared back and struck hard.

She wanted to move toward him, grab his wrists, and snap them in two. Instead, she stepped away.

"I think you need some time to think things through before you make a decision," he said. "You'll need to choose between the child you carry in your belly and the ones you've already given birth to. You can't have them all."

"There's only one choice I'm making, Asher. My girls and I are leaving together and you're not going to stop us."

"I'm going to send you home for a while, Layla-pup. When you come back, I expect you to have your mind made up. I'm ready to get on with our new life."

He was close to her now.

There was an unfamiliar sound, one she couldn't quite place. But when he raised his arm above her in a swift move, she knew the knife in his hand was going to come down hard.

She only had time to scream, "No!"

here's Mama?" Emma asked her father. She drew a picture of a happy family on a blank piece of paper with a crayon. "Did I hear her yell?"

"I don't think so. She had to run home, sweetheart, but she'll be back.

Mason stared at the girls talking with their dead father. Asher stood beside them, appearing just as he always had when he was alive. When Layla told him she had seen him in her dream, he didn't at all believe her. He didn't believe Dixie either when she said that Asher was in the house. Because ghosts weren't something you had to believe in. But here he was, right in front of him and more real than he ever would have imagined.

"Where'd you get these crayons?"

"Mister Mason had paper and crayons and kid scissors in that drawer for us," Anna Kate answered without looking at her father, and continuing to color. "For paper dolls and pictures."

Mason smiled when Asher turned to him. Not because

he was happy to see him, but because he hoped to set him off. If seeing their father act like a raging ass scared them enough to wake them, all the better.

He assumed that's what Asher did with Layla to get her to leave. He must have frightened her right out of her dream. She would never have left her children otherwise.

Her children.

Mason thought about the pregnancy. He had known it couldn't possibly be real, he had known that beyond any shadowy doubt because he had science on his side. And yet here he was with Layla's dead husband and their children in a part of the manor that didn't feel quite real. There was a stillness here that was almost tangible, and anything beyond the manor seemed not to exist.

The table in front of him was not the one that he had restored. This one was brand new, with only a few minor carving marks on the surface. Curtains in the kitchen window occasionally appeared to have white ruffled edges with tie-backs, which was unlike the straight-edged curtains they usually had.

"Well, well. You have been hiding a couple of secrets from me, *Mister* Mason," Asher said. "First, big baby news. Next, crayons and paper."

Mason tucked the piece of glass inside of his watch band so Asher wouldn't see it. When he'd directed the girls to the crayons and paper in the drawer, they had also found the broken pieces of glass he'd left there earlier in the night. In the real world, at least, and they had transferred over.

For the last few minutes he had been using the glass to slice away at the ropes. He was sure it created a bloody mess, but Asher didn't seem to notice.

Asher leaned close to Mason's face. "If you think you're going to replace me and take over my family, you should know you've already lost out. You see, Layla will be back here in a little while and we're going to be together again. Oh, and sorry that fatherhood won't work out for you this time." He clicked his tongue against the roof of his mouth. "But I know Layla won't give up her girls for the half-baked youngster that belongs to you. Bird in the hand and all that."

A shimmy of fear slid through Mason's stomach. "I have to hand it to you, Asher. I never thought of extortion and kidnapping as a way to pull a family together. So creative. I guess it was your only option, though."

He never saw Asher's fist heading toward him, but he did feel the sharp pain in his jaw and heard the loud crack when contact was made.

Just before it all went black around him, he heard the girls' screams, and he hoped he had done his job well enough. He hoped they were on their way home.

34

Mason lay asleep on the floor where Layla had left him. The cuts on his wrists were bloody and open and Layla smoothed ointment over them. She wrapped medical gauze around his wrists until the bleeding stopped and tried to pretend that everything was going to be okay. When his cheek swelled with a bruise, that feeling faded.

She checked her sleeping girls for injuries and, finding none, breathed a grateful sigh of relief and covered them with blankets. Then she ran to the kitchen and filled a plastic bag with ice.

She stared at the work table Mason had restored with his own hands. It was older than the one her girls were sitting at right now.

Somewhere close by, though not within easy reach, her girls sat at this table playing games with their dead father.

Mason was there too, the father of her next and youngest child. Tiny flutters flickered deep inside and she pressed her hand against her abdomen.

Had this been her first pregnancy she might have

discounted that sensation almost entirely. But this was her third time to carry a child, so she knew this wasn't some perfunctory reflex of the body. It was her baby, *their* baby. Stretching and reaching, maybe to let her know that it was there, the way children did when they wanted to connect with you.

The memory of Asher came to mind in a startling flash, how he forced her to choose between the children he had given her and Mason's child that grew beneath her heart.

She propped the bag of ice next to Mason's cheek and kissed the swollen area where she assumed Asher had punched him. She hoped his jaw wasn't broken. Asher had a gift for hitting people in just the right spot to inflict the most damage. Her own jaw still clicked and popped where it hadn't completely healed properly. He'd hit her particularly hard that time.

She stood tall in spite of the disgust that dragged at her center and she kissed each daughter before she walked out of the room.

She had seen movies about women who found a weapon in instances when they were attacked. They were knocked down or beaten up and miraculously found a pair of scissors or a knife to kill their attacker. But not Layla. When Asher punched her in the jaw, she was just grateful that he hadn't hit her near her stomach, because she had been pregnant with Emma at the time.

Why hadn't her anger motivated her to action when she needed it most?

"It's normal to lose your confidence in the face of this kind of bullying," Dr. Waters had told her years ago. "The lucid dreaming and our discussions will build your confidence. I promise." And it had. Until Alcott Manor intervened in her dreams and changed the course of her life.

Layla walked out the kitchen door and across the majestic green yard. The same great lawn that her mother thought would make a fantastic overnight camping trip for the church youth group.

"You'll be on private property and right next to the beach! There's nowhere else in Charleston where you could camp on the beach and be so safe at the same time!"

Yes. So safe. So perfectly safe that that trip nearly ruined her life.

She breathed in the warm salty air. Her mind's eye held tight to its vision of the people she loved most in the world, unconscious in the Alcott Manor living room. If anyone were to walk in and see them, they would think they were dead. Soon they would be, unless she could think of something to help them.

She needed a plan. What that plan was, she didn't know.

What is real? What is true?

Dixie's words floated up to her like a gift.

"The answer is always in the truth," Dixie had said.

"Okay." She exhaled hard. "What is true?" She began a mental list of truths about the situation:

One, Mason and the girls and Asher for that matter were in Alcott Manor's dead zone. That meant a lot of vulnerability for everyone.

Two, whatever happened in her dreams at Alcott Manor had an effect in the real world: Brooke died, Jordan was injured, Layla's neck was bruised by Mason's kisses, she got pregnant, and it seemed like she remembered Asher's arm being burned from a vacation dream a long time ago.

Three, anyone who died in her dream world would most likely die in real life. Whether that was true for Asher or not she didn't know. Ghosts were already dead.

Four, with a few exceptions, Asher was essentially the

same person he had been in life—arrogant and power hungry and needing to believe that he controlled her. Since attacking him with all out force didn't seem to be an option, she decided she needed to approach him more subtly. Make him think that she was under his control.

Her heart pattered with adrenaline—and not the good kind that motivated you. This was the kind that made you feel sick, made you panic, and made you think the end was near. In life he had a way of dominating her, saying or doing just the right thing that made her feel small and powerless. This time she would overcome that.

Hope.

Don't get your hopes up! her mother's voice echoed in her mind.

Make me a tea, would you, Lay?

She spied the various rose bushes, some varieties with rose hips in bloom and she had an idea: tea. She would start with tea. That would send the message that she was the old Layla he knew and used. His wife who wasn't a threat. The one who was on his side no matter what.

She picked rose hip blooms, rose petals, hibiscus, and several flowers. She gathered different blooms from this garden than she would have from her former garden, though her practice tonight was not unfamiliar. As she always had, she placed the petals for Asher's tea in the left hem of her blouse that she turned into a makeshift basket. The flowers for her girls, she separated to the right.

There was lavender and chamomile around the yard somewhere, she had smelled their soft scent the other day. Lavender did best in full sun, but chamomile needed some shade, so maybe they were among the herbs that were closer to the back porch. She searched along the darker shadows when she heard a knock on the back door.

"Mason!"

Layla looked to the back porch and her heart twisted with fury.

"Mason! Are you in there?" Jordan banged hard on the back door.

She couldn't have Jordan walking into the manor and finding Mason and the girls unconscious and non-responsive. Layla looked around for some place to put the tea ingredients she had gathered. But there was no place they wouldn't blow away. She decided to press her blouse to her stomach.

Jordan banged on the door in the middle of the night like she was on a rescue mission, like Mason couldn't do without her, and like she was *the* most important person in his life.

"What do you *want*, Jordan?" Layla's tone was angry and fierce. Her mama bear side put its best foot forward to protect her children from this intruder.

Jordan jumped away from the door, not at all expecting a call from the shadowy lawn. "Oh my gosh, you scared me. What are you doing out here?"

"I own this house. What are *you* doing here?"

Jordan smoothed her blonde hair and pressed her hand against her chest as she gathered her composure. But Layla thought that she was scheming, taking a minute to reorganize her plan. She hadn't thought Layla would approach her from the back yard.

"I'm looking for Mason, I think something's wrong. Is he here?"

Layla's heart tripped on its own rhythm. "Why would you say that?"

"Because he hasn't returned my calls or texts and that's unusual," she said it like the spoiled brat she was, with a strong air of empty entitlement. She swayed just slightly before she caught her balance and tried to act as though that hadn't happened. Her eyes were glassy and her reflexes were slow. She had been drinking.

"Maybe he doesn't want to talk to you." She hoped Jordan would be offended at her comment. She hoped she would huff and threaten to tell Mason and just walk away. Instead, her focus became laser sharp. Jordan stepped toward her.

"Let me tell you something, Layla. Whatever you think you have going on with Mason, it's a temporary thing. Just like your new figure, it will fade. What we had wasn't casual, it meant something."

Layla's stomach lurched at the mental image of the two of them together. For a moment, she felt like the overweight girl in high school again, discounted and ignored. She checked her watch. One hour to go. "It's the middle of the night and you shouldn't be here. It's time for you to leave."

"Mason's truck is out front, so I know he's here. I'm not leaving until I get to see him."

"I have children inside. You've been drinking. You're not going in. So you can leave on your own or I'll call the police and have you removed." Layla wondered where the cop was that should have been patrolling the property. Police attendance had been spotty in the evenings.

"You know, there's something wrong about you, wrong about this house. I don't know how you got away with it all those years ago, but I know you're the one who attacked Brooke. You're the reason she died and I fell." Jordan drove her finger into Layla's chest and she batted it away.

This was so close to what had happened in high school. This was how it started. Brooke threatening her with those pictures. Next morning, Brooke was carried off in an ambulance. "Go home, Jordan. For your own safety."

"I heard you talking with Mason's mother. All about dreams and Asher still being around. You're a weird one, Layla. I think you can do things. Bad things. I wouldn't be surprised if you've done something to Mason in there. Maybe you have him tied up because you want him all to yourself. Are you doing to him what you did to me? I would guess that's the only way you could get someone like Mason to stay with you. Maybe I'll be the one who calls the police."

"Whose side do you think the police will take when they find a drunk and aging beauty queen on my property?"

"You...jealous bitch."

"That's right, Jordan. I am a bitch and if you don't want to get hurt again, then you should get away from here. Far away."

"I'm not leaving until I get to see that Mason is okay and unharmed. Send him out or I'm going in."

Layla thought of the police barging into the manor and finding Mason and her girls unconscious, especially with Mason's bloody wrists and bruised face. They would think Jordan was right, that Layla had done something to them.

"He's asleep. In *my* family home. How do you think he's going to react to you when I wake him up to tell him you're out here on a drunken tirade?"

Jordan's head jerked slightly, involuntarily. The idea seemed to hit home with her. Maybe Mason wouldn't like that.

"You're up to something. I can feel it and I am afraid for his safety. That's reason enough to call the police."

Layla stood strong and resolute at the back door. She would tackle her if she had to, though she didn't want to.

That would be incredibly hard to explain to the cops and she didn't have time for this!

"Leave. Now. I'm not waking him up." That last part was true. She didn't know how it worked if someone woke you up from the bodily side of things. It might be okay. But what if he was protecting her girls and she took him away from that?

"You freak." Jordan shook her head and looked at her phone screen. "I'm giving you one hour and if I don't see him in good health by then, I'm calling the cops."

Layla didn't say a word.

Jordan said, "I'll be waiting out front in my car."

35

"Are you okay, Mr. Mason?" one of the girls whispered.

He awoke to Anna Kate holding a cool towel to his cheek and Emma standing beside her. It hurt to move his jaw. His mouth tasted like metal and blood.

"Yeah." He looked around the kitchen. "Where're your mom and dad?"

"Mama's not back yet. We don't know where Daddy is. He comes and goes but he told us to stay here and let him know if you woke up. But we haven't told him."

"Good." He turned and spit a half-mouthful of blood that spattered onto the floor.

"Gross!" Emma's mouth twisted in disgust.

"Listen to me. This is a dream, okay? I know that sounds strange, but you need to wake up, then you'll know what I'm talking about. It's easy. Just make yourself wake up."

The two girls looked at one another and then at him.

"We can't."

"Sure you can."

"We don't want to hurt Daddy. He says if we do that then we won't be able to see him anymore."

"Do you remember going to your dad's funeral service?"

They looked sad and nodded.

"But he's not dead anymore," Emma said. "We changed that."

"Anna Kate. You know that people can't come back to life, right? That's impossible."

Layla's eldest daughter looked at Emma, whose eyes begged her not to agree with him.

"But he's here. So—"

"Sometimes after people pass on, they can appear in our dreams. It feels real and it's even good to see them. But it can't last. We have to let them move on. We have to move on." He couldn't believe he was quoting his mother's wisdom, repeating words he had heard her say in her readings for other people. "We can't live in the past, it just won't work."

His eyes watered unexpectedly.

"Are you hurting Mr. Mason?" Anna held the towel to his jaw again.

"No, something just hit me—something I should have seen a long time ago. A mistake."

"I make mistakes all the time," Emma said. "Anna Kate points most of them out to me."

Anna glared at her sister.

"Think about your grandmother and how much you love her. Think about swimming with her again and how much fun y'all have together. If we stay in the past, here, then you won't be able to see her again."

"We won't?" Anna Kate asked.

Emma turned pale. She lowered herself to the chair. "I don't feel so good."

"What's the matter, butterfly?" Asher walked into the room.

"I don't know. I feel...tired and kind of spacey. Like I forgot to eat lunch." She laid her head on the table. "Did we eat lunch, Anna Kate?"

"We ate dinner. You ate too much cake, as usual. Then Grandma said we could lie down on those couches in the living room if we took our shoes off. Now we're here. So it's not really time for lunch, I guess. I'm getting confused. Seems like we ought to be asleep right now."

Asher wagged his finger at Mason. "Uh, uh, uh..." he sang.

Mason glanced at the antique clock on the wall he'd never noticed before. They were running out of time and fast. He was pretty sure he could wake himself up, but he was only making slow progress with the girls.

"Where's Mama?" Emma asked.

Her father stroked her hair and her eyes drifted shut.

"She's coming."

"How do you know?" Anna asked.

"I just saw her. She's on her way."

36

L ayla had to settle herself three times before she could keep her eyes closed. She fretted about Jordan and how she sat in her car in front of the manor. Which made Layla get up from her meditation spot on the couch near Mason and her girls and look out the front window.

There Jordan sat, the light of her phone occasionally illuminating her face. Layla wondered if she had already called police, was putting this play by play rescue of hers on her Facebook page, or was just talking to her dad, the mayor.

Layla wiped the fresh blood from Mason's mouth and covered her girls with an extra blanket. They felt cold to the touch.

Now she just needed to drop herself into a deep enough level of meditation to reach that dream state. The blooms she had gathered for her family's flower teas were safely stored in the kitchen. If all went as planned, those leaves would be waiting for her when she arrived. Hopefully this worked, hopefully this would soften Asher's defenses enough that he would think she wanted them to be a family again.

Hopefully.

She breathed deeply for a while, focusing on the people who waited for her. When she heard Anna Kate's voice, she opened her eyes. She was still on the couch, but the physical bodies of her loved ones were no longer there.

She found them in the kitchen.

"Hey," she said. Like she was just coming home from a shift at work. Like it was normal to find her dead husband hovering around her girls. Like it didn't mean anything that Mason was in the background, tied up and bloodied.

"Mama—" Emma lifted her head but she never left her chair. "I don't feel so good."

"Oh, baby." She rushed to her side and felt her forehead. She wasn't warm with fever. She bore a clammy sweat.

Layla could swear there was less of her there, like she had become a shadow of her normal self.

"It will all be over soon, butterfly," Asher said, "then you'll feel better."

He was playing his part perfectly again, as he did in front of the girls. The role of perfect Dad. Layla always thought he must have watched endless episodes of old family sitcoms to get the body language, tone, and inflection just right.

"What will be over?" Anna asked and held on to her mother from the side.

"Good question," Mason said and raised an eyebrow at Layla's eldest daughter.

Layla felt it coming before Asher even turned around to Mason. There was a shift in the energy, like the goodness in the room was sucked away.

Asher pulled his fist back, his whole body readying itself to land another punch on Mason.

"Daddy! No! Stop it!" Anna yelled. "No hitting!"

Emma Cath began to cry into her mother's side and Layla held her close.

"Wake up," she whispered to her daughters when Asher wasn't looking. "Hurry and wake up and all the bad goes away."

"I wasn't going to hit him." Asher lowered his fist. "I just wanted to scare him."

"You *were* hitting him," Anna said.

For the first time, Layla saw what she thought might never happen, a crack in Asher's perfect fatherly mask. Frighteningly, she also saw a change in the way Asher looked at his daughter.

She recognized that expression, the how-could-you look of betrayal, the one that preceded a physical attack. If he had given either of their daughters that look when he was still alive, she would have killed him herself.

She opened her mouth slightly and her jaw clicked.

"I'm sorry," he said with a vapid smile. One that made Layla's skin crawl. One that made both girls cling to her more tightly.

With their hands in hers, she led them to the other side of the kitchen.

"Emma, you sit here." Layla pulled a straight back chair next to her at the kitchen counter. "Anna Kate, get the cups and let's make tea."

"We're having tea?" Asher perked up.

"I thought we should." Layla reached for the two pottery-type canisters that she had filled with petals before she left reality. "As a way to celebrate our fresh start as a family. If that's okay with you."

His shoulders relaxed, his chest inflated, his chin tipped up. "I think that's a lovely idea." He leaned halfway to Mason. "I was just about to send you home with a few holes in you. But now I'd like for you to see me take away the mother of your child. She was mine first, she'll be mine last."

Layla shivered and hoped the girls didn't hear him.

Asher adjusted the chair at the end of the table so that he faced Layla and her girls. She forced a sweet smile. It turned her stomach.

Out of Asher's immediate sight, Mason raised a bloody hand from behind his back just enough so that she could see he had broken through the ropes.

Her heart nearly flew from her chest. She kept her smile steady.

Asher conjured a lit cigar and drew on it. "Make me a tea, would you, Lay?"

She cocked her head to the side as though he'd given her a compliment. "Happy to."

Anna Kate placed four mugs on the counter, then returned to the work table and shuffled through a deck of cards.

Layla placed the petals into separate cheesecloths, tied them off with string and poured hot water over them. She checked Emma when she didn't think Asher was looking.

"Wake up, my baby," she whispered.

Emma shook her head.

She served Asher first, then her girls and herself last. As usual.

"Mmmm." Asher licked his lips. "What is that flavor?"

"Lavender. With hibiscus. Some rose hips and petals."

"Delicious," he said.

"I'm glad you like it." The family drank sips of tea in the sickly quiet room.

Mason sat in the background like the elephant Asher was training everyone to ignore.

Layla struggled to think of a plan 3 in case this one didn't work.

How do you kill a ghost?

What is true? What is real?

Mason was free. Asher's defenses were lowering, both of which were good. Mason seemed to understand what she was doing with the tea, buttering up Asher. He'd seen how quickly Asher reacted with his black wings. By not attacking him outright as soon as his hands were free, Mason must have known that everything had to be timed just right. They may have only one chance.

Emma was fading. Anna Kate and Mason didn't look so strong either. Scare the girls home? Or try to kill a ghost and then go home?

"Asher, I'm here as promised. Tell the girls the truth so they can go home."

His lips pursed and his gaze drifted to the upper corner of the room, as though he entertained the idea.

"That was our agreement," she said.

"Mason?" a voice called from the front of the house. "Mason?"

Asher stood quickly. His chair scraped against the hardwood floor. "What's going on? Who did you bring?"

Her shoulders shrugged high. "No one."

She wasn't lying; she hadn't brought anyone, but she knew that voice too well. Everyone did.

Jordan appeared at the doorway of the kitchen and sucked in a loud breath. "Oh, Mason!" She stormed across the wide kitchen and pointed her finger at Layla. "I knew it! You did this to him. You kidnapped and beat hi—"

Asher waved to Jordan before she reached Mason. Layla watched the anger dissolve from Jordan's face and melt into a mess of confusion.

"What a nice surprise. Can we offer you some tea?" Asher drained his mug and left it on the table. "Can't say we were expecting you, though."

"I was waiting in my car, and—and I decided to come in and look for Mason. I knew she had done something terrible to him." Her expression shifted like she recognized something was wrong. "I thought you died."

"Everyone did." Asher slowly walked toward her until he positioned himself between her and Mason. "But surprise!" He ran his hand over his chest.

The closer he moved toward her, the further she stepped in the opposite direction.

"No, you're dead. I read it in the papers." Jordan checked behind her and continued backward. "I saw it on TV, it was a big story." She snatched the scissors from the table and pointed them at Asher. Then Layla. Then Asher again.

Asher laughed. "You know I was just about to tell my —" He looked at Mason. "Wife." Then he looked to Jordan again. "That rather than it being just the two of us rattling around in this old home, we should keep the kids with us."

"No!" Layla yelled.

Anna Kate ran to her mother's side and shared the wooden chair with her sister.

"I don't know what y'all are up to here, but I'm going to take Mason and leave. Do you understand? Just leave us out of it," Jordan said.

"Actually, I'm thinking it would be fun for you to stay

with us as well. Sort of an extra playmate for me. Maybe you'll be as good as your sister."

Jordan glanced quickly at Mason, panic glimmering in her eyes. "Shut up, Asher."

Asher grinned darkly. "How interesting...you're still protective of your long-dead sister."

"What are you talking about?" Mason asked Asher.

"That's right...I never had the chance to tell you what a lucky boy you were for a while." Asher glanced at the girls huddled with one another in the chair. "Let's just say that Brooke got overly friendly whenever she thought you might dump her. She needed reassurance that she was still desirable and I was happy to oblige. Especially at the end, when she was convinced that you were leaving her for Layla."

Mason's mouth drifted open, it seemed he was unable to say anything.

Jordan shook her head as if nothing made sense and she sidestepped her way toward Mason. "I'm just going to take him out of here. Okay?"

Layla focused hard on Asher, who moved toward Jordan.

"Stay away!" she yelled and jabbed the scissors at Asher.

"You're drunk, Jordan." Layla took her chance. "You're also dreaming."

"Layla!" Asher objected, his voice deep and threatening.

Mason rose up, fast and with blood red hands raised to her. "Wake up!"

Jordan gasped, her eyes wide with horror. Asher charged her, lunging and yelling, "No!"

She scrambled backward into a spectacular trip and fall and disappeared just before he reached her.

Layla leaned down to her girls. "You're in a dream. Do you see how Mr. Mason is hurt? You're in danger here, now think of your grandmother. Go to her. Wake up!!" She screamed loud and harsh and she threw her arms over them.

It must have been frightening enough, because they disappeared.

Layla didn't have time to breathe any relief. Asher stalked Mason step by step, his cartoonish smile lacking humor and soul. His steps faltered and he leaned against the table.

"What's the matter, honey?" Layla asked.

Mason moved further away from him.

"Rapid heartbeat. I've never had that feeling before." He struggled to inhale deeply and patted his chest.

"That's because you've never had this kind of tea before." She nodded to his mug that rested at the head of the table.

He followed her line of sight, his eyes dark and flat. "What do you mean?"

She focused her intent again. Just as she always had when she swam beneath the ocean or flew with her own wings. Just as Dr. Waters had taught her so long ago. "It's too late now, Asher. What's done is done."

He grabbed the mug and sniffed where the tea used to be. "Did you make a mistake?" His voice was thin and panicked.

"Do you remember the oleander plants we had in the back yard of our old house? The one the bank owns now?"

"You put oleander in my tea?"

"When I was gathering herbs and flowers a little while ago, I found some oleander bushes at the edge of the property. And yes, I put the blooms in your tea. Quite a few, actually."

He hunched over with apparent stomach pain. "You poisoned me?"

"I poisoned you," she said calmly.

"What about the girls?"

"They didn't get any oleander tea. I saved it all just for you."

"Oh, I feel sick."

She didn't feel conflicted as she thought she might. Instead, she felt hopeful, and adrenaline zinged through her, giving her strength. "Good."

Asher's face bloomed with red fury, so much so that he seemed to shake.

She looked around for a knife, anything she could use as a weapon, but there was nothing. Asher charged her. He grabbed her around the neck with both hands and squeezed.

Layla struggled to breathe. She focused her intent on what she had wanted for a long time now: Asher dead and gone from her life.

Mason lunged for him and pulled him off of her.

Asher writhed and groaned like something worked at him from the inside. He flipped to his back, arching upward.

"Watch out!" Layla yelled to Mason and they jumped back.

A blaze of fire erupted from his midsection, causing him to release a scream, high-pitched and shattering.

The fire spread, encompassing his entire body until his screaming gurgled and finally stopped.

The flames finally burned out.

And all that was left were the charred remains of a human form.

37

M ason awoke on the floor of the Alcott Manor living room.

A soft glow of early morning light drifted through the windows. A distant charred scent filled the air.

Layla held her crying girls on the couch. "It's all over now. It was just a dream, it was just a dream." She rocked them just enough to be a comfort. All three of them held tightly to one another.

Their closeness would be the one gift that came from this nightmare, he decided. Mason's jaw ached. He stood quietly, hiding his bloodied wrists and hands so the girls wouldn't be alarmed. He turned to close the pocket doors. Layla caught his eye.

"Thank you," she mouthed to him.

He nodded. He couldn't at all explain what had happened the night before. He only knew that he and Layla had fought her now-completely-dead husband within her dreams. They fought him for custody of her children, custody of her life, and custody of her future.

They had won.

That much he knew for sure.

He stopped in the kitchen, expecting to find Asher's burned body in the middle of the floor. He didn't. In its place he found a large black spot where the hardwoods had been charred.

He made his way outside for the ibuprofen and the long-sleeved shirt he kept in his truck. His shoes crunched against the mixture of gravel and shells that made up the front drive. When he opened the heavy passenger-side door of his father's old red truck it creaked with weight and age.

Jordan's black Porsche was parked several feet ahead. He thought he saw her blonde head on the driver's side. That must have been how she ended up in Layla's dream the night before.

He arrived at her open window. He smelled alcohol. She was drunk and passed out, as she had been that night when they were teenagers. The subtle scent of vodka rose from her open mouth, a half-empty bottle on the passenger floor board.

"Jordan." He reached through the window and jostled her by the shoulder. With her mascara smudged beneath her eyes and her hair spread across her face, she looked as he had seen her before in New York, after she'd had a night out with the girls. "Jordan!"

Her eyes shot open. She blinked several times. She reached for him.

He removed her hands from his arms. "You need to go home."

"You're bleeding. It was Layla who did this, wasn't it?" She examined his bloody wrists with the gashes that were left by the broken piece of glass. "And your face. Oh, bless your heart. Do you remember this? You were there. And her girls. And Asher! Mason, he's alive. He's in the manor somewhere." She pointed to the manor that no longer appeared threatening with its fresh coat of white paint glowing soft and gentle in the morning light.

"I don't have any idea what you're talking about. Go home. You've been drinking." He nodded to the bottle of vodka on the other side of the car.

"That's not mine."

"Of course it's not."

"I've been here all night trying to help you and I think it's this dreaming thing she talked to your mother about. She's dangerous, Mason. She has to be stopped."

"You're right. She is dangerous. So here's the deal." He leaned on the open window ledge of her car door. "As long as you keep those city inspectors away from the manor, and as long as my company continues to prosper, I'll keep her away from you. If you get in our way again, I'll set her loose on you in a way you'll never forget. Got it?"

Her eyes widened. In her expression he saw the same sad girl he'd felt so sorry for all those years ago. Only now she was an adult and the years of unaccountability and entitlement gave her story a depth of disgust.

He leaned close. "And let's be honest. The only person you've ever tried to help is *you*. So do yourself a favor—stop drinking, get some therapy, and move on. Most of us have to work from a plan B at some point in life."

Mason buttoned his shirt and walked back to the manor.

The sound of her car engine starting was a welcome noise, but the music of Jordan's car tires crunching over rock and shell made him smile. He didn't turn around but when she hit the gas and the engine roared, he knew that was the last he or Layla would ever see of her.

He opened the heavy iron door of Alcott Manor and it groaned.

He never looked back.

He made his way through the majestic home that felt strangely empty. He found Layla and her girls on the porch that faced the water.

The sun hadn't yet risen over the horizon, though the sky was bright with oranges and yellows in announcement of its coming. Soon, its reflections against Alcott Manor would mark it as a sign of hope for Layla and her family. Its final restoration would be an accomplishment and a path forward for the Alcotts who had paid a significant price for their ownership.

Emma and Anna Kate whispered to one another on the porch swing and sipped on apple juice. Layla leaned against a pillar and faced the shifting colors in the sky. The swing squeaked its early morning back and forth, an even melody that marked the time of their movement. Mason thought it sounded a lot like peace.

"Is your tummy okay, Mama?" Emma asked.

"Yeah, fine. Why?"

"Because you keep rubbing it."

Layla didn't smile when she saw Mason standing in the doorway, but in that moment he did feel an entire lifetime pass between them.

Yes. From now on, he was only looking ahead.

38

"Where *is* Daddy?" Emma lifted her head from the oversized blanket Mason had spread on the grassy hill near the lake. This was the third time Layla's daughter had asked since early yesterday morning when she woke up from her mother's dream. She answered plainly every time, "He's dead, honey. He's not with us anymore."

"But I know I saw him and he was angry."

"In a dream, yes." Layla brushed her daughter's long bangs to the side and watched her process what very few adults could have understood.

"Mr. Mason says that sometimes when people die, they can visit you in your dreams. Do you think that's what Daddy was doing?"

Mason swam to the shore and handed Anna Kate the rope swing. Winston yipped and jumped on the grassy bank like he wanted a turn. Anna Kate swung over the still lake and squealed with joy. She landed with a loud splash.

He had insisted they come out to the lake for a swim. "Give the girls a change of scenery. Let 'em run free for a while." Something they both knew they couldn't entirely do at their grandmother's house. She refused until the girls overheard his offer on the phone and begged their mother into submission.

She and Mason would have to learn to coexist and co-parent anyway, she rationalized. Might as well start today.

"Maybe. I think those visits are happiest after our loved ones have crossed over."

"Has Daddy crossed over?" Emma pursed her lips in all seriousness.

"I think so. Yes." She thought of Asher's charred body that she had left on the kitchen floor of the dead zone. He was definitely gone from this Earth. Gone from her life.

Emma looked in the direction of her sister's laughter. "Is he going to be happier now?"

"I hope so, darlin'."

Emma nodded, her mother's answers were sufficient for the moment.

"I like your bikini, Mama. Red's my favorite color."

"Thank you, love.'" Layla had decided that she should enjoy the bikini she had bought for inspiration several months ago. Soon enough she would look like she was storing a watermelon in her belly.

"Can I go play with Anna Kate?"

"Go on, sweetheart."

She took off toward the tree and the rope swing. She took off to make memories with her sister. Memories, Layla hoped, that would overpower and replace the ones she'd gotten the other night.

Layla didn't want her to tell her girls that their experiences were just a dream. But that was the truth. She would add to the story later, when they were older.

Mason pulled on a T-shirt and walked Winston and both

girls to where Dixie stood at the back door of his house. She held a large green basket filled with various things. Toys, Layla supposed. She waved to Dixie, who waved in return.

They had had a good visit when she first arrived. Dixie was very excited about becoming a grandmother and Layla was feeling less anxious about babysitting support. Neither Dixie nor Jayne Ella worked full-time and they both wanted babysitting rights. She thought she might have to work out a schedule between the two of them to keep the baby time evenly divided.

"They seem to be doing well." Mason sat next to her and ran a hand through his wet hair.

At the sound of his voice, the butterfly wings took off in her belly.

Neither of her girls kicked or danced in recognition of their father's voice until Layla was in her second trimester. Nevertheless, this happened today.

"Yeah. Definitely better," she finally said and turned to Mason.

"They think it was all a dream?"

"A bad dream, yes. I'll tell them more when they're older."

Mason opened his mouth to say something but didn't.

"Thanks for letting my girls swim out here today, they needed this. What are they doing with Dixie?" she asked quickly.

"She wanted to do some games with them. Hopscotch, I think. She's never had girls, you know."

Layla's heart ached with bittersweetness at the sight of her daughters being welcomed by Dixie and graciously so.

She realized she didn't know when she and Mason would talk again. It might not be until the first prenatal appointment and that would be awkward. So she decided to share something she couldn't say when the girls were around.

"Thank you for your help last night with Asher, for going into my dream—I know that was incredibly strange. You could have just left, gone on about your business. Instead, you risked your life for us."

He pulled at a thread from the blanket.

"I would do it all again in a heartbeat." He reached for her hand and interlaced his fingers with hers. "I owe you an apology."

She couldn't catch the tears. Pregnancy hormones, she thought. They dictated when you were strong and when you would cry. She knew she would have absolutely no control for several more months. At least she had been able to keep her face from crumpling, she reasoned. That was so embarrassing.

Mason squeezed her hand in a be-strong-I'm-with-you kind of way.

"A couple of things occurred to me when I was tied up in that dream with Asher. Things I should have realized a long time ago."

"Oh?" She wanted to tell him to just leave it be. He was off the hook. She didn't need anything. Except for partial custody of his mother, that is.

"First, my mother told me a long time ago that I needed to forgive the people who nearly ran us out of town. At the time, I didn't really see the value of that. I thought the revenge of success and a life well-lived was a better option. It occurred to me the other night that that has left me rooted in the past. It's kept me a prisoner to all that anger. So, I've let that go." His expression was serious but peaceful. He had finally reconciled with the past and it made her want to do the same.

"Second, I've lived in a very different reality from you and Dixie. It's easy to deny that something exists, especially when you don't want it to be real. Or because you don't want your loved ones to be a part of it. I think I've built up a type of allergic reaction to all things paranormal and I shouldn't have put that off on you. I'm sorry."

She noticed a sadness in Mason's eyes that she hadn't seen earlier. A kind that came from carrying a burden, a regret. She had an intimate familiarity with this emotion and could recognize it at fifty feet.

"Makes me a little sick to think that I acted like the people that came against Dixie and our family all those years ago. I'm really sorry."

She nodded with gratitude.

"Whatever influence the manor has over your dreams, you obviously wouldn't have asked for any of that to happen. Just like Dixie never asked to see people's personal business." He sat upright.

"I certainly never expected to lose control over my dreams. I never wanted them to intersect with reality, let alone Asher." She hated saying his name. "Or Brooke. I'd dreamed hundreds of times before that night and the only reality I'd ever affected was my own state of mind. Which was the way the dreaming was supposed to work. I hope you can forgive me. I know you must have loved Brooke."

He touched her hand, tenderly, gently. "You couldn't have known Brooke and Jordan were going to be hurt. No one could have predicted that." He turned his wrist, where partially healed scars covered rope burns and glass cuts. "Besides, had they not been drunk that night, maybe they would have woken up before they hit the ground." He shrugged.

They would never know for sure, but Layla had suspected the same thing. She appreciated the validation that came with hearing Mason say it aloud. Something inside of her settled and strengthened.

"Hindsight being what it is, I can confidently say that I was never meant to end up with her. Whatever she and I had was all just high school and youth and—that's been over for me since the first kiss you and I shared. Before that, even."

A tingling warmth spread through Layla's chest.

"Strange things happen at Alcott Manor. I hope you can let yourself off the hook for that," Mason said.

She thought maybe she could. Finally. She felt an unfamiliar and yet comforting peace inside of her. She breathed relief that her secret was no longer her own and that the guilt no longer carried any power over her.

"Come here. I want to show you something."

She threw on her black crocheted cover up, the one with the goddess sleeves. They walked to the dock. Along the way, Mason pulled several papers from his bag and tucked one into his pocket.

"These are just some rough drawings, but see here. This is the deck," he pointed toward the house. "And here's my solution to the afternoon sun dilemma."

She examined the hand-drawn plans that she thought might have been to scale. "A retractable roof?"

"Yeah. Depending upon where the sun hits, you can close it or leave them parted. These are shades along the top to keep out the heat."

"It's perfect," she said and giggled quietly at her use of the word.

"It's possible." He smiled. Not the winner's smile that she had found so intoxicating, the one that created a ripple inside of her that could morph into a wave and sweep her off her feet. No, this one was sweet and soft and she thought she might cry again.

He must have sensed the shift in her emotions, because he rubbed her arm with a gentle touch. "There are so many reasons why you have always been one of my favorite people in the world. One of the best is that you have this way of guiding me beyond my own world, beyond limits I thought I had to live within. A way beyond other people's rules."

He held her hands in his.

"You were right that I needed to open my mind to possibility instead of perfection. There was this moment in your dream where your girls wanted so desperately to stay with their father and make that work, and it just hit me how that wasn't possible. I remember saying, 'We can't live in the past.' I think that's when I realized that I had been. Somehow, ever since the Milligans ousted Dixie, I got more and more intent on everything needing to be a certain way. Just so." He made an imaginary box in the air with his hands.

"Right angles," she said.

"Right angles. I wanted certainty and order and the false sense of security that gave me. But the more I pushed for that, the more Dixie explored her gifts. And as you know, there's nothing about that that's easily explainable. It's all very loose and that stuff just freaks me out." He waved his hands in the air and she chuckled.

"I didn't want her or anyone I cared about to be hurt again. I didn't want your dreaming to be real because I couldn't protect you from what might happen with that. In general, I can't stand it when things don't go according to plan. Misplaced good intentions, I guess. I'm sorry I put that on you. I ought to have been more open-minded." His sigh was heavy and final. "Can't fix the past, as I'm learning. So, I've forgiven people instead."

His fingertips grazed her belly, and the warmth in her heart intensified even more and spread, filling her chest like a balloon.

The first time she felt that warmth, she had been a teenager. A senior in high school, graduation just around the corner. All grades were in and the only thing left were the parties. In fact, her own mother had organized a campout on the great lawn of Alcott Manor for that weekend.

She and Mason were at the lake, this lake. They had skipped the entire day of school to swim and hang out. They sat on the dock, maybe the very one they stood on today, and they talked about their future. Warm breezes swirled around them that day, as soft and sweet as a memory. The scent of oleander hung close to them. Their ideal future seemed within their grasp.

He had all kinds of plans. When he asked her what she wanted to do, she said she wanted to be a nurse. And then there was that warmth in her chest and she said that she knew something good was coming. She knew she was going to be happy. He kissed her. With their feet dangling in the water, his tongue grazed against hers in the most perfect kiss.

She let her hopes soar that day, higher than they'd ever been. Because she just knew. In a flash of inexplicable insight, she knew. They would marry and they would have two girls and a boy—the youngest with dark hair and ginger eyes just like his Daddy.

Tears slid down her cheeks. There was no stopping them.

His expression was clear and confident. Not at all conflicted as it had been at their last discussion.

She recognized that feeling in her heart now: love. It was love. She had been in love then, with Mason. At the time, she thought that he loved her, too. Now she knew she was right.

"If there are any more dreams, though, I can think of one that I'd like to repeat." He winked and smiled, and the warmth in her chest spread to her cheeks.

He pulled a loosely rolled set of documents from his pocket and stared at it for a long moment. A gentle breeze blew through the pines and skated across Layla's back.

"This is for you." He handed her the papers.

"What is it?"

He nodded to the scroll in her hands. "Open it."

She unraveled the papers and scanned the legalese. DEED was the only word that made sense. "Deed? Deed to what?"

He gestured to the house behind him.

"Your house?"

"Your house now."

"No, Mason. This is your home!"

"I was happiest here because of you, because of the times we shared. I don't want to be here without you."

"Mason—"

"Layla, I promise that if you will give me the chance, I will do everything I can to make you as happy as you make me." More tears fell as quickly as he wiped them away.

"We don't have to do this. The baby was unexpected and you were in a dream. My dream. We would have handled ourselves together differently if either of us had been awake. I don't want you to feel obligated."

"Ha!" He laughed loud enough to cast an echo across the lake. "Obligated? I left an entire life and a career in New York just to be near you. That's not obligation, that's—this is—" He gestured to her midsection. "I can't believe I'm going to use my mother's words here." He sighed with another laugh. "Guidance. This is just meant to be. I don't know how you feel and obviously this is your choice. But in my world, Layla, all roads lead to you. They always have. I'm standing right here, with you, on this land that used to be our favorite place, because I followed my happiness. I followed my heart. I'm right where I want to be. Where I've always wanted to be."

He reached into his front pocket and offered her a ring from bended knee—a large oval labradorite center stone set in gold and surrounded by square diamonds. "It's not traditional, but I thought—"

"The stone," she gasped.

"I found it the morning after the dream with the cave." He pointed to the other side of the lake. "In my hand, oddly enough. There are two more and I thought we might have necklaces made for the girls."

"This is the same stone from the cave, the one from my dreams." She spun around and looked across the lake to the cave where they had swam, where he had proposed. It was nothing more than a wide arch of tree roots over a section of the lake, nothing like her dream. "It's not there, it never was!"

His winner's smile broadened and the wave hit her hard. "You have to believe in possibility," he said. He slipped the ring on her finger. "Marry me, Layla."

The blinding glare of the sun on the water reflected on her face. In a blink, she circled to the past and back again. She and Mason on this dock so many years ago and now again today, the future she'd known was theirs, finally within reach.

Although they weren't alone. Because the butterfly wings moved fast against the inside of her belly, as if to applaud her decision, as if he knew how happy she finally was, and as if he had known all along that this was the way it was meant to be. She pressed her hand against her abdomen and felt the joy of a dream fulfilled.

CONTINUE THE ADVENTURE WITH A STRANGER AT ALCOTT MANOR

To continue the adventure with Alcott Manor, turn the page and keep reading for an excerpt from: A STRANGER AT ALCOTT MANOR ...

SNEAK PREVIEW, A STRANGER AT ALCOTT MANOR
CHAPTER ONE

Ancient water oaks swayed in the warm, salty breezes and threw their inky shadows against the front pillars of Alcott Manor. Peyton Alcott stood next to the passenger side door of the rental and dropped the car keys onto the seat. She stared at the front of the house, tracing the outline of the bottle of Xanax bulging in her small soft-sided purse.

The manor's first floor windows were warped with age, and the darkness inside was deep and cold and formless. The home's secrets were palpable, but unseen. They shifted like forgotten spirits, hidden memories and old nightmares.

This visit to her family's ancestral estate was her first alone in twenty years. The prescription bottle lid flicked open with a pop. Just one dose would cushion whatever memories came to light. She glanced at her overstuffed computer bag in the backseat. Remembering the mountain of work she had to do, she reluctantly recapped the bottle.

She lifted her work satchel, filled well beyond its unzipped brim with a laptop, client files and instructions from her mother. Rounded oyster shells crunched beneath her Jimmy Choos.

At a long squeal of brakes, she spun, squinting at the black car with its round headlights and narrow front grill. She lowered her bag to the ground, her stomach clenched. The car's white-haired driver was a ghost from her past she'd hoped to outrun.

An oceanic updraft caught her work papers and they scattered. She snatched at them, catching only one. The rest danced and twirled down the stark white drive and away from Alcott Manor. She envied their ability to escape.

She cursed the wind and the lost papers, the manor and the land it was built on, and her own attendance at this godforsaken place.

The old Plymouth rattled to a rolling stop behind her rental car with another long screech of brakes. The elderly woman exited with a slowness that made Peyton wonder if it was wise for her to be driving.

"Mrs. Miller?"

"Hope those papers weren't important." Her smile was broad and welcoming, a gesture Peyton knew better than to trust. Her eyes were moist, more from age than emotion. One was glassy.

"My goodness, it's been years." Peyton leaned down to hug her. Mrs. Miller was frailer than she remembered, but her perfume was the same. The delicate scent of roses infused with Mentholatum.

"Well, let me take a look at you." Mrs. Miller cocked her head to the side. She raked her good eye in a slow survey from the top of Peyton's jeweled hair combs to the tip toes of her polished heels.

Peyton stood trying to hold her smile, feeling like the

blue-ribboned pig at the county fair where winning made you the blue plate special.

"Still have your daddy's good looks, I see. Let's hope you kept his temperament. Your mother says you're a big city girl now, but coming home to get married?"

"Yes, ma'am. I live in Boston, and the wedding is in four days." Peyton wished she had remembered to spin her large diamond engagement ring to the inside of her hand. But Mrs. Miller caught sight of it and Peyton saw her lips tighten.

"You still take all those pictures like you used to?" Mrs. Miller asked.

"No, I haven't had the time for much photography these days."

"I thought as much." She patted Peyton's shoulders twice. "I've got just the thing for you. Carry these inside." The rear car door groaned when she pulled it open. Mrs. Miller pointed to two large gray containers and instructed Peyton to be careful.

"These are more of the estate's cameras and tintypes that we had at the museum. We're bringing much of it here, now that you're organizing the house for tours. You'll need them for exhibits and whatnot. Jayne Ella insisted I bring these. You know how your mother is." She raised one eyebrow.

Yes. She knew exactly how her mother was.

"Are you still working at the museum?" Peyton hoisted the first plastic carton from the back seat and directed the small talk away from herself.

"Lord, yes, honey. I'll probably die in the place. No one else in Charleston knows as much about the city's history. Or Alcott Manor's history. Except for you, of course. I taught you especially well."

"Yes ma'am." She put the container near the double

front door, and the tintypes shuddered with a metallic clatter. She stared at a sign that was pasted to one of the front pillars, and her stomach dropped to the floor.

Beau Spencer
Missing
Last Seen at Alcott Manor
REWARD

Beau was in his early twenties, with bed-head-sexy blond hair and light blue eyes that were striking enough for a double take. The camera had caught him with his devil-may-care smile that won him a free pass whenever he wanted. Too many emotions knocked at the back door of her memory bank.

"Sad about Beau, isn't it?" Mrs. Miller said.

Peyton started at the closeness of Mrs. Miller's voice that squeaked like an old chair.

"He was such a wild child. Lord only knows if he's really missing or if he just hopped a plane and left. Did y'all ever speak after he stood you up at the church?"

The question hit her like a slap, Peyton squeezed her eyes shut to stem the angry tide of memories: Waiting for an hour in the church parlor in her full-skirted wedding dress, her mother ultimately telling her they had waited long enough, that Beau obviously wasn't coming. Her father saying he would make the announcement to the guests.

"No," she finally said. "Do you know who posted this here?"

"His daddy, I'm sure. Austin Spencer has them posted all over town. He stuck one right on the museum's front window."

Beau had been gone for nine years, long enough to be

declared legally dead. His parents had even held a funeral for him and erected a gravestone with his name on the front as if he were buried there.

Peyton peeled the tape from the white paint, folded the flyer in half, and half again.

Mrs. Miller's phone rang like an old telephone bell. She retrieved it from one of the patch pockets of her cotton dress and tilted her head to look through the bottom half of her glasses. "Just a minute, honey. I have to take this." She walked to the far end of the wide porch, her low-heeled shoes scuffling along the painted wood.

Mrs. Miller looked and moved like a woman far older than she actually was. She used to be a vibrant and beautiful woman, not much older than Peyton's own mother, Jayne Ella. But when Mrs. Miller's daughter went missing over twenty years ago, her hair turned stark white and everything about her physique withered and slowed and sagged.

Peyton loaded the other container to the front porch to keep herself distracted. Mrs. Miller was still talking on the phone. Peyton's directions for the combination lock were gone with the wind, so she decided to wait. Maybe Mrs. Miller would have the access code.

She opened one of the containers and found seven neat rows of dusty tintype photographs. She hadn't touched a tintype since college. The first captured memory—several Alcott family members posed in front of the grand staircase —sent a pang of anxiety from her head to her heart and back again. The threat of an old nightmare.

"Stop it," she whispered to the fear like she was the one in charge. She licked her dry lips and held a different glass plate to the light.

This tintype was a traditional wedding photo from the

1850s, and Peyton recognized the bride. She was a niece of the original owners of the manor, Benjamin and Bertha Mae Alcott. The wedding party had gathered in the ballroom and Peyton scanned the faces one by one. She knew them all, and their stories, thanks to her internship with Mrs. Miller at the museum.

One man at the side of the gathering sent a shiver of cold dancing across her back. His hair was shorter in length, though the layers had grown out. His light-colored eyes fixed straight ahead as if he looked right at her. The charm-filled smile he had often used as his ticket to get what he wanted was gone, but his lips were the same full shape she remembered.

It was impossible, though undeniable. The guest in the 1850s tintype was the man she almost married. He was the man who was missing, Beau Spencer.

Sign up at www.AlyssaRichards.com or follow her on Amazon or BookBub to receive a new release alert!

ALSO BY ALYSSA RICHARDS

THE FINE ART OF DECEPTION SERIES

THE FINE ART OF DECEPTION, UNDOING TIME

SOMEWHERE IN TIME

LOST IN TIME

THE FINE ART OF DECEPTION, BOXED SET

THE ALCOTT MANOR SERIES

THE HAUNTING AT ALCOTT MANOR

A MURDER AT ALCOTT MANOR

A STRANGER AT ALCOTT MANOR

THE CHASING SECRETS SERIES

CHASING SECRETS

FORCED PERSPECTIVE

Be the first to know about Alyssa Richards' next novel, sign up here: www.AlyssaRichards.com

and follow her on Amazon or BookBub to receive a new release alert!

ABOUT THE AUTHOR

ALYSSA RICHARDS is the USA TODAY BESTSELLING
AUTHOR of romantic suspense and mystery thriller novels.
She loves living in the South with her husband and two
children. She also loves good espresso, her rescue dogs,
magnolias and gardenias, and, of course, reading a great
book. She grew up running barefoot in the Blue Ridge
Mountains of North Carolina, where her favorite weekly
adventure was a trip to the library with her mom.

Sign up for Alyssa's newsletter at www.alyssarichards.com
to receive special offers, and news about her latest releases.

For More information
www.AlyssaRichards.com
Contact Alyssa at:
authoralyssarichards@protonmail.com

instagram.com/alyssaauthor

amazon.com/Alyssa-Richards/e/B00S1IGJ9O

bookbub.com/authors/alyssa-richards

goodreads.com/alyssarichards

ACKNOWLEDGMENTS

My deepest gratitude...

...to my husband and my boys for their encouragement and support. You are the best blessings in my life.

...to my editor, Peter Senftleben, for his expert guidance and invaluable input.

...to Yvonne for critiquing the earliest version of this book.

...and to Lucinda for her gracious friendship and feedback.